Wishing you a good read,
Nicci Kadilak

WHEN

WE

WERE

MOTHERS

Nicci Kadilak

Cover art by Kari Brownlie.
Illustrations by Ryan Webb.
Print Formatting by Nicci Kadilak.

Visit the author's website at www.niccikadilak.com.

ISBN 979-8-9860647-4-1

1st edition 2022

For my daughters and yours.

1

IT'S BEEN SIX YEARS SINCE LUCINDA LIVED UP HERE WITH Zavi, passing the most conspicuous months of her pregnancy under lock and key as they waited for Serafina to be born. But she's no stranger to these rooms; she returns often and gives what she can to whatever Sister is in residence. A checkup, some company—anything to add some color to three long months with nothing to do but watch her belly grow and wait.

"Celeste?" she calls, and the insulated walls drink in the sound.

"Just a minute!" says Celeste from the bedroom. She sounds in good spirits. Must not be too far along.

Lucinda rounds the burgundy sofa, pacing her usual path around the living area while she waits. The network of flowers embroidered on the drapery draws her near, a surrogate for the open air on the other side of the picture window. The tapestry is a controlled chaos of blossoms, but in the rectangular halo of moonlight spilling in around the edges, only the purple lotuses shimmer.

Lucinda traces a petal with her fingertip. The flowers are supposed to suggest comfort and peace. But to Lucinda, they only ever signaled isolation. An old whisper urges her to rip open the curtains and thrust her head out, sucking in deep gulps of cool autumn air, the scent of the river in the distance.

But Lucinda is free to come and go as she pleases. Celeste is the one tucked away in here now, though maybe not for long.

The message chimed through Lucinda's darkened bedroom an hour ago. *Maybe you should come.*

She threw on leggings and an oversized black sweatshirt from the pile in the closet floor, finger-combed her hair, and cursed the autochef for being out of coffee. Even uncaffeinated, she must have set a record for fastest trip to the greenhouse. "Come *on*," she said as the elevator's authenticator took far too long to scan her in. She hardly registered the canopy around her, inky black in the dim light of emergency exit signs, as she rose through the glass tube to the secured birthing floor.

Can it be time already? Celeste's body offered no hint yesterday evening as they and their Sisters worked the ground in their Family garden plot on the lower level, or as she ambled away toward the elevator that would return her to her temporary home up here. Things change quickly, though, as her mother never fails to remind her. It's important to always be prepared.

The bedroom door opens, and Lucinda turns to see Celeste in the doorway, bracing herself against the wooden frame. Her eyes and nose scrunch up. "Ooh!" She stands there for a moment, her breathing deep and deliberate, and Lucinda looks her over. Her belly hangs lower now; her stance is wider. Celeste was right to call Lucinda. There's a good chance this baby will be here today.

Celeste straightens and takes a deep breath, then blows it out through pursed lips.

"You okay?" says Lucinda.

Celeste's smile is radiant, as always. "Yeah," she says. "It's been coming and going for a while now. That was a good one, though." She glides toward Lucinda, more graceful on the brink of labor than Lucinda's been in all her life. Celeste settles onto the sofa after much shifting, and Lucinda sits opposite her. Their bodies angle comfortably toward each other like when they were twelve years old and gossiping about the gym teacher or the cute boy who winked at Lucinda in math class.

"Babe," Martin's voice sounds from the bedroom. "You forgot your electrolyte water," He comes over and hands Celeste the glass, kissing the blonde curls piled on top of her head. "Hey Lucinda," he says with a nervous wave. His eyes are clear, considering the hour. Quite a contrast to Zavi, snoring in a tangle of soft sheets and heavy blankets when she left. "Thanks, babe," Celeste says. "Now go back to sleep."

Martin grins. "How could I sleep at a time like this? Not gonna happen. But I'll leave you to talk. I'll be in the bedroom watching those old documentaries on childbirth if you need me." He kisses Celeste again and is gone.

Celeste chuckles and rolls her eyes. "Hope you catch something you missed the first twenty times," she says after him.

When the door closes behind him, Lucinda says, "How's he been coping with the seclusion?"

"Are you kidding?" Celeste laughs. "You know Martin. He's so worried something will go wrong, he's been trying to wrap me in a bubble for nine months. I think he secretly loves having me locked in here." Lucinda has seen her fair share of nervous partners since she had Serafina, the first natural birth in a hundred years, but Martin wins the award for most anxious. Celeste glances back at the door. "I'm sure once the baby comes and we get back home, things will go back to normal."

Lucinda smiles. "Soon enough," she says. But the word rings in her ears. Normal. When have things ever been normal for them? In her earliest memories, she kneels next to Celeste and their Sisters in the Garden as the Mothers' murmurs drift through the empty space. Though they were too young to grasp most of the conversation floating around them, certain words were unmistakable. *Different. Special.* Never once were they called *normal.*

"I almost slipped up today," Celeste says, the words seeming to fall out unexpectedly. The memory dissipates, and Lucinda's eyes focus on her Sister. Celeste, in turn, twists the pendant of her necklace and looks anywhere but at Lucinda.

"Slipped?" says Lucinda.

Celeste drums her fingers on her belly. "On the phone," she says, finally making eye contact. "With Martin's mom. Little stinker kicked me in the bladder, so hard I thought I peed a little. I almost said something."

"But you didn't," says Lucinda, letting out a breath she didn't realize she'd been holding.

"Barely caught myself. Told her I stubbed my toe or something." Celeste lets out a mirthless chuckle. "I think I just need to stop talking to people until she's born."

"Maybe a good idea," Lucinda says, and immediately she wishes she hadn't. There's no room for careless mistakes. Still, Celeste is one of her oldest friends, and Lucinda hates sounding like her overbearing mother.

Celeste's smile fades. "I was joking," she says. She stares past Lucinda at the covered window. "I'm already stir crazy enough. I think I'd die if I couldn't even talk to anyone."

Lucinda pats Celeste on the knee. "I've been there, trust me," she says, recalling her urge only moments ago to break free. "But the end is in sight! Seems like she's getting ready for her grand entrance." Lucinda can almost feel the warm bundle in her arms, the tiny fingers encircling her thumb.

"The wait is killing me," Celeste says. "I don't know how you did it."

Does she mean the unbearable anticipation of waiting for the baby or the torture of being locked away for three months? Either way, the answer is the same. "No choice," Lucinda says with a shrug. "Anyway, anything that happened before the baby is just a blur now. You'll see after she's born." She leans towards Celeste's belly, close enough to catch the aroma of rose-scented lotion. "And I can't wait to meet you, little girl. You're going to be beautiful, just like your mama. Do you have a name yet?" she says, raising her eyes to meet Celeste's.

Celeste grins. "Maybe. But we're not sharing until after she's born, just like I told you last time you asked. Oh!" She holds a hand to her belly and her smile widens. "There she is. She knows your voice already."

They sit together, giggling as the lumps in Celeste's abdomen pop up, rearrange themselves, and disappear. Those little movements were Lucinda's favorite part of pregnancy. Even six years later, she still feels phantom twinges in her belly from time to time, Serafina's body forever impressed upon her insides.

Celeste stiffens and takes in a sharp breath.

"You okay?" Lucinda says again.

Celeste nods, closing her eyes and settling back into the deep breathing rhythm from before. Lucinda finds her own breath mirroring Celeste's, and after a moment they both relax back into the sofa. Lucinda looks at her watch. "Ten minutes since the last one, 30-second duration," she says to Celeste. It's early yet.

"She would keep it a secret, you know," Celeste says.

Lucinda raises her eyebrows.

"Martin's mom. She wouldn't say anything."

"Celeste," Lucinda says. "You know you can't—"

"Right, yes, of course," says Celeste. "I never would. I just think sometimes, you know, maybe it's not such a big deal. If it's someone we trust. I mean, we tell our partners, don't we?" Celeste searches Lucinda's face, looking for reassurance Lucinda can't give.

"It would be pretty hard not to tell our partners," Lucinda says. "But we don't vet their family members the way we do with them. No matter how much you trust someone, no matter how well you think you know them, people change when they have this kind of information. And it only takes one. You know we can't risk it."

The Mothers never told them what would happen if the wrong person found out they weren't safeguarded—How could they know?—but that didn't prevent the girls from making up their own stories. They turned it into a macabre game sometimes, taking turns thinking up increasingly worse punishments for their crime. The Mothers would be arrested. Or maybe the Sisters would be kidnapped, safe-guarded by doctors, and sent to live with families that followed the rules. Or perhaps they'd be sent to some kind of jail for kids, never to see their friends or family again.

When they were children, it was all make-believe. Nothing would happen, of course. Because the girls and their Mothers would keep quiet, and no one would ever find out.

But now they're all grown up. As more Sisters be-come pregnant and give birth instead of using the required nursery wombs, protecting them from being discovered has become much harder. The danger that was once theoretical is now very real. If one Sister were found out, the others wouldn't be far behind. Would their children be taken from them? Maybe they would be arrested, their families disman-tled, or worse. Lucinda blinks away an image of Serafina being pulled away from her, crying the animal screams of a child ripped from her mother. And, though she was the first, Sera is far from the only one. The Garden is full of natural-born, unaltered little girls. One slip could tear countless fam-ilies apart.

Lucinda's fingers are digging into her thighs through the fabric of her leggings. She flattens her palms, rubbing away the sting. It's no use getting her imagination running. Yes, her job has gotten more difficult, and the stakes are higher than ever. But she's been preparing for this work since the day she was born. As long as she follows her mother's guidance and keeps leading the way for her Sisters, they'll all stay safe.

And right now, Celeste's face reminds her, there are more pressing things to attend to.

Another ten minutes.

"Getting worse or staying the same?" she says when Celeste pushes the air from her lungs.

"That one wasn't great," says Celeste. Her lip is still curled up in discomfort.

"Want me to call the others?"

"Nah," says Celeste. "It'll be a while, won't it?"

"Probably," says Lucinda.

"This is the boring part, then." Celeste's grin is back, and it makes Lucinda smile, too. If any part of birth could be considered boring, this is it.

"You think I could sneak out for a coffee?" says Lucinda. "My autochef was out. I'll just be over at Bel's. I'll see if I can get Astor out."

Celeste laughs. "Yeah, of course," she says. "Like I said, boring. I'm sure Martin will be thrilled to keep me company." As soon as Lucinda stands to leave, Martin appears in the bedroom doorway.

"Wow. Were you watching that doc with one ear on the door?" says Lucinda. Both women let out a laugh.

Martin's cheeks redden. "Multitasking," he says, not bothering to deny his eavesdropping.

Lucinda leaves the couple with a list of instructions: Walk; Hydrate; Bounce on the big ball; Have a snack now, while Celeste can keep it down; Rest; Watch something on the wallscreen.

"Maybe don't call your mother-in-law, though," Lucinda says with a wink.

Celeste's cheeks flush.

"Kidding!" says Lucinda, giving Celeste's shoulder a squeeze. "I'll check you out on the monitor when I get back."

Martin walks her to the door. "Everything's good, right?" he asks. He's smiling, but Lucinda could reach out and touch his anxiety.

Lucinda squeezes Martin's shoulders. "It's fine." She lowers her voice. "Do me a favor and at least pretend to be relaxed, okay? Your nerves will rub off. Be cool."

Martin chuckles, shaking the hair back from his face. "Be cool. Got it. Cool is my middle name. Now, go and get caffeinated. We need you at your sharpest."

When Lucinda pulls the suite's door closed behind her, Celeste is standing next to the tapestry-covered window. If she's anything like Lucinda, she's counting down the hours until she can be on the other side again.

The nerves set in as the elevator doors slide closed. She's attended a dozen or more births, but the emotional stew of nervousness and excitement never lessens. As she holds out her hand to the scanner next to the button panel once more, goosebumps move over her skin. A bright purple projection unfurls in her palm—a lotus blossom, opening one petal at a time, that she can see only through the overlay enhancement in her glasses. *Slow down and breathe.* The scanner verifies her photogram, and the platform begins to glide down through the clear shaft.

Lucinda's heart gradually slows. Everything about Celeste's pregnancy up to now has been textbook, and the birth most likely will be, too. So what if it's a week or two early? She's still in the range of normal. The best thing Lucinda can do is to follow her own advice. Be cool. Birth is natural. Before the laws changed, people had been having babies this way since the beginning of time.

Besides, they won't be alone. With the tap of a button, Lucinda will summon the rest of the Family to Celeste's side when the time is right. She smiles at the thought of huddling with her Sisters around a laboring Celeste, as they've done with every Society birth. And, of course, Mother will be there. She was there when Sera was born, and she's helped Lucinda deliver all the others. And she's a doctor. If something out of the ordinary did happen, she would know what to do.

Lucinda can't imagine ever having that kind of confidence in herself.

She takes out her mobile and brings up her message thread with Astor. *At the suite w C,* she types. *I think today's the day. Coffee @ Bel's?* As she waits for Astor's response, the garden plots below come into greater relief. The gardens up here mirror those on the secured lower level, where the Garden Society has been gathering since Lucinda was just a collection of cells, incubating in a nursery womb in her childhood bedroom.

The squeals of Serafina and the other children filled the air just hours ago as they ran around and through their Family garden plot, playing chase like Lucinda, Celeste, Astor, and the rest of their Sisters did when theirs was the only Family, the only plot, a single oasis in the stretch of barren soil. Lucinda smiles. The Garden has grown into a lush greenscape. After decades of planning, she and her Sisters are bringing the Society's vision to life. And soon, there will be another little Sister running through these garden paths.

The elevator opens onto the public gardens of the greenhouse's main floor. In the dark, the paths she's traversed countless times look foreign, and it takes all her concentration to see the clearings below her feet and avoid stepping on a creeping jasmine or zucchini plant.

She crosses toward the exit, closing her hands at her sides and straightening her shoulders as she walks. The sliding doors open, and she steps onto the sidewalk and into the outside world. The streets are deserted at this hour yet still bright with overhead awnings and streetlights. Is this what Celeste was imagining, standing by that window upstairs?

Lucinda hugs herself and takes a sharp breath. What was a playful breeze last night when she left this building has transformed into a biting wind that chases her long, black hair in a never-ending circle around her face. And, of course, in the rush to get to Celeste, she forgot her coat. She squints against the cold and walks three endless blocks through the tunnel of skyscrapers. The hazy blue lights of Bel's entrance come into relief just before she freezes in place on the sidewalk.

Down the concrete steps, she hefts open the riveted metal door and steps inside. A last gust of wind whips at her as the door slams closed, and she reaches up with both hands to smooth her hair back into place. She stands in the entryway as her eyes adjust, trying to defrost from the outside in, lungs filling with the sweet, yeasty smell of beer that never quite leaves a place like this.

Her mobile buzzes in her pocket. Astor: *Shit. Just left that place. Fine, be there soon.*

The bright neon light behind the bar is almost as loud as the heavy bass thump pouring from the speakers. A man and woman, clad in matching white dress shirts and black bowties, are wiping down the bar, getting ready for the changeover to the breakfast crew. Neither pays Lucinda any notice as she bypasses them and takes the stairs at the far end of the room.

Up on the automated level, Lucinda sits at a high table in the corner. Her mobile buzzes again: *Hot Coffee > 2 Cream > 1 Sugar. Repeat order?* She taps *Yes*, then replays Serafina's good-night message from her parents' place last night. Sera's shaky hand brings Lucinda around the apartment where she grew up, and then the frame steadies as Sera hands the phone over and proudly holds up the new game Grandma and Papa bought for her visit. Lucinda smiles at her little girl's glee as she pushes down a twinge of resentment. There are more toys and games in her parents' house now than when a child actually lived there.

"Good night, Mama! Love you!" says Serafina, and then Ruma's face appears in the frame. Lucinda flicks the message off.

"Yeah, Mom. I get it," Lucinda says under her breath. At the gathering last night, Lucinda made the mistake of oversimplifying an explanation for the children while her mother was within earshot. She's already heard the reprimands twice—once in front of the rest of the Sisters, and again at the end of Serafina's message. No need to subject herself to them again.

The silver door in the wall opens onto a steaming mug. Her thawing fingers burn against the ceramic, but warmth seeps through her body as the coffee moves down to her stomach. As the heat creeps in, she sits back and surveys the floor. A soccer game from across the world plays on the wallscreen for a single viewer, a droopy middle-aged man grasping a pint glass at the long bar. A young couple sits in a booth, both men on the same side of the table, touching foreheads and nuzzling their noses together.

"How cute are they?" Astor says, sliding into the seat opposite Lucinda. Her hair is blue today, shaved on one side and braided over her other shoulder, though nothing holds it in place and it's already loosening at the ends. Her eyes are a startling shade of red.

"Have you gotten any sleep at all?" Lucinda asks.

Astor grins. "Not much. Stayed out late with some of my new work friends. Turns out lawyers really know how to party." She lowers her eyes to her mobile and types in her order. "So, you think this is it?" she says, gesturing toward the space where Celeste would normally be seated.

Lucinda and her Sisters have known each other forever, attended each other's births and weddings and graduations. Eventually they will grow old and die together, leaving their children to keep their shared secrets. As the originals, Astor, Lucinda, and Celeste have shared a special closeness. Play dates during their elementary school days, bowling and movies as teens, exercise classes and dinner parties as they've grown. Subdued, unfrequented, all-hours Bel's is the latest place they've settled—the perfect place to talk without being overheard. Maybe next time they're here, things will be back to normal, and Celeste will be able to come.

Normal. There's that word again. She shakes the echo from her mind and turns to Astor. "I think it might be. You excited?"

"Sure, I guess," Astor replies, retrieving a glass filled with ice and a dark liquid from the compartment and taking a long pull. Whether it's coffee, bourbon, or both, Lucinda can't tell.

"What's that supposed to mean?" Lucinda asks.

Astor shrugs, her upper lip curling. "You know how I feel about this shit, Lucinda. I'll never be comfortable with it."

Sisters begin preparing for what the Mothers call "the beautiful and natural act of childbearing" from their earliest days. Astor, though, has never been very enthusiastic about the idea, and it's always felt like Lucinda's job to convince her their path is the right one. Lucinda was certain after watching their Sisters give birth, Astor would warm up to the beauty of it all. But if anything, the opposite has happened.

Lucinda leans close and keeps her volume down. "Astor. After all we've seen, you don't think it's amazing what our bodies can do?" Why ask it as a question? She already knows the answer.

The silence between them stretches. The wallscreen flashes with an advertisement, the sound combining with the bar's ambient music in an unintelligible jumble. Astor shrugs. "Sure. It's amazing. But it also seems, I don't know, unnecessarily hard."

"What does?" Lucinda says, as if this conversation hasn't played out in a hundred different ways over the years.

"Come on, Lucinda. The hiding. The isolation. Knowing the agony you have waiting for you at the end. The risk to your life and the baby's. If you just did things the modern way, you'd avoid all that."

It's not that Astor's points aren't valid. Nothing about this life has been easy. Lucinda has spent most of her years terrified and lonely, from having monthly cycles when all the women around her were safeguarded, to being the first person in generations to become pregnant and give birth, going through every step without the support of someone who had been through it before—because there was no one still alive who had.

But their work is important. Bringing this essential function back to humanity, taking back their natural-given capabilities, and helping others do the same—that has validated the struggle a hundred times over, and she knows their Sisters would agree.

Lucinda can't wait until Celeste can join them again. She's the perfect buffer, always keeping the peace even when Astor wants to fight.

"Astor," Lucinda says slowly. "Birth is a natural part of life. And we both know that ninety-nine percent of the time, things go just fine."

"Ninety-nine-percent is not one hundred percent." Astor empties her drink and, after a few taps on her mobile, another appears. "Why risk it if you don't have to? Look at Myles and Peter. They go to an appointment, pick a gender, combine their DNA exactly how they want, then pop the cartridge into the nursery womb and watch the whole thing as it happens. Nine months later, the baby comes out. Perfect and completely risk-free."

"You sound like an infomercial. Yes, okay. For them, that's a great solution. But what about someone who wants to feel her child grow inside her?" Lucinda can't help touching her belly, remembering the fullness and promise of

Serafina growing within. "Shouldn't she be able to make that decision on her own?"

Astor presses her fingers to her temples and stares down into her drink. "Lucinda. Unexpected things happen all the time in nature. Just look at what happened with—" Astor stops abruptly. "Sorry," she says.

Lucinda doesn't need a reminder from Astor to call up that day. It's always there, close enough to touch. *Selective termination,* her mother called it, her voice sickeningly flat and emotionless. *There can only be one.* Lucinda can still taste Zavi's tears mingling with hers, can still feel the cramps and the bleeding and the unrelenting grief for who Serafina's twin might have grown to be.

Lucinda swallows, irrationally angry at the cheering fans on the wallscreen, which continues playing though the middle-aged man and his beer are gone. She sniffs. "So, because things might, maybe, possibly go wrong, we should take the decision out of a mother's hands?" she demands.

Astor's eyes rise to meet Lucinda's. "And because someone might, maybe, possibly want to carry a baby we should break the law and make a decision for her that she will have to carry around forever?"

"At least then she'll be able to choose for herself," says Lucinda.

Astor suddenly looks half her age, indignation plastered on her face. "Well, I'd prefer not to have to live a life of secrecy. The monthly bloodbath, the secret meetings, the—"

Lucinda blinks. "The sisterhood? The community? The *truth*?"

Astor sighs and looks past Lucinda, toward the couple in the booth. "It's all fine and good for the rest of you. You're perfectly happy to incubate humans inside your bodies, and you have partners to help you make these humans. It's not like that for me. No thank you, on both counts." Another dark drink has appeared in front of Astor, and she raises it to her lips. Her eyes are still puffy, but the redness is fading.

Lucinda thinks of all the women, ignorant to what the Governing Council decided on their behalf before they were born. Women who have been made to forget what their bodies are capable of. Astor can choose to have a baby or not, with or without a partner. That's the whole point. How does she not see that? "You might be upset the decision was made for you," says Lucinda. "But it's better than the other way around."

"Says you. Our mothers made the unilateral decision to condemn us to a life of hiding and risk and pain, and now we are expected to do the same to our daughters. How fair is it to thrust little girls into this situation? To force them to lie, to hide, to break the law, without giving them a choice?"

Lucinda stares in disbelief. Astor knows the history as well as anybody. She couldn't possibly think it's right to sterilize infants who don't have the capacity for consent. "Choice? Astor. Don't you realize the irony of what you're saying? After all these years, I would think you would understand that the Society *gave* us choice. They didn't take it away."

Astor looks down. "I should have just kept quiet," she mutters. "Like usual. Forget I said anything. Blame the drinks I had earlier tonight."

Lucinda opens her mouth to speak but closes it again. Astor has always been different from the others, but she's never been this blunt about her feelings before. They both grew up saying the same pledge, learning the same history. How could they have such different views on the very thing that binds them? And why now, when they're about to help bring a new life into the world?

The music plays on, oblivious to their silence. One song ends and another begins, and Lucinda watches Astor, whose eyes stay fixed on the icy drink cupped between her hands. When she finally looks up her face is placid. "What's done is done," she eventually says, her voice wooden. "There's nothing I can do about it. I know that. It's just—I care about you and Celeste and the others. I don't want anything to happen to you."

"I know, Sister," Lucinda says, reaching across the table and taking Astor's cold fingers in her own. "But we've been safe and careful so far, haven't we?"

Astor nods, blinking. "Yeah. I guess we have."

"Then there's no reason to think this time will be any different."

No sooner have the words escaped her lips than her mobile buzzes with a message.

It's Celeste.

Can you come back? Please? I think something's wrong.

Rising once more through the gardens, this time with Astor by her side, Lucinda tries to shake off the unease of Celeste's message. Labor has a way of making everyone panic. No reason to get worked up before she knows what she's dealing with. Just breathe, she reminds herself as if she's the one in labor. In, out. Things will be fine.

Martin's face through the cracked door suggests things are not fine. He moves aside and pulls his fingers through his hair as Lucinda and Astor step in. Not an hour has passed since Lucinda left, but his face has paled by a couple of shades.

"What changed?" she asks.

"I don't know," Martin says, his voice shaky. "She just said something doesn't feel right."

Lucinda lets out a breath. Sounds like she's transitioning to active labor. "Okay. That's actually a pretty common feeling toward the end of labor."

"I thought you said it would be a while," says Martin.

Lucinda shrugs. "Some labors progress more quickly than others. We'll get her checked out and see what's what." She scans the living area. Empty. "My mother's not here?"

"Not yet," says Martin. Lucinda pushed the beacon out to the Family before leaving Bel's. They should start arriving any moment now.

A whimper sounds from the sofa. Celeste. Lucinda rushes to her side and kneels, while Astor stays near the door, instinctively keeping Martin and his anxiety away for now. Celeste is curled up on one side, holding her belly with both hands, a sheen of sweat covering her forehead. "Hey, Sister," Lucinda says. Despite her assurances to Martin, it takes everything she has to sound focused and confident.

"Lucinda," Celeste groans through gritted teeth. "What's going on? This doesn't feel right. It's not supposed to happen this fast."

Lucinda brushes Celeste's golden curls back. Celeste and Lucinda have been to dozens of births together, and no baby has ever come so quickly before. But that doesn't mean it's not right. "Remember what we always say? All babies have their own plan," says Lucinda. "Apparently this baby's plan is to meet us all as soon as possible." She gives what she hopes is a natural-looking smile. "It'll be okay, Sis. The others are on their way. We'll all be right here with you."

"No," Celeste says, shaking her head. "Something's wrong."

"If there is, we'll figure it out." She flicks her eyes toward Martin and Astor at the door and then back down to Celeste. "Promise."

Celeste's eyes close and her face twists up in a grimace.

"Come get her through this contraction," Lucinda says to the others. "I'll be right back."

Martin's eyes are half-panicked, but he replaces her at Celeste's side. While Astor is filling a cup with crushed ice from the dispenser in the autochef, Lucinda ducks into the bedroom and tries her mother. Voicemail. "Mom, where are you? Get here now," she whispers. She hesitates and then adds, "Something might be wrong." Immediately, she hates that she said it. Everything is going to be fine. Ruma is probably on her way and can't talk. Still, the silence makes Lucinda uneasy.

She punches the code into the keypad on the equipment cabinet, and the door swings open. Obsolete pregnancy monitoring equipment, scavenged from storage rooms of clinics and hospitals before it could be discarded, sits in neat rows on the shelves.

"Mom, are you sure that stuff even works?" Lucinda asked her mother when she first saw the ancient-looking devices. She and Zavi were sitting on the bed right there, the same bed where Serafina would eventually be born.

"Don't be silly," Ruma said in her low, milky voice. "Of course they work." But Lucinda wasn't so confident. These kinds of tools hadn't been used for decades.

Lucinda's doubts were soon put to rest when, after a few tense moments of searching, a tiny flicker appeared on the black-and-white monitor. "That," said Ruma, pointing with a manicured finger, "is my grandchild's heartbeat."

Lucinda breathed a sigh of relief. Her mother slid the wand around her belly, explaining each landmark on the display and its significance. Lucinda had seen them all before, but only in hundred-year-old e-books read in staccato bursts over the years. Seeing them in person, in connection with her body and her baby, was more surreal than she'd imagined. She squeezed her mother's hand, her heart warming at sharing this rare moment of intimacy.

And then the air left the room.

"Ruma," Zavi said slowly. "Is that another one?"

Their smiles faded. Lucinda let go of her mother and tightened her other hand around Zavi's. Ruma said nothing at first. Maybe she wasn't sure, or maybe she just didn't want it to be true. But there it was—there *they* were—two undeniably beating hearts, two tiny humans, growing inside Lucinda's womb.

Ruma wiped the imaging wand with a sterilization towel before replacing it in its holder. The clinical indifference in her gaze turns Lucinda's stomach to this day. "I'm sorry," she said. "But you know there can only be one." Tears filled Lucinda's eyes as Zavi squeezed her shoulder. But they both knew her mother was right. Twins were a thing of the past. It would be impossible to explain a second baby.

She'd been vibrating with nervous excitement in the days leading up to that moment. Now, she'll never be able to give expecting parents a glimpse at the life they're carrying without remembering what was torn away from her.

A knock on the suite's main door brings her back to the present. That must be her mother.

Back at the sofa, Lucinda settles on the floor with the imaging machine while Martin gets the door.

"Mind if I check you out?" Lucinda asks.

"Okay, yeah," says Celeste, gingerly shifting. Her delicate voice is barely audible.

Adi appears around the end of the sofa as Lucinda is positioning the monitor, and they exchange nervous smiles as Adi collects her long microbraids and ties them with a loose elastic at the nape of her neck. Adi's daughter, Micah, will be sour when she wakes to find her mother is attending yet another birth. Micah won't be allowed until she's had her first cycle, and she doesn't hold back from voicing her opinions about the rule.

If anyone understands Micah's eagerness, it's Lucinda. She longed for an example to follow when she was younger, someone who had been through it all and could understand her fear and uncertainty. That's the blessing and curse of being the First Daughter. Periods, pregnancy, birth.

She got through everything on her own. And now she is the example her Sisters, and eventually her daughter, will follow as they experience what the rest of the world has forgotten.

"I'm sure by the next birth you'll be ready," she said to Micah last night as they knelt around their Family's garden plot. She tucked a long, black-and-purple twist of hair behind the girl's ear and leaned in so their foreheads touched. "Just gotta be patient." It's probably not much comfort now, but Micah will have plenty of chances to see the Society's work in action.

The monitor beeps in Lucinda's hand. One look at the measurements tells her what she already knew. This is happening, ready or not. She levels her eyes at her Sister. "Okay, Celeste," Lucinda says. "You're almost fully dilated and effaced. I know you don't think you're ready, but your body knows best. And your body says it's time to have a baby."

Celeste's voice is urgent. "No. No, it's too fast. Make it stop."

"Trying to stop it now would be dangerous for you both," Lucinda says. "The baby's in a good position, and your body is telling us it's time for her to come. All we can do is help her arrive as smoothly as possible."

Where is Ruma?

"We're right here with you," Astor says, squeezing Celeste's hand.

Her mobile buzzes, and a tentative relief tempers the fear rising in Lucinda's chest. That must be her. She unlocks the device and hands it to Adi before pulling on some gloves. "Can you check this? It's probably my mother." She presses her forehead against Celeste's. "Listen to me, Sis," she says.

"Your baby is coming. You've got to get your mind around it. Otherwise, you're going to fight it, and that's not good for either of you."

Celeste searches Lucinda's face. The tears clear from her eyes, and she takes a shaky breath. "Okay," she says, nodding. "Okay. Everything will be fine. Right?"

Lucinda gives her most encouraging smile. "Yeah, it will. Everything will be fine. Just let your body do its thing."

Celeste takes another breath, smoother this time, and a new resolve settles over her. She's ready.

"Are you comfortable?" Lucinda asks. "Do you want to move to the bedroom, or maybe the tub?"

Celeste squeezes her eyes closed, clutching her belly once more. "No," she says. "No, I can't move. I want to stay here. Is that okay?"

All the supplies are in the bedroom, but it's best to keep Celeste comfortable. "Sure," says Lucinda. She turns to Astor. "Can you grab some absorbent pads and towels?"

Adi passes Lucinda's mobile back as Astor heads into the bedroom. "It was Zavi," she says. "Just checking in. I told him you'll hit him back later."

Lucinda's heart beats faster every minute her mother doesn't show. She's delivered plenty of babies from all different Families in the Society, but never without the reassurance of having Ruma there.

Celeste shrinks up once more, whimpering with the pain of a contraction. Martin crouches by her side, holding her hand and brushing away the hair that's pasted to her forehead.

Lucinda stands to excuse herself and try Ruma again, but she's interrupted by a low, guttural sound—a sound that could only mean one thing.

"She's pushing," Adi says, kneeling near Celeste's feet. Her voice is level, but Lucinda can see the question in her eyes. Why is this baby coming so quickly?

Lucinda drops back down to the ground.

Astor is back in an instant, slinging an armful of white supplies onto the table next to them.

"Where's my mother?" Lucinda murmurs into Astor's ear.

Astor shakes her head as she unfolds one of the absorbent pads. She doesn't know any more than Lucinda.

The sound coming from Celeste tapers off, and she relaxes into the soft burgundy upholstery. "Celeste? Sis? How are you doing?" Astor asks.

"My body just wouldn't let me not push," she responds, her voice even smoother and more airy than usual. "She wants to come out."

"Okay," Lucinda says. "It's okay. Just let me check you first. We need to be sure you're dilated enough so you don't hurt yourself."

"No," Celeste says, breathless. "No time. The baby's coming." And with a gurgling groan, she pushes once more.

Martin kneels at Celeste's side, looking from Celeste to Lucinda and back again. His eyes amplify the pleading voice inside Lucinda's head. Please let everything be okay.

Adi takes one of the towels from the pile of supplies and dampens it in the kitchen. "Here," she says, handing the towel to Martin. "For her forehead."

He reaches out a tentative hand and dabs at the droplets of sweat. "Is that okay?" he asks.

Celeste nods. "Leave it there," she says. "That feels nice."

"How are you doing?" Lucinda asks.

"I'm okay right now," says Celeste. "But when I push, it feels like I might die."

Lucinda can't help smiling. At this stage with Serafina, each contraction felt like it would split her in two. "That's normal," she says. "You can do it, Mama. You're strong." It was silly to worry. Some babies just come more quickly than others.

A throaty, animal sound comes from Celeste. Her head and knees lift, and she bears down. The baby's head comes into view, slippery dark hair plastered to pink skin. Celeste leans back, panting. "Do you want to feel?" says Lucinda.

"No," Celeste's voice is strained as her body struggles to let go of the last contraction. Astor whispers into her ear and they both take deep breaths. Four seconds in, four seconds out. A peaceful smile passes over Celeste's face.

"The next one's going to be it," Lucinda says. "When you feel the urge to push, I want you to imagine your little girl coming out to meet you, and I want you to push as hard as you can. You're both working together here."

"Okay," Celeste says. She and Astor inhale and exhale together one more time before her eyes clench and her breathing becomes shallow again.

"Take a big breath in," says Lucinda. "And then one long push until you feel the baby's head come out."

More moans from Celeste as her body crunches to-gether. Within moments the baby's head is through. Her face is squished and perfect, traces of red and white streaking her skin. With one more push, her entire body is out, sliding eas-ily into Lucinda's waiting hands. The baby takes a deep breath and lets out a yell, like she knows better than to make these people worry. She's perfect.

"You did it!" Lucinda says. She hands the tiny, pink baby to Astor for a checkup and gives Celeste's shoulder a squeeze. "Good job, Mama," she says, and Celeste nods back at her, smiling faintly through droopy eyelids.

"Here you go, Mom," says Astor, passing a bundle of loosely wrapped blankets to Celeste. The baby quickly settles in her mother's arms.

"Hi, baby," Celeste says, smiling down at the tiny face peeking out of the blanket. Her voice has that breezy, blissful sound of someone who has just given birth.

Martin kneels next to the two of them, beaming. "She looks just like you, babe," he says through tears. He pushes Celeste's hair off her brow once more, kisses first Celeste and then his new daughter on the forehead. He looks up to Astor. "Is she ok?"

"Yeah," Astor says. "When Ruma gets here, she'll do a more thorough checkup. But it looks like your baby's doing just fine."

The unease has left Adi's eyes. She moves from Celeste's feet to the back of the sofa, peering over at the newly completed family with a warm smile. Even Astor, while she stays out of the way, perched on the edge of a nearby chair, seems to have loosened a bit. But where is Ruma? How could she have missed the entire birth?

"Want to try and feed her, Mom?" asks Lucinda. "Then maybe you can finally tell us her name."

The same faint smile still turns up the corners of Celeste's mouth. "I wasssssss…" she begins, but her words fade as her eyelids flutter closed. Her body contracts.

"Celeste?" Martin asks. He barely grabs the baby before she rolls out of Celeste's limp arms.

"Celeste?" Lucinda echoes, voice high with alarm. She looks down under Celeste's dress just as her body contracts again and the placenta delivers itself. The blood comes out in an unmistakable gush before disappearing into the sofa's upholstery. "Oh no," she whispers. "No, no, no, no, no." Panic rises from her belly into her throat. She jumps up and edges Martin out of the way. "Celeste?" she asks more urgently this time, shaking Celeste's shoulder. Tears blur her view, but she can tell all she needs to know from the sickening lack of resistance Celeste's body offers. Please be okay, she thinks. Where is my mother?

"Towels!" she shouts. "Get me every towel you can find! Shit! How am I supposed to—"

The others are yelling Celeste's name, attempting to bring her back as Lucinda tries in vain to stop bleeding that was out of control long before she recognized it was happening.

Martin and the Sisters keep shouting, over and over, until their voices become hoarse and their screams give way to sobs and, eventually, to bleak, desperate, puffy-eyed silence. After what seems like an eternity of yelling and screaming, soaking and massaging, pleading and sobbing, the only sound left in the spacious apartment is the cry of the baby, doubtless hungry and with no milk to drink.

The new day's light shines through the windows of the suite. More Sisters arrived some time ago, and one by one they joined the bloody vigil around Celeste's body. Aside from the mewling of the baby, swaddled in Martin's arms, no one has moved or made a sound in what could be minutes or hours.

Lucinda gives her head a shake, forcing her eyes from Celeste and trying to clear the fog from her mind. She needs to move. She unfolds herself and rises from the floor, careful not to disturb Celeste's body or the unfathomable pool that has grown around it. In the kitchen, she snaps off her useless gloves and rinses her hands under scalding water. A rust-colored outline remains on her left forearm, and she runs a finger along it, numbly feeling its ridge before pumping some soap into her hands and scrubbing it away. When the water finally runs clean, she pulls back from the sink, arms covered to the elbows with red stripes the width of her fingernails.

Her mobile rings. She answers with a hiss, turning her back to the living room. "Mom. Where—"

"Not now, Lucinda," says Ruma before she can even finish the question. "Are you still at the suite?"

"Of course we are," Lucinda says, exasperated. "The baby came, and Celeste is—"

"Yes, I know. You all need to get out of there."

Lucinda blinks. "Out of here?" She glances at the others, eyes blank, faces still angled toward the grotesque scene before them.

"Lucinda, listen to me," Ruma comes back, even more urgent than before. "Listen very closely. You and your Sisters need to clean up, as quickly and as thoroughly as possible, and then you all need to leave the suite. All of you, including Martin and the baby. Get that baby registered, retroactively, as of some reasonable time yesterday evening. Yvette Blair will be by to…to pick her up."

Blair. Lucinda recognizes the name but can't place it through the haze in her mind. "Mom," she manages to choke out. "How are we supposed to—"

"You'll figure it out, Lucinda." Easy for her to say from a safe distance. "There's no other choice."

She begins to argue but her mother interjects once more, her voice a near whisper. "Imagine the questions, Lucinda," she says, "if the suite is discovered, if Celeste is found inside…" she pauses, clears her throat, "…dead and with a newborn. We need to protect Celeste and her family, and we need to protect everyone else in that suite, and we need to do it quickly. The authorities will want to question Martin. He must be at home for that to happen. The more time you spend at the suite, the more dangerous it is for us all."

Lucinda takes a slow, deep inhale and blows it out. Her mother won't be winning any prizes for tact. But she's not wrong. "Okay," she says, her voice hollow and empty, disconnecting the call without another word. She turns to her Sisters, a collection of vacant faces gathered around Celeste's body. "We have to leave," she says. The glossy-eyed Sisters begin to stir, and eventually their eyes settle on her. She directs them to clean up as best they can with the tools they have, and they begin gathering, spraying, wiping, arranging. From time to time there is a sniffle, the swipe of a hand across a cheek, but otherwise they work in silence. Even Astor, while her face is twisted more in fury than in sorrow, doesn't say a word.

Martin sits on the floor, slumped against an armchair, facing his dead partner. The newborn in his arms grunts as she roots fruitlessly for anything that will provide her some nourishment. Martin stares straight ahead at Celeste's pale, empty face.

Lucinda cannot see Zavi in Martin's face. He has taken up the greatest part of her heart since the day they met at the Engineering Library, each expecting to meet a tutor that didn't have the chance to arrive before the two of them ditched the books and went out for a drink. She cannot think about what would have happened to her partner and her daughter, of what would be today, if this had happened to her instead of Celeste. If Sera's birth had gone differently, maybe Celeste wouldn't be here right now, a pool of congealing blood surrounding her.

"Martin." Dead eyes stare ahead.

The sounds of a plastic trash bag being shaken open, of soaked towels being slopped inside, drift to her as if through pudding.

"Martin." He blinks but doesn't move. She kneels close to him and repeats his name, more forcefully this time. She doesn't have the time or energy to feel guilty about her tone. He flinches and looks her way. "We need to get you and the baby home."

He stares at Lucinda, looking but not seeing.

"Martin, your baby is hungry. You need to feed her, and there's nothing here for her to eat. Did you keep the formula that came with the nursery womb?"

"I think so?" he answers feebly after a moment. His gaze settles once more on Celeste's lifeless body, only averting when her Sisters wrap it in one of the waterproof sheets from the bed.

Lucinda places her hands on Martin's shoulders until he raises his eyes to meet hers. "Martin, I need you with me right now. Your baby needs to eat so she can stay healthy. The girls will take care of Celeste. I promise. But right now, we need to get you and the baby home."

Martin's eyes moisten, but he shows no sign of moving.

"Martin, Look at your daughter. Look at her." He slowly obliges and, when he sees her face twisted up in hunger, something inside him seems to awaken. He cradles the baby awkwardly, standing in slow, halting movements. "Okay," he says through the oily curls hanging in his face. "Let's go, then."

Lucinda holds the baby as Martin cleans himself up, changing clothes and washing the blood from his skin. She has to fight against muscle memory and the instinct to offer her breast when the little girl's cheek rubs against her chest.

Lucinda's black clothing is forgiving, disguising stains Lucinda would rather not consider. After returning the baby to Martin and splashing some water on her puffy face she determines she can pass as a sleep-deprived new mother, though hopefully there will be no need.

Lucinda leads Martin down the stairs to the building's back exit rather than through the gardens. Though the other Sisters weren't called to receive them as they usually are for a birth, it wouldn't do to cross paths with anyone. The car she summoned is waiting in the loading area. Behind it parks a large black van, and a short, stocky woman, vaguely familiar, gets out. From the back of the van, she pulls a long red board with black straps fastened at each end and around the middle. She rushes into the building behind them, acknowledging Lucinda with a glance as she passes. With her arm around Martin's shoulders, Lucinda gently steers him away from the van and toward the back seat of the car.

"Anabel," Martin croaks once they're on the road. With effort, Lucinda breaks her gaze away from the window and focuses on him. He clears his throat. "When we found out she was a girl, we decided to name her Anabel. It's good she's a girl," he continues with a wan smile. "We never could agree on any boy names." The tears stream down his face so easily, he's probably not even aware of them.

"Oh, thank goodness," Lucinda mutters when she finds the formula stacked on the top shelf of the closet in Celeste and Martin's nursery. She brings a box into the kitchen, trying to focus over baby Anabel's cries as she runs her finger along the instructions. As the first bottle is warming, she programs the autochef to make regular bottles and the mini-dishwasher to clean and sterilize them.

Martin's tears fall onto the blanket wrapped around his daughter as he feeds her for the first time. Lucinda squeezes his shoulder, then turns and walks back down the hall.

The womb is set up in the nursery, a flimsy decoy to keep up appearances. Lucinda punches in a birth time of 7:50 yesterday evening, enters the baby's name, and waits for the acceptance message. Then she finds the disassembly instructions and follows them as if Celeste and Martin's baby has just come out of it. She drains the fluid into a bucket and then pours the bucket into the bathtub in the hall bathroom. She rinses and dries the pieces and replaces them into the bin in which they came, ensuring all the components are packed before sealing it up for shipment back to the medical agency. There, it will be sterilized and sent to another family who's been granted permission to have their baby. What are the chances the womb will go to another Society member, sitting unused for another nine months? Will that family, too, be mourning a tragedy as they pack the bits and pieces away? Probably not. But maybe.

In the dim light, she can see the mural Celeste had been painting for the nursery, the intricate garden scene she didn't have the time to finish before leaving for the birthing suite. "I want it to be just right," Celeste said as Lucinda helped pack the necessities for Celeste and Martin's leave. "I'll finish it while the baby naps," she said with a wink. It was a joke, meant to poke fun of the big plans new parents always have for their child's naptime—plans that never fail to be frustrated by babies' own plans—and the three of them laughed.

Tears begin to fill Lucinda's eyes as she runs her fingers along the outline. She sniffs and blinks them away. So much will remain unfinished now that Celeste is gone, and Anabel will never know her goofy, kind, amazing mother.

Lucinda turns away from the mural and there is the bin once more, sitting dumb in the middle of the room, ignorant of her pain. She walks toward it, rage coursing through her veins like acid. In her mind she howls and picks it up, heaving it onto the ground and smashing the nursery womb into a million tiny pieces. She wishes she could destroy every single one of these machines—these shameful substitutes for growing human life, these instruments the world has used to rob women of what they were born to do. It is this womb's fault that Celeste is gone. The culture that created this womb made childbearing—the most natural thing in the world—burdensome and obsolete. With both hands, she moves to lift the heavy container, but instead, her knees buckle underneath her.

Her head is resting on top of the bin, her shoulders heaving, when footsteps enter the nursery. She stands abruptly, swiping at her eyes as Astor enters.

The Sisters must have finished cleaning up the suite. Celeste is surely gone now, taken to wherever Yvette Blair takes bodies when they're finished living. Astor's cheeks are red and swollen. "Hey," she says. "I came to see if you needed anything. Looks like you got everything settled, though."

"Astor," Lucinda says, but it's all she can get out. Astor moves closer and wraps her arms around Lucinda, an unspoken invitation to let it all out.

After a minute Lucinda's sobs have slowed, and she takes a hitching breath. "Who the hell do we think we are?" she asks, her voice muffled in Astor's shoulder. Astor pulls back and their eyes meet. "Who are we," Lucinda says, "to think we can do this, without any real training, without support, without any damn experience? Nobody ever said it was going to be this way."

"They didn't know how it was going to be." Astor's arms fall to her sides and her icy eyes pierce Lucinda's. "They only knew what they read in some books from a hundred years ago. They're not any better trained than we are. And now our friend—the woman we've been told to call Sister since the day she was born—is gone. A baby is going to grow up without a mother because some old women decided to write their own rulebook and then dump the responsibility onto our backs. You're asking the wrong question, Lucinda. We're not the ones to blame for all this. You should be asking, who do *they* think they are?

2

EMEKA HANGS HIS SUIT JACKET ON THE BACK OF THE kitchen chair. He leans down and kisses Abigail on the forehead, just where white hair meets smooth brown skin, as he's done every morning for the better part of a lifetime. Her smell drifts into his nose, and he smiles. "Good morning, gorgeous."

"Hello, darlin'," she says, cupping his hand with her own and leaning into his kiss.

His coffee is waiting for him, steaming in his favorite *#1 Papa* mug. He and Abigail sit in a familiar silence as the sun gradually seeps in through the windows. Emeka sips his coffee, smooth and sweet, while Abigail does the day's word puzzle on her mobile. Little by little, natural light illuminates Abigail's skin. Her face turns up into a mischievous grin as she pretends to ignore Emeka's admiring gaze. Even after all these years, this is still his favorite part of every day.

"We still meeting Adi and Micah tonight?" Emeka asks.

"Mmm-hmm," Abigail says. "What about dinner at Sofu's before the show? Micah's pick."

Emeka's mouth waters reflexively at the suggestion of Nigerian flavors. Sofu's is the only place he's ever had bitterleaf soup that lived up to his grandmother's, and the fact that his granddaughter suggested it makes his cheeks flush with pride. She's at that age where they don't get too excited about anything, where their connections with adults begin to thin. He smiles, remembering Micah's weight on his lap as she tried bites of his boyhood food from his fork. "Well, how could I turn that down?"

A notification from Emeka's mobile announces the arrival of his car. He tips his mug, savoring the last milky sweet drops, then shrugs on his jacket and squeezes Abigail's shoulder. "Have a good day, sweets. I'll pick you up at the shop."

"You too, darlin'," she says. He closes the door on his way out, but not before he takes in that sweet smile of hers.

On the drive, his content aggregator warns him to expect rain later in the week and catches him up on the weekend's news headlines, holding his work messages until he's at his desk. The closer he gets, the larger and more imposing the surrounding buildings become, until the car stops in front of the tallest of them all, the steel-and-glass-grid that houses the Bureau's downtown office. He checks his reflection in the mirror before getting out. Creases outline all the places touched by his smile, and he finds fewer black hairs and more gray ones each day. Signs of a full and happy life, Mama always used to say.

Emeka walks into the building with a nostalgic smile touching his lips, picturing his mother's round face and gap-toothed grin. She'd be proud if she could see the life he's made for himself here. A beautiful family. A long career upholding the law, working for what's right. His life has been very full and happy, indeed.

The offices and cubicles on the 72nd floor sit darkened, empty, and silent, reluctant to let the weekend go just yet. Maybe he'll have time to get oriented to the week before the drop-ins start. Motion-sensitive lights follow behind him as he makes his way past the conference rooms and the cluster of snack machines in the corner, finally arriving at his cubicle.

His messages this morning are sparse: a commendation from Director Araleus for a quick case closure and a notification of reassignment for a couple of junior agents—a promotion for each. He sends a quick congratulations to Agents Cane and Neruda, and then his eyes linger over the last message.

Bureau Gala: Important Update, it reads. After a moment's hesitation, he clicks the link, scanning down until he finds the words he's looking for: Keynote Speaker, Detective Emeka Abuto. His heart pounds. Is he nervous? Excited? A little of both, maybe. It's not something he'd volunteer to do. He'd much rather be in the audience listening to some other old man talk about his long career in law enforcement than to be the old man talking.

"What would I even say?" he said to Araleus when she asked him about it for the third time.

"I don't know, Abuto. Some inspirational words for us youngsters. Surely you can think of something. You've been a detective longer than half of these agents have been alive, probably closed more cases than all of them combined." She wasn't pleading, exactly, but her voice was higher-pitched than usual. It was important to her that he do this. He'd feel guilty not doing it, especially after letting the invitation sit unanswered in his inbox for so long. Who knows? Maybe he'll enjoy it. He'll have to ask the girls for ideas for the speech at Sofu's tonight.

Inbox cleared, he begins reviewing his case files one by one, creating a to-do list for the day. Looks like it'll be a slow start to the week.

"You know the work day doesn't start for another half-hour, right?" The voice of Director Araleus snaps his concentration away from his work. This is exactly why he likes to get here early.

"At my age, I'm going to bed when the rest of you are finishing work," Emeka says with a wink. "Gotta come in early to make up for it."

The director's smile is without humor. She takes a step into the cubicle. "May I?"

Emeka gestures to the chair next to his desk, and Araleus sits. Emeka turns away from his work. "What's on your mind, boss? This about the speech?"

Araleus sets her mouth in a grim expression. "I wish it was. New case came in this morning, premature death of a thirty-four-year-old woman, a Ms. Harlow. Medical examiner says it looks like an aneurysm rupture. I want you to close it out."

Emeka's eyes soften. "Thirty-four," he says, shaking his head. That's a few years younger than his daughter. Such early deaths are almost entirely unheard of these days. But every so often, there's a case like this. The human body is complex. Even with the implants monitoring just about every aspect of health, sometimes the body does something unexpected, and then…gone.

"I've got it," he says.

"Great. I'll send you the case file."

"Okay, boss," Emeka says, and the conversation is over. Araleus has never tried to micromanage him as other supervisors have done. She trusts his process and experience. That's why they get along so well.

Emeka picks up the photo frame on his desk as he waits for the file from Araleus. Abigail, Adi, and Micah, three generations of beautiful Abuto women, at Micah's fifth-grade graduation a couple of years ago. Matching dresses, yellow with white flowers, stand out against their smooth, dark skin. The silver earrings he bought them all for the occasion glint in the sunlight. His heart sinks. This Harlow woman's family must be crushed. If anything happened to his girls, he doesn't know how he'd get through it.

Emeka's mobile beeps with an incoming message, and the case file appears on the screen. He puts down the photo. So much for coming in early and organizing his day. He's going to have to put the rest of his investigations on hold while he clears this up. No bother. He wouldn't have made it this long at the Bureau if he couldn't handle a speed-bump or two.

He's walking out of the building before many of his colleagues have arrived, and a car stands waiting to take him across town for his first interview of the Harlow case. This investigation should be short. They always are. Just the crossing of *t*'s and dotting of *i*'s. With any luck, he'll be wrapping it up and back to his other cases by the end of the day.

The door to the medical examiner's office is tucked away in the back corner of the hospital. Emeka stands in front of it, waiting for the door to open. He's projected the Harlow file to the overlay on his glasses, so he doesn't hurt his old neck staring down at his mobile, and he's reviewing the file for a second time. He's about to press the buzzer again when the lock finally clicks open.

"Detective Abuto," the medical examiner greets him. Her dark hair is pulled back into its usual neat bun, but today her eyes are rimmed with red.

"Good morning, Dr. Blair," Emeka says. "Nice to see you again."

The doctor doesn't return his smile. "You as well. This way," she says, turning before he can offer a hand. He catches the door before it closes on him and follows the doctor through the network of deserted hallways to the examination suite. He last saw Dr. Blair after those two teenagers were killed trying to cross the train tracks a few months back. They've worked some tough cases together, but she's never been this gruff.

"Sorry if you had to wait long," she says. "I was in the middle of an exam when you buzzed."

"Not a problem, Doctor," Emeka says, attempting a smile once more. Blair doesn't seem to notice. It's not the most uplifting of professions, but usually she at least makes an attempt at small talk. Not today. She sits atop a high stool on one side of the peninsular countertop she uses as a desk and gestures for him to sit opposite her.

Before Emeka can ask anything, she brings up a file on her computer and begins to read. "Thirty-four-year-old Celeste Harlow, sudden death by apparent aortic aneurysm rupture." She pauses and swallows. "She died in the middle of the night in her living room. Her partner declined a detailed autopsy, and the body was cremated within twenty-four hours per DPH regulations. Her implant was, of course, retained. I have it here for you," she adds, holding out a small vial with a chip inside, so tiny it's nearly invisible.

A pop of bright purple flashes in her hand as he takes the vial from her. He must have forgotten to turn off his overlay when the doctor greeted him at the door. Though he's never felt inclined to get a photogram tattoo, he's seen plenty of them. Tiny microchips embedded just below the skin's surface project an image that can only be seen with enhanced viewing technologies like augmented reality visors and overlays like the one in his glasses. This one disappears from view before he can tell what it is.

"I see," he says, securing the vial in a pouch inside his small handbag. "Did anything stick out during the examination?"

Dr. Blair shakes her head. "No. You can read everything in her history, though. She was attended by her family physician on the scene, who certified the cause of death, and our office concurred, from what we can tell without an autopsy." Her lips press together. "So sad."

Sad is right. How awful for this woman and her family. Thirty-four is far too young. "No sign of harm? Entry or exit wounds? Bleeding?"

"No wounds," she says. "And most of the bleeding was contained inside her body, aside from some regurgitated blood we found in her mouth. No reason to suspect foul play."

"But the partner declined the autopsy. Why?"

The doctor shrugs, shifting her eyes from the Harlow file to Emeka and back. "He said he trusts the doctor's conclusion, based on her health data."

"Anything else of note from your office?" Emeka asks. There's no need for an extended interview. The analysts at the office will extract any important information from the implant.

"No, nothing," she answers, looking down at her hands. "Everything was routine, aside from Ms. Harlow's unfortunate age." She lowers herself from her seat and moves toward the door to show Emeka out.

"Thank you, Dr. Blair," he says. She turns once more in his direction, and he searches her face. She looks past him rather than at him, and her eyes seem to be redder than they were even a few minutes ago when she opened the back door for him. "Doctor, are you feeling okay?" he asks.

She finally makes eye contact with him. "Yes, of course. I'm fine. Why?" she asks.

"It's just—I can't help noticing how red your eyes are." His voice conveys his genuine concern. But his professional curiosity is also piqued. Dr. Blair sees dead people every day. Why would she feel especially strongly about this one?

"Oh. No," Blair answers. "It's just the reagents. The chemicals we use. I was using a particularly irritating one just before you arrived. I should really go wash my face."

Emeka nods. "Thanks for your time, doctor. If anything comes up, don't hesitate to give us a call." He reaches out a hand.

She accepts his handshake this time, and he catches one more glimpse of the curious photogram in her palm. Something animated. He can't tell what. "Sure thing, Detective Abuto."

Back in the car, Emeka sets the address of his next visit. Item one, done. One more stop and, if all goes as expected, he should be able to close out this case and get back to his others.

As soon as the thought crosses his mind, a voice in the back of his head pipes up. Not so fast, old man, it says. Something doesn't seem right here. Sure, family members have the right to decline an autopsy. But why, especially when the deceased was only thirty-four? If it was Emeka, he'd want answers, if only to confirm the doctors' guess about her cause of death. Then there's Dr. Blair. He doesn't buy her excuse about the reagents—this case affected her emotionally in a way he's never seen before. He's been a detective long enough to know not to ignore the small stuff.

He'll figure it out, though. He'll follow the story where it leads, and the answers will come. Hard or easy, fast or slow, Emeka's job is to close the cases. He'll close this one just as he's closed all the others. If it ends up taking a little longer, so be it.

3

SHE IS FALLING.

Down off the bank and into the river. Through the water, until she should have reached the bottom by now. She bobs back up and takes a gulp of air but keeps falling, rushing downriver. Mama's face falls away, and soon it's gone.

She's still awake when the rushing stops. She lies face up in the calm shallows, trying to tell if she's got any injuries. In just a few minutes, the river has brought her to a place she doesn't recognize, farther than she's ever explored before. She crawls on bruised knees to the water's edge, walking toward the place where she fell. Or she hopes so, anyway.

Her shoes have disappeared, and she wears only one sock, soggy and useless. She takes it off and squeezes out the water, then ties it around her wrist. Her sundress, a gift from her twelfth birthday just last month, is soaked, but when the sun comes out from behind the clouds it kisses her brown skin and she is warm, for now. Her braids have fallen out, and her long, shiny hair is matted with sticks and leaves. She doesn't bother trying to take them out. Aunt Elle will brush it out for her when she gets home.

Home. Upriver. She walks.

No bears out here, or at least she hasn't seen any in all her exploring. Nothing that bites worse than a mosquito. The plants are more dangerous than the animals, she thinks, scanning the tree trunks. Poison ivy. She'll need a scrub when she gets back.

She stops hard and weaves, avoiding a huge nettle. Maybe that's what caught her hand. When she rubs the tiny bump in her palm a sharp pain pokes into her flesh. The photogram, she remembers. Mama put it there before they left the city, a quiet celebration between the two of them. Lucinda stands a little straighter. She's a woman now. And all her Sisters will know it.

She needs to get back. The sun is already below the trees, and it will just keep sinking until it's too dark for her to find her way. That's when the real monsters come out. Lucinda tells herself she's not hearing them, breathing and waiting all around her.

Mama will be looking for her, at least. She'll know which way the river carried Lucinda, and she'll come find her. Aunt Elle, too. They'll probably be just over that hill. Or the next one. But not Uncle Clark because he's on a camping trip with Daddy and Myles.

She doesn't call out, embarrassed she let herself fall, ashamed to need help getting back. Afraid calling for her mother will be proof of her weakness, a failure of some test she didn't know she was taking.

She walks, barefoot, until it's too dark to trust her eyes. Is there a sharp rock up ahead? A pointy twig? She drags her feet a little, just in case, and keeps walking.

And walking.

Mama's not coming.

Tears well up in her eyes, but she refuses to let them fall.

Twinkling ahead. Eyes? Her pulse quickens. No, lights. The house. She sighs with relief.

Her feet ache and her limbs are streaked with scratches and smears of blood from the brush. Yet as soon as she hits the clearing, she speeds up, picking dried leaves out of her hair as best she can as she runs.

Nobody is waiting outside.

She stops at the water pump next to the old greenhouse where Aunt Elle's grandma GiGi used to keep her plants. She unties the sock from around her wrist and rinses it, then dampens it and dabs at her wounds, soaking up the blood from the scratches on her shins and forearms. She could wait and shower inside. But she doesn't want Mother and Aunt Elle to see her like this, weak and bleeding.

She walks through the back door and into the kitchen, squinting against the bright lights. Her mother is sitting at the table. Places are set for the three of them, though Elle is nowhere in sight. In the center, next to a vase of fresh-cut flowers, sits a pot of something steaming and smelling of onions and garlic and hearty meat.

"You didn't come for me," she says.

"And yet you made it back," Ruma says with a smile that anyone else would mistake as warm. "Now get cleaned up. It's time for dinner."

The scene winks out until her mother's hard, expectant face is the only thing she can see.

Someone is shaking her shoulder. Her eyes squint in the dim light.

"I hate to wake you," Zavi says, "but it didn't seem like you were sleeping all that soundly."

She's at home, in her bed, and in that split second between sleeping and waking, she is blissfully unaware. She doesn't remember getting home, or falling asleep, or what day it is, or why her head feels like it's encased in concrete.

The dream—the memory—comes back first. She can still feel the way her feet and knees ached when she finally reached Aunt Elle's house that night, and for days afterward.

"Where were you?" she asked her mother, only once.

"There was nothing I could do," Ruma said. "The river took you. You got yourself into a situation. I knew you could get yourself out of it. And now, you know it, too."

The pinks and yellows of sunrise have faded to the dull blue-gray of mid-morning. Lucinda would normally be in the office by now, but she can't bring herself to focus on work after all that's happened. Maybe she'll feel more like going tomorrow.

She shares a blanket with Zavi on the balcony sofa, hands cupped around a mug of steaming lemon tea. The heat lamp radiates down upon her. All the hot tea and heat lamps in the world, though, couldn't warm up the tight, cold ball Lucinda feels in the pit of her stomach.

Her eyes are on fire. From exhaustion, from crying, from reading and responding to countless messages. Her Sisters want to check in, see how she's holding up, even commiserate with her feelings of guilt and shock. Other friends, who couldn't know any differently, offer condolences about Celeste's freak accident. It seems everyone she's ever known has reached out in the last couple of days. Everyone except Astor.

Her eyes run absently back and forth over the mini garden she and Serafina have managed to cultivate out here. To the left, to the right, and back again. She's always felt better on the balcony, freer and closer to nature among the basil and tomatoes, the strawberries and rosemary.

Today she feels untethered.

The wind's howling covers the din of the city, but one is no better than the other. Both just add to the jumbled mess inside her head. Opposing viewpoints play on an endless loop like one of those political argument shows she grew up watching with Uncle Clark.

Her Sister is dead. Lucinda was responsible for her care, and instead of caring for her, she watched Celeste die. And she was powerless to stop it.

But no one could have done anything to stop it. These things happen—rarely, but they do happen. It's a part of the nature of things.

If she'd been in a hospital, though, or if a doctor had been there, or if she'd just used the nursery womb like every other woman in the world, then maybe she'd be just fine right now. Lucinda wouldn't be suffocating under this blanket of guilt and grief, and neither would the rest of her Family. *If she'd just used the nursery womb*, she thinks again. Lucinda hates the nursery wombs, but Celeste would be alive if she and Martin had used one.

But the Garden works for the good of the many. She and her Sisters aim to take back reproductive choice for all, and that will never happen if everyone keeps using nursery wombs.

Around and around she goes, the pendulum swinging from one side to the other. How can she feel grief and guilt for Celeste at the same time that she views the loss of one Sister as an acceptable sacrifice?

Acceptable when it's someone else's Sister, she finally allows herself to think. Her stomach turns over.

Zavi is studying her. She runs her eyes over his smooth skin, the curls that have escaped his ponytail, and finally settles on his violet eyes. His brows are raised, expectant. Shit. It must be her turn to talk.

She sighs. "Sorry," she says, tapping her temple. "Stuck in my head."

"It's okay," he says, and his understanding makes her feel even worse for not having heard him in the first place. How many times has this scene repeated since Celeste died? And each time he's responded with unflappable patience. "Are you headed out today?" he says.

"Oh." She straightens. "Oh. Yeah. I'm going to go check on Martin. Then I'll pick up Sera for dinner with my parents, and then we're off to a gathering. Can't wait for that," she says, pumping her fist in mock enthusiasm. She is not looking forward to facing her Family.

"Today?" he asks.

"My mother called a special emergency gathering," she says.

He doesn't take his eyes off her. "And you're sure you're up for it?"

"Up for planting some vegetables, watering some flowers, or pruning some bushes? No big deal," she says. "Every gathering, without fail, we plant something new and tend the growing plants. Out of the dirt, from what seems like nothing, grows new life." She realizes she's slipped into her First Daughter voice, reciting something she's heard—and said—a hundred different ways since she was a child. She drops the character and looks Zavi in the eye. "I'm sure. In a way, it's more important today than ever. I need to be there for the others."

"So, after Celeste, you're not, um, having second thoughts about things?" His concern surprises her. He's never questioned her involvement in the Garden. Not that he's had a choice. "It doesn't make you worry for Serafina at all?"

Does it? No. It can't. She can feel her eyes harden, and she looks at Zavi without really seeing him. "Before Celeste, before me, before the Garden Society, billions of mothers gave birth without intervention. What happened with Celeste is terrible. But it's not the norm. By the time Serafina is old enough, we'll have more support and more experience. If the Sisters in the Governing Council do their jobs, hopefully the laws will be different by then. Even now, though, ninety-nine percent of the time, things turn out just fine." She doesn't regret saying it. It might be a script, but it's also true.

Zavi nods and takes a deep breath, placing his drink down on the table next to him. He reaches out and pulls her close to him. "I know," he says into the top of her head. "It's the other one percent that scares me."

"Sit," Lucinda says to Martin. "Eat something. And then go lie down. Get some rest."

The smell of shrimp lo mein and sweet and sour chicken wafts from the takeout cartons on the dining table. Lucinda stopped at the tiny corner restaurant on the way here, and it's a good thing she did. The autochef has seen better days.

"I've never seen both the orange and red warning lights go off at once," she said when she arrived. "I'm impressed."

"Oh, yeah," was Martin's vague reply as he wiped crust out of one eye. "Low on dry ingredients. Low on liquids. Low on everything. I keep meaning to do an order."

Some color returns to his face with what might be his first meal since she last saw him. He's in the kitchen, staring blankly at the autochef's display, when Lucinda shoos him away. With the press of a button, she clears the errors and schedules the grocery delivery for early tomorrow morning. She'll have to come back and unpack so the food won't go bad before Martin gets around to it.

She doesn't blame him; that's why she's here. She remembers how hard it was to take care of the basics when Serafina was a newborn, and she had a partner to help her with it. Martin is on his own.

A cry erupts from the nursery.

"Don't you dare," says Lucinda, grabbing a warm bottle from the autochef before Martin can. She gently moves him to the side and brushes past. "I will take care of Anabel. You, take a break. You'll have plenty of time to take care of her after I leave."

He sighs behind her, but he doesn't protest. Either he's too worn down to fight or he knows it would be no use anyway. Whichever it is, she'll take it.

In the nursery, Anabel wiggles in the bassinet, all balled fists and scrunched face.

The room already smells like baby, like gentle detergent and unscented diapers and spit-up cloths. Lucinda picks up the little girl and holds her close. She inhales, and it's like breathing in Anabel and Serafina and all the babies that came in between.

Lucinda feels Celeste's absence profoundly in this room. The flowers stare back at her from the half-finished mural as if asking her, "What now?" She sits in the rocking chair and angles the bottle into Anabel's mouth. As the baby eats, Lucinda loses herself in green eyes that are a perfect match for Celeste's.

A message comes in from Adi. *Didn't see you in your office. You okay?* Lucinda mostly keeps to herself at work, but Adi is different. She probably doesn't want to be there today, either.

Meant to tell you I took the day off, she responds. *Checking in on Martin and the baby. See you tonight.* She snaps a quick photo of Anabel and sends it with the message. It's a bittersweet feeling, holding the soft sweetness of Celeste's daughter while only memories of Celeste remain. She wonders if Adi feels it, too, though she wasn't nearly as close with Celeste as Lucinda was. Her only response is a thumbs-up.

When the baby is full and settled, Lucinda changes her and wraps her in a soft fleece blanket. Cradling the baby in the crook of one elbow, she pads into the living room. Martin is reclined on the sofa, snores blaring from his open mouth. On the wallscreen, the menu offers a selection of programs. Poor guy didn't even pick a show to watch before he fell asleep.

She sits, gently rocking Anabel in a baby seat in the living room, batting a toy from time to time to catch the baby's attention. In the silence, she begins to wonder about things she hasn't had the time to consider yet. What happened to Celeste after Lucinda left the suite with Martin and Anabel? How was her death explained? The death of a thirty-four-year-old is more than just unusual. It's a near-impossibility. Surely there will be some follow-up, some questions. Questions which, if Martin's not careful, could lead to answers she and her Sisters can't risk being revealed.

It's an hour before Martin wakes up. "Oh, shit, Lucinda. I'm sorry," he says when he sees the clock, squinting against the afternoon light pouring in through the windows.

"Nonsense," Lucinda says. "I was having a delightful time with your beautiful daughter." She lays a hand on his arm. "Plus, you looked like you needed the rest. Feel better?"

A weak smile turns up the corners of his mouth. He nods. "A little."

"Good." She hands Anabel over to Martin but doesn't move to leave. She watches Martin instead as he looks into his daughter's face, remorse wrapping like a vise around her heart. It wasn't supposed to be like this. It's minutes before she draws up the courage to say what comes next. "Martin," she begins.

He flicks his eyes up to meet Lucinda's.

"I hate to bring this up," she says.

He says nothing, just keeps looking at her with those half-absent eyes.

She should just leave it alone. Martin just lost the love of his life. He's got a newborn to take care of all on his own. There's enough on his mind. But she must be sure the Garden is protected. She takes a deep breath and forces herself to go on. "You and my mother talked about the official story, right?" Regret stabs her in the stomach as soon as the words are out. "I'm sorry, Martin. I trust you. I just…"

"You want to make sure no one ever finds out how she really died," he says. He doesn't lift his eyes. "I understand."

No one talks for a moment. Anabel yawns and looks around the room. Lucinda really should be picking Serafina up by now, but tension hangs in the air as if Martin has more to say.

At last, he takes a deep breath and relaxes his shoulders. "I don't want to get the rest of you in trouble," he says. "I already had my words with Holly. I don't know that we'll be speaking again." It hadn't occurred to Lucinda that Martin might blame Celeste's mother for her death. Now that he's said it, though, it makes sense. It was Holly who made the decision not to safeguard Celeste when she was a baby, after all. "There's no reason to drag the rest of you into it, though. I don't know what I'd say anyway," he adds. "Celeste never really gave me many details."

Relief washes over Lucinda. Sisters are warned not to share any more than the necessary information with their partners, and this is why. She stands and hugs him. "Thank you, Martin," she says. "I've got to go pick up Sera, but I'll be back in the morning to help with the groceries. You take care of that beautiful girl."

Anabel has fallen asleep in Martin's arms. Lucinda kisses her on the forehead. "Good-bye, little one," she says, closing her eyes and taking in one last breath of baby scent before rushing out the door and down the hall.

4

THE ELEVATOR OPENS ONTO CELESTE HARLOW'S FLOOR, and Emeka moves to step out. At the same time, a young woman waiting to step inside nearly bumps into him. The woman was holding her open palm in front of her when the doors opened. Seeing Emeka, she thrusts both hands into her pockets.

"Oh! Excuse me," he says.

"My fault," the woman says. She looks to be in her thirties, with long, black hair. He catches barely a glimpse of her golden eyes before she lowers them and hurries onto the elevator. Just enough for him to be certain he's seen them somewhere before. Emeka searches his memory banks for the woman's face as he follows the placards on the wall to the Harlow apartment.

He knocks, five quick raps, a habit he's held since the Academy. He hears rustling on the other side of the door, and then it opens wide. "Did you—" a man's voice begins, but he stops when he sees Emeka. "Oh. Sorry, I thought you were somebody else," he says flatly.

"Martin Granby?" Emeka asks.

"Yeah," the young man says. He's around 35, pale skin and scraggly brown hair. Dark circles surround his wide, sunken eyes, and his chin sports several days' growth. He holds a clump of fabric to his chest. Some kind of comfort object, maybe the late partner's favorite shirt. But when the unmistakable sound of newborn grunting drifts up from the bundle, Emeka's perspective tilts. Araleus never said anything about a baby.

Emeka clears his throat. "Detective Emeka Abuto," he says, extending a hand. "I'm so sorry to know of your loss, Mr. Granby, and I apologize for the intrusion. I just have a few questions for you, and then I'll be on my way. I'm hoping to close your partner's case as soon as possible."

Martin stands, unmoving and expressionless, for so long Emeka is about to repeat himself. Finally, though, he nods. "You want to come in?" His voice is gruff, his expression vacant. He looks like he hasn't slept in days, and no wonder. Emeka remembers plenty of sleepless days and weeks after Adi was born.

"That would be more comfortable, yes," says Emeka, offering the man a good-natured smile.

"Please," says Martin, standing to the side and gesturing widely with the arm that isn't holding the baby. "You can, uh, just sit at the counter, okay?"

"Certainly," says Emeka. The entryway smells of Chinese food. The dark wood table near the door holds a collection of open takeout containers and two glasses, one full of water and one nearly empty. The kitchen is to his right, separated from the dining area by a raised counter. He perches himself upon a stool and surveys the living area as he waits for Martin to join him.

Straight ahead, beyond the dining area and kitchen, stands the bright white back of a sofa sitting atop a white marble floor, met obliquely with a matching armchair. A column in the middle of the room contains a fireplace, and beyond that, a wall of oversized windows looks out over the street and into the next building over.

"Drink?" Martin mutters from the other side of the counter. He's addressing Emeka, but he's looking out the windows and into nowhere. This man is in quite a state. Emeka's investigated plenty of premature deaths, but this is the first investigation he's conducted with the newly widowed parent of a newborn. Will Martin be able to answer any questions at all?

Emeka offers a sympathetic smile. "No, thank you," he says. "You've got your hands full. Why don't you come and have a seat?"

Martin walks around to the side of the counter where Emeka is seated but doesn't move for a chair. "I'll stand if it's okay. She's only quiet when I'm moving," he says, halfway between apology and explanation. He runs his finger along the baby's cheek and rocks from one foot to the other. "I just can't stand to hear her cry." A tear falls down one side of his face and he makes no effort to wipe it off.

"Of course," Emeka says. "How old?" he asks, gesturing to the collection of blankets in the man's arms.

Martin looks to the ceiling as if counting. "Two days, I guess."

Emeka has to catch his breath. That would mean the baby was just a day old when her mother died. How terrible. "I'm so sorry, Mr. Granby. If you don't mind, I'll go ahead and begin, so you can get back to your day. You might be aware it's standard Bureau policy to investigate any untimely or suspicious deaths. Usually, these meetings are a mere formality, to get the firsthand story on record. I don't want for you to feel nervous at all."

"Sure, okay," Martin says. His voice is as hollow as his eyes.

"Can we just start with your recollection of what happened the morning of your partner's death?"

"Yeah, okay," he says. "Sure."

"Take your time." Emeka touches his glasses, whose camera can capture his visual field. "I'll record our conversation so that we have the record, if that's okay."

"O—Okay."

Emeka taps to begin recording. "Whenever you're ready, Mr. Granby."

"Okay, well, Celeste—and I—*we*—we had the baby, Anabel, just a few hours before."

"And everything went as expected with the birth of the baby?"

Martin looks past Emeka, at the doorway. "Sure. I mean, it's all science, right? She came out of the nursery womb just like the instructions said she would."

"Okay," Emeka says. "And what happened next?"

Martin speaks haltingly. "Well, the baby was up a few times, and we decided to alternate nights at first, and Celeste was taking the first night. She got up with the baby, I'm not sure what time it was, because, you know, because I went back to sleep, and then a little while later I heard the baby crying—like, really crying, hard. Celeste wasn't in bed, and when I checked the nursery, the baby was alone in the bassinet. So I came out into the living room, and that's when I found her." He chokes back a sob here, his face twisting up with agony. Emeka imagines finding Abigail on the sofa in the middle of the night, lifeless. He shudders.

"I'm so sorry to ask you this, Mr. Granby," says Emeka, placing his large hand on Martin's frail elbow, "but can you describe what you found?"

Martin gestures to the living room. "She was sitting on the couch, kind of slumped over, and she was so pale." He chuckles ironically. "Even more pale than usual, I mean. I went to her and tried to get her attention—" he can't go on after this, and Emeka gives him a moment to recover. Martin swallows thickly. "She was cold. Her eyes were open, but she wasn't there."

"What time would you say it was when you found her?"

"I don't know, maybe six?" Martin brings the baby up to his shoulder, rubbing her back and nuzzling her cheek.

"But you're not sure," Emeka says.

"I'm not sure of much of anything," Martin says, almost to himself.

"Was anybody else here at the time, Mr. Granby?"

"No," Martin says, his voice empty. "It was the middle of the night. She was all alone."

"And can you tell me about how it came to be that the doctor arrived?" Emeka asks, ever-so-gently.

"I don't know, I guess I tried to get Celeste back, and then when I went to call for help, I saw a missed call from the doctor. I guess she got an alert. I called her back. Eventually she showed up. I don't really know what happened after that."

"You didn't call for an ambulance?"

Martin shrugs. "I knew it was no use. Dr. Das knew she was gone too. She saw the health logs. She told me to just hang tight until she could get here."

"You declined an autopsy at the coroner's office," says Emeka.

"Right," Martin says. "I didn't want them cutting open her body to find out what we already knew. She'd already been through enough," he adds, looking at the ground. The baby has started to fuss, and he bounces her, whispering, "Shhh, baby."

"Had Celeste complained of any pain lately? Had she been ill at all?"

"No," Martin says. "We'd been on leave together before the baby came, and she seemed great. Just—" he doesn't even blink as the tears fall from his eyes onto his lounge pants. "Just beautiful." His shoulders hitch, and he reaches for a towel from the other side of the counter.

"When did you both take your leave?" Emeka asks.

"Couple months ago, I guess? Maybe two and a half?"

That doesn't sound quite right. While it varies from one family to the next, most expecting parents take twelve weeks of their parental leave before the baby arrives and another forty afterward. He nods, though, because he knows better than to press Martin any further; the man is clearly close to his breaking point. Emeka stands, giving Martin's shoulder a gentle squeeze. He would be larger than Martin on an ordinary day, but he gets the sense that a few days ago, his hand would not have enveloped the younger man's shoulder entirely. "I think that's all for today, Mr. Granby. You should have my information in your messages. Please get in contact if you need to, and I'll be back in touch if I have any more questions."

"O—Okay," Martin says, swaying with the baby, whose fussing has grown more urgent. "I—I should get her a bottle, anyway."

"Right," Emeka says. "Of course." He squeezes Martin's shoulder once more and lets go. "You take care of yourself, Martin, okay? Call some friends, some family. Get some help around here so you can get some rest. So you can grieve."

Martin goes into the kitchen, taking a bottle from the autochef. "Thanks. I'll do that."

"Oh—one more question," Emeka adds over his shoulder as he reaches for the door. Martin looks up at him and mumbles his consent. "Has anyone been by to visit since Celeste's death?"

"Oh, sure," Martin says, and there's a bitterness there that surprises Emeka.

"Friends? Family?"

"Sure. Both. Celeste has—had—a lot of friends. Family, well, we have as much family as anyone has, I guess, and we didn't see them much while she was — while we were expecting Anabel. But our parents and grandparents have all come by at some point to meet the baby, and to pay respects." He removes the bottle from the autochef's delivery compartment, squeezing the nipple onto his forearm and rubbing in the drop of formula before reclining the baby. "I'm going to take her into the nursery now. I'm hoping she'll take a little nap after she eats. Do you mind letting yourself out?"

"No. No, of course not," responds Emeka. Martin disappears down the hallway and Emeka decides to take the scenic route toward the exit, sweeping his eyes from side to side as he makes a circuit around the central fireplace. He lingers at the sofa, running his eyes over the spotless white fabric. It seems incongruous that such a tragedy could have happened in such an immaculate place.

Emeka bows his head and sends peace to Martin and Anabel as he leaves the apartment, softly latching the door behind him.

5

RAP-RAP-RAP. LUCINDA'S KNUCKLES SOUND AGAINST HER parents' apartment door just as they always have. Today more than usual, though, as she holds Serafina's hand in her own, she feels the strangeness of knocking at the door to her own childhood home. Decades of shared experiences combine strangely with the secrets standing around and among them. Celeste's death and the circumstances surrounding it sit like one more shim, compartmentalizing the family further into a collection of individuals, each unable to fully know or be known to the others.

"Enter!" her father sings from the other side of the door.

She pushes the door open to find her dad sitting on a stool, guitar in hand, clumsily picking out a tune. In a week's time, he'll have composed a full instrumental arrangement and probably written vocals as well. During the project's painful infancy, though, ears will bleed as the notes travel from the recesses of his mind to be assembled at his fingertips.

It takes a moment for her to notice her mother on the other side of the counter. She stands in suspended animation, knife poised over a cutting board full of garlic and vegetables, watching Josiah at work. A distant, sad smile touches her lips.

"Papa Jo!" Serafina says, racing toward her grandfather and throwing her arms around both him and the guitar.

Josiah chuckles and lays the instrument on the table, taking the little girl into his lap.

Ruma's head turns in Lucinda's direction. "Hello, girls," she says. Her wistful expression has disappeared, leaving her usual practiced warmth in its place. Always on guard.

"Hi, Mom," says Lucinda. She leans down to kiss her father on the cheek. "Hi, Daddy," she says, resisting the urge to sink into his embrace as she would have done at her daughter's age. Back when there was nothing she couldn't share with him.

She circles around to the kitchen and stands next to her mother, removing a knife from the block and a head of cauliflower from the refrigerator. Josiah lifts Serafina onto the stool next to him and goes back to his guitar.

"Don't mind him." Ruma points her chin toward Josiah. "He's just busy trying to write the song that will change the world."

Lucinda chuckles.

"I heard that," Josiah says. "Kids, don't listen to her. I do not write ordinary *songs,*" he says, speaking in an exaggerated baritone, "I use my musical genius to write extraordinary *compositions*. You should be honored simply to witness such greatness." He winks at a grinning Serafina.

"So sorry, your musical majesty," says Ruma, bowing her head in Josiah's direction. She wipes her hands on a towel and rounds the counter toward where he sits. She tousles his sandy hair; he reaches out and snags her around the waist, pulling her close, the two of them separated only by the guitar. She leans in, giving him a brief peck on the lips before attempting to back away. He doesn't loosen his grasp, though, and she falls sideways into his lap in front of the guitar, laughing and wrapping her arms around his neck.

Josiah loves to tell the story of how he and Ruma met at one of his shows, back when Josiah used to play at bars and clubs, and Aunt Elle used to drag Ruma out to those same places. "She's the only thing I could see that night," her father always says. "Those golden eyes cut right through the stage lighting." And Ruma chimes in, "Your Aunt Elle was busy chatting up this handsome military guy she'd just met—who turned out to be your Uncle Clark—but to me, everything fell away and your father was the only other person in the whole club."

Lucinda smiles to see them like this even after so many years of marriage. Still, she wonders how her parents' love could seem so effortless and genuine despite the skeletons that have piled up between them. Her father is an innocent, a goofy old creative with a grin that turns wide, earnest eyes into squinting slits. He's never kept a secret in his life. He deserves better.

Lucinda is not bitter like Astor. She's not upset with her mother for putting her into this situation. She doesn't mourn her so-called ability to choose. But she does regret, fiercely, the secrets she must keep from her father.

"Apology accepted," says Josiah, his eyes following the sway of Ruma's wide hips as she returns to the kitchen next to Lucinda. Lucinda shakes her head and smiles faintly as she watches her father continue to piece together the melody on his guitar. Despite the exaggerated bluster, he has a real gift. When he finally finds what he's looking for, he catches Lucinda's eye and winks. The two exchange the kind of well-worn-in smile that only two people who share a heart can. Then, he hops from his stool and disappears down the hall.

Serafina darts behind him. The music room is her favorite room in her grandparents' apartment. She's got little instruments and headphones in there, and she loves pretending to make music alongside her Papa Jo. Lucinda knows she won't see either of them again until they're called for dinner.

She stands next to Ruma at the cutting board, rocking her knife back and forth with a practiced hand. They work in silence for interminable moments as the familiar sounds of music-making drift toward them from the other end of the apartment.

Lucinda swallows. The last thing she wants is to confront her mother. But she owes it to Celeste and her family to find out why Ruma—a doctor; someone who could have intervened and possibly even saved Celeste's life—didn't show up until it was too late. She opens her mouth to speak at last, but Ruma speaks first, as if to head her off.

"Have you been to see Martin?" Ruma asks, keeping her honey-thick voice even lower than usual.

"I went this morning," she says. "I ordered him a grocery delivery, stayed with Anabel for a bit while he got some rest. He looked like he hadn't slept at all since…" she lets her voice trail off.

"He's having a hard time," says Ruma. What an understatement.

"Of course he is. One day, he has a happy and healthy partner. The next, he has this tiny baby to raise by himself. Wouldn't you be a mess?" Lucinda can't help the bitterness that creeps into her voice, though it's directed as much inward as toward her mother.

Seconds pass. "Would you say he poses a threat?" asks Ruma.

Lucinda stops chopping. She sets the finely-honed knife down and turns toward her mother. "A threat? Is that really what you're concerned about? Not, how is he coping with the loss of his partner and the responsibilities of fatherhood and the guilt of watching the mother of his daughter die in front of his eyes and not being able to do anything about it?"

"Lucinda, please. Lower your voice. Do we really need to have this conversation right now? I feel for Martin, I truly do, and I am just as devastated as you are at Celeste's death. But we've already lost her. There will be many more lives at stake if Martin doesn't…" Ruma sighs but doesn't finish her thought. "There will be an investigation," she says. "There always is in the case of premature death. Martin will be questioned. It's essential for all our safety that he keep quiet about what happened."

Lucinda resumes chopping. "Of course he's not a threat," she mumbles. "That's like asking if Zavi's a threat. He knows what's at stake just as well as we do." After a moment she adds, "Besides, I already talked to him about it earlier today."

"And?" Ruma asks. Just the question. No acknowledgement for anticipating her mother's concerns and trying to protect the Society. But why should Lucinda expect any different?

"And I'm as certain as I can be that he'll keep quiet." How certain can she be, though? She wants to believe Martin wouldn't expose the Society. But, as much as Celeste's death was an unpredictable tragedy, who knows what will happen in Martin's mind once he's left alone to think about it. Celeste would still be alive, after all, if not for the Garden Society. And it seems he's already said as much to Celeste's mother.

Ruma's eyes pierce through her daughter for a moment, and Lucinda meets them as coolly as possible. "Start the oil, will you?" Ruma finally says.

Lucinda obeys. She wouldn't know how to cook at all if not for these regular dinners; Ruma is the only person she knows who makes her own meals rather than having the autochef prepare them. "It's just not the same," Ruma has always said, "having a machine cook your food. Where's the love in that?"

Lucinda's never been able to taste a difference.

"Where were you?" Lucinda murmurs when she's back at her mother's side. Her twelve-year-old voice echoes in her mind. All these years later, she's still asking her mother the same question.

A moment's hesitation, no longer than a breath. "I was held up."

"At three in the morning?"

No response.

"You're her doctor of record. Didn't you get an alert when she started losing blood?"

"That's none of your concern."

"Not my concern?" Lucinda hisses. "Not my concern that the one person who could have helped her didn't show up and then left me to deal with the fallout? Do you think Evie would have approved of that?"

Ruma has turned her back to Lucinda and is sautéing the onions, waiting for the right moment to dump in a small dish of minced garlic. Her shoulders stiffen at the mention of the Society's leader, the mysterious guiding figure who no one in the Society ever seems to have met. Lucinda doesn't even know if she's alive anymore. "It's more complicated than that, Lucinda, and now's not the time to get into it. It happened so fast, anyway. There was nothing anyone could have done." Barely audible, she adds, "She was gone before you ever arrived."

The elevator is waiting when Lucinda and Ruma approach through the tunnel of foliage on the greenhouse's main floor. Serafina ran ahead so she could do her customary trail of cartwheels through the tunnel, and she's already pressed the button to open the door. "Come on, turtles!" she giggles.

"Coming, little rabbit," Ruma calls with a smile, though there's no way Lucinda would have gotten away with saying something like that when she was a girl.

"Can we go up? Please?" Serafina asks once they're all inside. She gives Lucinda her most persuasive smile, big golden eyes looking up through long eyelashes. Some days, they ride up to the mezzanine and hold hands, looking out over the immense indoor landscape and trying to identify as many species as possible from the high perch.

"Not today, kiddo," says Lucinda. "We're already running late."

The pout is instant and intense, but it just as quickly fades when Lucinda opens her hand to reveal the purple lotus photogram that grants them entrance to the hidden gardens below. Sera doesn't have overlay glasses with her, but she bounces with anticipation all the same. When the scanner's LED turns green, Lucinda nods. A reluctant grin shines through Sera's frown and she presses the down button. She's always been delighted by this shared secret, the photogram possessed only by Sisters of the Garden Society, and the access it brings to hidden worlds.

The others are already at the Family plot when the three of them step off the elevator. The familiar smell of earth infuses the space as pairs of mothers and their unaltered daughters cultivate and plant, water and trim. Lucinda remembers when their plot was the only spot of green in the expansive greenhouse. As more women joined, more Family plots were cultivated, and now purple lotuses appear and vanish all around, signaling the opening and closing of hands hard at work.

Serafina wiggles away, joining the other children at a rose bush where they take turns clapping each other's hands in rhythm. For a moment Lucinda's mouth moves absently along with theirs, reciting a chant from another lifetime, blonde curls and green eyes flashing in her mind.

Celeste's absence echoes painfully here. Lucinda can almost see her Sister as she was just days ago, feet folded beneath her and a tray of seedlings at her side, surrounded by a trio of young girls clambering to place their hands atop her bulging belly. She was so patient with the curious youngsters, describing everything from her changing energy levels to how baby hiccups feel from the inside. Their mothers, too, soaked in every word. Outside, childbirth is a matter of predictable convenience. A cheek swab, a trait-selection session on the BabyMaker app, and nine months watching the baby grow in a nursery womb. Only inside the Garden can these

Sisters witness the incredible life-giving work a woman's body is capable of. Work that their bodies will one day carry out, as well.

If it doesn't kill them.

The adults exchange subdued greetings and embraces. She can almost touch the raw, unspoken sorrow hanging in the air. An enormous gray rain cloud, draining life rather than nourishing it.

Ruma's eyes scan the Family once, and then again. Her brow creases. "Astor?"

Lucinda avoids her mother's eyes. "I haven't heard from her since Celeste." She winces even as she says it. Such a beautiful name, fitting for the most delicate and graceful person she's ever known. And now it's shorthand for the worst trauma she could imagine.

No one else has seen Astor either; even Astor's mother hasn't heard from her, though that doesn't surprise Lucinda considering their strained relationship.

"You need to find her," Ruma says, and Lucinda's stomach clenches.

No, she thinks reflexively, surprising herself. But then she looks around at the others, a collection of mirrors returning her gaze. Eyes wide, expectant. Of course this is now her responsibility. Why should she be surprised?

Lucinda begins to protest but thinks better of it. She's it. She's always been it. The one to get things done. The one to just take care of it. The one who knows what to do, what to say, where to shine the light when the path is unclear. And even though any number of other Sisters *could* find Astor, figure out where she's been, talk some sense into her,

Lucinda knows that she's the one who ultimately will. And she suspects it won't be pleasant when she does.

Ruma takes her place at the head of the group, her bright pink dress flowing like water as she moves. She brushes back a strand of hair that has escaped her long braid, and the jingle from her gold bracelets reverberates through the greenhouse. The women and girls stop working their garden plots and turn toward her. Ruma smiles. "Welcome, Sisters."

Ruma extends her hand to reveal her photogram, and the other women follow. Lucinda feels a familiar swell in her heart at the sea of matching purple projections, at the full scale of all the women who have come of age alongside her. Here with her Sisters, she has always felt at home. How will it ever feel the same without Celeste?

"Let's begin," says Ruma.

A hushed chorus sounds. "We are the Sisters of the Garden Society. We are the seeds of the next generation. We are the few who remember how the human seed is planted and grown, and we will pass our knowledge down to our daughters and theirs. We support and rely only on one another, for our lives and our daughters' lives depend on it. Evie's words guide us for the good of the many."

The Sisters recite their parts, but the words barely register. Days ago, everything was normal. Now Celeste is dead, Astor is absent, and Lucinda is the sole pillar upon which the entire Family balances. Is this what she wants? With everyone leaning on her for support, does what she wants even matter?

The air around Lucinda, usually alive with smiles and hugs and life updates, is tense and thick. Last week,

Micah was beginning rehearsals for the school play. Astor started a new job as an Assistant Council Attorney. Adam, the first baby Lucinda helped deliver, was learning to read. Now, the empty space where Celeste last knelt speaks more loudly than any of their voices.

The women don't turn to the Family plots like they usually do when the mantra ends. Instead, they remain facing Ruma as she announces what Lucinda and her closest Sisters already know. It's a devastating loss, she says, but it's important to keep things in perspective. It's incredibly rare for such a thing to happen, after all. It was just bad luck. Ruma's eyes do their best to look sad, but her voice is as solid as ever. Lucinda is glad it's her mother up there and not her.

When Ruma finishes, the other Families file out, solemn faces offering condolences to Lucinda and her Sisters as they pass the central garden plot. It's all Lucinda can do to keep her face from cracking into a thousand pieces.

After a few minutes, only Lucinda and her Family remain. The greenhouse is quieter than Lucinda has ever seen as the women look over their plot, avoiding each other's eyes.

After a minute, a voice pipes up. "Why isn't Astor here?" It's Alice, a young teen whose hair is twisted up in pink spirals. She showed up with her mother at the birthing suite, after Celeste was already gone. Her eyes are still haunted by the horror of that morning.

Lucinda steels her gaze with the practiced confidence her Sisters have come to expect. She could cover for Astor, but what would she say? Nothing is as important as Garden Society gatherings. "I don't know," she says instead.

The rest of the children snap their heads up to look at Lucinda, while the adults keep their eyes down and fuss with the plants and the soil, listening but not interjecting. Lucinda realizes, not for the first time, just how blurry the line between parent and Sister has become over the years. Everyone is responsible for everyone else, and Lucinda is responsible for them all. She never asked to be the teacher, to be the protector. It just happened over the years. Being the First Daughter of the Garden Society has brought with it the responsibility for all those that came after her. And now, she's stuck with it.

"But missing the gathering isn't allowed," says Alice.

"Except in extraordinary cases," Lucinda reminds her. There's always an asterisk.

"How is Astor's case extraordinary and mine's not?" the girl fires back. "We were both there. I saw it, too."

"Alice!" hisses her mother, suddenly looking up from her work and shooting an apologetic look at Lucinda and Ruma. It's a fair question, though, and one Lucinda can't answer. Even Holly is here, after all, and it was her daughter who died. Alice sends a venomous look to her mother, but she says nothing more.

"Celeste is dead," says Micah, staring intently at the handful of braids she's twirling between her two fingers.

"Yes, she is," Lucinda says.

"She died having her baby."

Lucinda glances around at her Sisters' faces, still gazing at her. "She did."

Micah finally makes eye contact and Lucinda sees terror in her eyes. Lucinda's heart aches. Micah was so excited about Celeste's birth, so upset about missing it. But it's a good thing she did. It would have broken her.

Lucinda runs her eyes over each girl in turn, carefully measuring their expressions. Fear. Sadness. Bewilderment. They deserve answers. Ruma has always emphasized the importance of Sisters believing they know the truth—that they can trust their Mothers and Sisters to never, ever lie to them. As long as they believe the Garden is where they will find the truth, they will keep coming back. Because out there is a world ruled by those committed to erasing the past, while in here exists a world devoted entirely to preserving it.

And so, while it's tempting to do what her mother did and recite the lines they all know by rote—that this was a rare occurrence and no one could have anticipated it and ninety-nine percent of the time, things turn out just fine— she instead tells the girls the story of Anabel's birth and Celeste's death.

"The baby came earlier than we expected, and we think the placenta caused some internal bleeding," she explains. "Astor and I were right next to her, holding her hands. She wasn't in pain. And she got to hold her daughter, Anabel, before she died." Her expression remains steady as she speaks. She fends off the crack that creeps into her voice and the dampness that seeps into her eyes. Micah still fusses with her hair; the other girls pick at the ground; the youngest climb into their mothers' laps. "Do you have any other questions?"

Fiona, one of the smallest, speaks. "I—I don't want that to happen to me." Her freckled face crumples and it's all Lucinda can do not to fall to pieces right along with her. Instead, she squares her shoulders and reaches out to take the little girl's hands, caked with dirt from working in the vegetable rows. Fiona looks down at their clasped hands, then back up at Lucinda. Her eyes seek a promise Lucinda could never make.

"Of course, Fiona. Of course—we never want this to happen to anyone. I can see why you would be afraid—" She frees one of her hands and makes a sweeping gesture towards Micah and the rest of the girls. "All of you. It's natural for us to be afraid after this kind of…incident." *Us,* she thinks, seeing her mother nod in her periphery. Yes. They are *all* afraid, aren't they? Even Lucinda. Maybe even Ruma.

She can't make promises, but she can put their fear in context, use it to motivate them. "You all are experts on the amazing things our bodies can do to create life. It's just that sometimes, something goes wrong in the process. But even though it happened to our Sister, Celeste, there's almost no chance it would happen to any of you. I wish I could promise you that all the bad things in the world are behind us, but it's not that simple. What I can promise you is that, as our Society grows even bigger and stronger, we will have more help. Our adult members work in places where we can help all our Sisters be safe and healthy. The bigger the Society grows, the easier things will get."

The Garden Society encourages its members to go into a handful of professions, and each one is engineered to provide cover for the Sisters. Programmers, like Lucinda, can study the health monitoring implant system and hack into it, masking data that would otherwise alert health authorities to the intact status of the girls. Sisters are paired with Society doctors who falsify the required safeguarding procedure that would sterilize their infant daughters. They support each other through the issues modern women don't experience like menstruation, pregnancy, and childbirth. Someone is stationed at nearly every gateway, from the Office of the Medical Examiner to the Council Attorney's Office.

The girls stare at Lucinda, eyes wide. They're too young to have considered the Garden's inner workings before; some can't yet understand. The idea that the Society exists outside the greenhouse must seem almost magical.

"The more people we have on our side, the better we will be able to respond when things go wrong. We'll have more doctors, more education, better preparation, better equipment and more experienced people"—here, she casts a glance at her mother—"in the birthing suite."

The girls still look at Lucinda, but the worry seems to have left their faces. Do they feel comforted, that there is a plan guiding them all? She, for one, is comforted, having said the words aloud. Even with all her years in the Society, she's never seen the big picture in the way she's beginning to see it today. Reminding herself of the endgame—even if it is so far away, she may never witness it—makes her feel even stronger in her convictions.

"Remember that having a baby is usually safe—ninety-nine percent of the time, things go just fine. And by the time you are all old enough to be having your own baby, chances are it will be even safer."

"But will we always have to keep secrets?" Micah asks. "Will we ever be able to just, like, be who we are, and not be afraid of getting caught?"

Lucinda pauses. She's spent her entire life simultaneously wishing she didn't have to keep this secret and understanding it had to be so. Her mother has hinted at the consequences—for Lucinda, Ruma, the rest of the Sisters— if they were to be discovered. She's suggested there might come a day when the Society would no longer have to hide. But Lucinda has never let herself imagine that day coming during her lifetime.

"Sometimes it takes a new generation to change things," Ruma says, and all heads turn in her direction. "When Evie and her partners wanted to move from educating women about their potential to helping them achieve it, our founder, Annette Gordon, didn't want anything to do with it. She wanted things to stay as they were because she feared what would happen once women started taking action. But Evie convinced Annette that women deserved the right to choose, and we would never get that right back unless we took it. She was the voice of the new generation, and it was her planning that moved the Garden Society forward.

"That was many, many years ago, and since then we have welcomed not one, but two, generations into our ranks. Evie, the other Mothers, even me—we represent the old guard." She points at Micah. "You all are the voice of the new generation. You might decide one day that it's time for another change. And if you do, you could have a tremendous impact on the world." Ruma pauses as the girls look to their mothers and around to each other. "For now, though, we must move on. For the good of the many."

The Sisters all echo Ruma's words, and in their chorus, Lucinda finds immeasurable comfort.

A renewed conviction sweeps through Lucinda as the Sisters clean up the area, composting trimmings and sweeping up excess dirt from the surrounding pathway. After their work is finished, Lucinda looks over her Family's plot. In the center stands the dogwood her mother planted the day she was born. Her eyes drift from the tree, along the grasses and tufts of tiger lilies, to the seedlings planted today. Lucinda, Astor, and Celeste used to play tag on these stone paths when they were girls, back when the rest of the gardens were just bare stretches of dirt. Now there are so many of them—here and throughout the network of public greenhouses—she can't see where they end.

They've come so far, built so much. Celeste may be gone, but the rest of them are still there. Maybe, like Ruma said, it's time for another change.

Though tonight's was an emergency gathering, outside the usual meeting schedule, Ruma readily gave in to Serafina's request for a sleepover. Of course, Lucinda knows how her mother expects her to be using her child-free time.

"Navigate to Astor's place," she sighs when she's in the front seat of a car outside the greenhouse. She's got no choice. Astor hasn't responded to the messages Lucinda has sent, and each time she tries calling, either the connection cuts off abruptly or the line rings and rings until Lucinda finally gives up.

As the car moves between the tall buildings, mirrored and dumb, left, then right, then straight for ages, she realizes she has no idea what she'll say once she gets there. She could chastise Astor for being so stubborn, so ungrateful, for rebelling for the sake of rebellion. She could threaten her—but with what leverage, if she doesn't respect the Society's influence? Beg her? As if that would work.

She just needs to talk some sense into her. Astor is an attorney. Logic is what she does. Surely if Lucinda just explained it in the right way, Astor would understand. They could move on from this and things would go back to the way they were supposed to be. She just needs to make Astor see.

When Astor's face appears in the cracked door to her apartment, she lets out a sharp breath. "Right on cue," she says when she finally opens the door to allow Lucinda in. "Your mom send you?"

"No," Lucinda says, then more quietly, "Yes. Kind of. We're worried about you."

"Worry? About me?" Astor scoffs, retrieving a drink from the autochef. The air around her smells like gin and tonic. "Worried I'm going to go around telling people all our dirty little secrets, maybe. Drink?"

Lucinda shakes her head. "Why didn't you come today?"

"I needed a break." In the living room, Astor sits in a black leather armchair. Lucinda sinks into the matching sofa and turns her body to face her Sister.

"You can't just do that, though. You can't just—"

"I did, though, didn't I?" Astor says, unblinking eyes boring into Lucinda's. "And what happened? Nothing. They sent you here to fish me back out into the open where they can keep an eye on me."

Lucinda is taken aback by Astor's paranoia. "Astor, what are you even talking about?"

Astor points toward Lucinda's shoulder. There's a spot of dried spit-up on her shirt. It must have been there for hours. "Been to see Martin?" Astor asks, her tone accusatory.

"Yes. Why?"

"Did your mom put you up to that, too?"

Anger rises in the back of Lucinda's throat. "What? No, of course not. I went over to check on him and the baby. To help him out, give him some time to rest. His autochef was empty today, Astor. Do you know how hard it is for an autochef to get down to empty? The man can barely keep it together, and he's got a baby to care for on top of it all. Why haven't you been to see him?"

"Oh, no," says Astor, placing her half-consumed drink on the round table at her side. "Don't start the Most Devoted Sister Contest bullshit with me, Lucinda. I stood and watched my friend die—a senseless death she didn't sign up for—for a cause I don't even believe in. So you'll forgive me if I don't want a constant visual reminder of what I'm already having nightmares about when I finally dare to close my eyes. And don't even pretend you've never thought about what would happen if Martin started talking about how Celeste really died."

Lucinda swallows around a knot of guilt. "Fine, okay, if that's the way you feel. But you can't just not show up at the Garden. We need you there. Especially the younger girls, and especially now."

A humorless smile turns up Astor's lips. "'Yes, girls, when Celeste was born, we signed her up to do this dangerous and illegal thing, whether she wanted to or not, and it killed her. And surprise! We did the same for you. And if you die like her, we'll all be right back here pretending it wasn't our fault. Oh, and you can never tell anybody. And you have to choose from a list of approved professions so you can perpetuate this bullshit for another generation or until we all get arrested or die.' Sounds like a great pitch, right? You sure you want me on that sales team?"

"That's enough," Lucinda says. "It's not like that, and you know it." But she should have known better. Logic may be Astor's love language, but cynicism is her default state. No matter what Lucinda says, Astor is going to spin it around. In Astor's mind, the Society ruined their lives; the rest of them just don't see it yet.

A sudden despair settles in Lucinda's chest. She's lost Celeste, and she's beginning to fear she'll lose Astor, too. She looks up, eyes pleading. "Astor. You were there when Serafina was born," she says, recalling the line of Sisters standing around the bed. With every contraction she had to resist the urge to scream at them all to *getthefuckout!* But she couldn't deny them the opportunity to witness the fruit of their work together—the first natural birth in generations.

Astor wasn't with the others, though, was she? She was tucked away in the corner, arms folded in front of her, magenta hair falling limp over her eyes. The expression beneath that swath of pink stood out against the earnest awe on their Sisters' faces. It wasn't exactly indifference, but it certainly wasn't joy.

But that was six years ago. Surely between then and now she's been able to find some beauty in the Society's work.

"You've been there for plenty of other births, too—births that went completely normally. Listen, I understand this is not what you'd choose for yourself. And you don't have to. But after you've seen what the human body is made to do, how beautiful the bond is between mother and child—after experiencing it all with us—how can you still think what the Society does is wrong?"

Astor shakes her head. There's a sadness in her eyes that borders on pity. She does not reach out her hand, does not embrace Lucinda and comfort her. "I don't want to be a part of it anymore, and I don't think you should, either," she says, standing from her seat and knocking back her drink. "I've already told you my reasons. Come back when you're ready to listen."

6

THE OFFICE OF DR. RUMA DAS IS WARM AND INVITING, A stark contrast to the hospital-white lighting in the corridor. The decor is homey, and it feels more like a living room than a medical office. It even smells comforting—lemongrass and honey, if he's not mistaken.

Dr. Das herself has an equally grounding presence. She's much shorter than Emeka, and she's got a curvy figure under her bright-blue flowing skirt and black top. Something about her reminds him of his mother, a warm comfort he last felt a lifetime ago. Her long black hair hangs down her back in a French braid, and she wears large, intricately made golden earrings and bracelets which make faint music when she walks.

"Thank you again for making the time to see me," he says. She sits in the lounge area of her office and motions for him to do the same. "Mind if I record?" he asks, tapping the arm of his glasses.

When she speaks, her voice feels like molasses in his ears—smooth and thick and melodic. "Of course," she responds with a warm smile. "How can I help you, Detective?"

"I'm here following up on the death of one of your patients—"

"Celeste Harlow," she interrupts, her eyes downcast. "She's the first patient I've lost in a dozen years or more. And so young. I'm happy to help in any way I can."

"I appreciate that, Dr. Das. As you may know, it's protocol to investigate any premature death. Usually, it's just a formality and these things wrap up quickly."

She gives a nod. "I'm happy to answer any questions you have. I'm afraid I wasn't present when she died, though, so I'm not sure how much assistance I can be."

"That was going to be my first question," says Emeka. "You arrived at the scene at what time?"

"I'm not sure exactly, but it was quite early in the morning. Maybe around seven?"

"And can you describe the events up to that point?"

"Sure. Well, I was—I was here, actually, performing my morning meditation, when an alert came in that Celeste was having a health crisis." She gestures to the oversized canvas on the wall to his left, an abstract burst of yellows and oranges that resembles the sun. "During meditation, I turn off all distractions. So, I didn't see the notification until I'd finished. I attempted to contact Martin Granby— Celeste's partner and emergency contact—as soon as I saw the alert. In checking the health monitoring logs from her implant, I saw that she had lost blood volume and blood pressure and that her pulse and respiration had been flat for several minutes already." Her face twitches and she swallows effortfully. "She was already dead by the time I knew anything was wrong. When Martin didn't answer, I rescheduled my morning appointments and headed over to their apartment as quickly as I could."

"And can you describe what you saw when you arrived?"

"When I walked in, she was lying on the sofa, lifeless." She shakes her head. "It must have happened so suddenly. I can only hope that it was peaceful for her."

"What, exactly, did happen?" Emeka asks. "In your clinical opinion?"

"My best clinical opinion is that she had an aneurysm—a weak spot in a blood vessel—that ruptured. Judging by how quickly her blood volume decreased, I am led to presume the rupture occurred in the aorta. The medical examiner confirmed my assessment."

"Mm-hmm," says Emeka. "And did you consider any other possibilities?"

A shadow passes over her face, disappearing almost before Emeka can take notice. "Like what?" she asks.

"You tell me, Doctor. Are there any other conditions that could cause a sudden loss of blood like you saw in Ms. Harlow?"

She looks up and to the side, and Emeka follows her gaze to the digital photo frame on the shelf behind him. "No, Detective," she says after a moment. "I can think of no other explanation in an otherwise healthy woman of her age who takes no medication and sustained no injury."

Emeka nods. "You're the family physician to Ms. Harlow and her partner—and their new child—is that correct, Doctor Das?"

"Yes."

"How long had you been seeing Ms. Harlow?"

"I knew Celeste all her life," she says. Her eyes go glassy for a moment, but she blinks and straightens herself against the emotion. "She was more than just a patient."

"You would have performed her safeguarding and health monitoring implantation procedure as a newborn, then, correct?"

"Yes, that's correct," she says.

"Would you be able to tell me if there are any implant settings that might have provided some warning ahead of an event like this?"

There it is again, that same darkness passing over her face so quickly that he could easily have imagined it. Except that he didn't. "The implant is no more than a data collection and transmission device," she says. "It picks up chemicals in the blood and mechanical vital signs such as respiration and heart rate, but detecting an imperfection in a blood vessel is beyond the device's capabilities. Without imaging, there would have been no way to know the aneurysm was there. And, of course, there was never any reason to perform such imaging."

"I see," Emeka says. "So, in your professional opinion, this was an unpredictable, unpreventable death?"

"Yes, definitely," says the doctor. After a moment she adds, "I'm sure you retrieved her implant from the medical examiner."

"Yes, of course," Emeka responds. It's routine procedure to retain and review the content from health monitoring implants.

"Oh, good," she responds, though she doesn't look relieved. "I am happy to review the data with your office if you'd like. I could run them through the process Dr. Blair and I used to analyze the information."

"Thank you, Doctor," says Emeka. "But that won't be necessary. Our analysts are very skilled at this kind of thing. Now, I'd like to go back to the day of Ms. Harlow's death."

"Sure, okay, but there's not much more to tell. I called the authorities when I arrived and confirmed her death. They sent the medical examiner and some police investigators. I gave a statement to the police and certified the cause of death with the M.E., and they took it from there. I came back here and resumed my work."

"Did you advise Mr. Granby not to call emergency personnel until after you'd arrived at the scene?" asks Emeka.

"I don't recall advising Martin one way or another," she responds. "But I might have. She had been dead for more than a half-hour before we spoke, and if my recollection is correct, I was almost to the apartment by the time Martin returned my call. Paramedics wouldn't have been able to help, and it would have just added to an already chaotic situation for Martin and the baby."

"Are you aware that Mr. Granby declined an autopsy?"

She straightens in her chair once more, her arms crossed in front of her midsection. "Yes. He did mention that to me, yes."

"Did you advise him to do that, as well?"

"Again, I don't recall advising him," she responds, "though there didn't seem to be a need. Celeste was already gone. As I said before, additional intervention would have only added chaos to an already heartbreaking situation. To the best of my recollection, I just gave him my medical opinion about the cause of death, and he made his own decision."

Emeka nods. "I see." Placing one hand on the arm of the sofa, he rocks his tall frame upward and stands. Dr. Das follows suit, standing with her hands clasped until he reaches one of his towards her. "Thank you so much for your time, Doctor," he says as they shake. Her hand is soft and almost limp, his least favorite kind of handshake.

"Of course, Detective Abuto," she says. "Hopefully this matter will be concluded soon, and we can put this tragedy behind us."

She sounds casual, but his senses are on fire. Her responses are seamless on the surface, but she flinched too many times for it to be a coincidence. The more he listens to her smooth and smoky voice, the more certain Emeka feels that there's something this doctor isn't saying. What about her relationship with the Harlow woman has Dr. Das on edge?

He activates the overlay in his glasses as he walks down the corridor, ever more certain there's more to this case than a fluke of human biology. Maybe if he reviews his conversation with the doctor, re-examines her facial expressions and word choices, he'll see something he missed before, some clue about where he should look next. As he boards the elevator and turns, his eyes drift back toward the doctor's office. Just before the doors close and the elevator begins descending, he catches a glimpse of a familiar bright-purple hologram on her nameplate.

7

LUCINDA'S MIND SWIRLS. SHE SLEPT FITFULLY LAST NIGHT, and the unbearable mix of grief, distrust, and anger in her gut has only gotten worse as the day's gone on. As she sits at the dinner table, all the feelings have settled into one unsavory ball at the pit of her stomach and it's all she can do to pick at her chicken and broccoli.

"Mama?" Serafina asks, breaking through her wandering thoughts.

"What?" Lucinda snaps back.

Sera's bright smile fades. "Never mind."

"Sweetheart, why don't you get ready for bed?" says Zavi, ushering Sera out of the kitchen. "I'll come tuck you in when you're ready."

Lucinda looks down at her barely-touched plate and smashes her fork into the pile of mashed potatoes.

Zavi reaches out a hand. "Let's talk," he says.

She doesn't want to talk. She wants to curl up into a ball and never have to talk to anyone again. But the look on Zavi's face tells her he's not going to leave it alone. She sighs and stands, following him to the balcony with her arms crossed.

They sit and Zavi takes her foot into his lap under the thick blanket. "What's up?" he asks. Like his touch, his words are warm but firm. He's always known just how to challenge Lucinda without pushing her away.

"Sorry," she mumbles. She should be apologizing to Serafina instead. She will, before her baby girl drifts off to sleep.

The Sisters are counseled from the beginning to share nothing about the Society with anyone outside it. Once they begin preparing to have children, their Mothers warn them to share only the minimum information necessary with their partners. The more Zavi knows, the more danger he could be in—and the more he could endanger the Society and the rest of its members—if anyone ever had occasion to ask him questions.

She needs this, though, to connect with someone outside the Garden about these confusing feelings. And while Zavi's not exactly impartial, he can be more objective than she or Astor, or anyone else from the inside. Everyone in the Society has their own expectations for Lucinda. The First Daughter must always be composed, self-assured. After all, she's the compass for the rest of them. If she voiced her doubts and fears with her Sisters, they might begin to have some of the same feelings.

The right path has always been clear: it was the one laid out by Evie and walked by Ruma. Lucinda was the chosen one. The Garden Society was started to give back something that was stolen generations ago. As First Daughter, she was the one who would mark the new beginning.

And mark it she did. As the first intact female infant in ages, she later became the first natural-bearing mother. All her life, she has served as the mentor, guide and teaching case to her Sisters. The Society wants to restore a choice that was stolen away. This mission isn't just for her; it's for all the others who will eventually follow in her footsteps. It has always felt right.

And Lucinda's always assumed the rest of the Sisters feel the same way. Why wouldn't they? Their mothers' secret rebellion was also an act of love, was it not?

Everything was clear when all her Sisters were still alive. Now she's not so certain.

Zavi sits up and pulls her close to him. She's been blubbering her stream of consciousness through hiccuping sobs. At her core something fundamental has begun to tear, and it threatens to split her in two.

"Fucking Astor!" she finally says, tears giving way to anger as she breaks from Zavi's embrace. "Why does she have to fight everything, every step of the way? Why can't she just do what she's supposed to, like all the rest of us? All she's doing is making things more difficult."

Zavi studies her face. He wants to say something. And if he hasn't said it yet, it's probably something she won't want to hear.

And so she keeps talking. "You know when she criticizes them, she's criticizing me, right? I made the same decision for Serafina that our mothers made for us. I'm one of them now."

"And you know it was a decision I fully supported," he reminds her.

"Yeah, but why?" she says, leveling his violet eyes. "Was it because my mother had already made the decision for us?"

"I don't think that gives either of us very much credit, Lucinda. We are both smart, educated people who believe the government has no business deciding what people can and can't do with their bodies. Regardless of the supposed benefits."

"And Astor?" says Lucinda.

"What about Astor?"

"What if she's right?"

Zavi shrugs. "Astor's going to do what's right for her. What's right for you may be different."

"Okay, but what if what's right for her puts the rest of us in danger?"

"Did she tell you something that made you believe she'd endanger the rest of you?"

Lucinda thinks for a moment, then shakes her head.

"Consider, then, how hard it must have been for her to speak up to you, knowing how firm you are in your beliefs."

"Hard for her to speak up?" Lucinda chuckles. "You must not know Astor as well as I thought you did."

"I know she values your relationship as much as you do," Zavi says. "I know she calls you Sister and really means it. And I think, as prickly as Astor can be sometimes, she loves you and doesn't want to fight with you. So, if she's saying something of this much consequence, something with the potential to destroy the bond the two of you have, don't you think she's put some thought into it?"

Lucinda stands and walks to the edge of the balcony. The river is barely visible in the distance, past the park where they take Serafina to play—the same one where, a lifetime ago, she used to ride the carousel with Astor and Celeste.

She searches the hazy maze of streets and alleys, high rise apartment buildings and storefronts, as if they can answer the question she can't even put into words.

Suddenly Zavi is behind her, encircling her in his arms and resting his chin on top of her head.

"I don't know what to do," she whispers at the wind.

"You don't have to do anything right now," he says, his voice vibrating in her head. "You can be sad for Celeste, and thankful for our daughter, and sorry that you and Astor aren't seeing eye to eye. But it doesn't have to be your responsibility to act on any of it. Right now, you don't have to *do* anything. You can just be."

She turns and kisses him then, because of course he's said the one thing she needed someone to say, giving her what she'd never have allowed for herself. Permission, for a moment in time, to exist outside what everyone else has come to expect of her. Permission to turn off the questions and just *be*.

Back inside, Lucinda kisses Serafina good night. "I'm sorry, baby girl," she says. "I didn't mean to snap. I love you."

The little girl smiles and wraps her arms around her mother's neck. "It's okay, Mama. I love you too."

She's just sitting to watch some mindless television with Zavi when her mobile lights up. Letting out a groan, she reaches for it and reads the message. *From Mother: We need to talk. Come as soon as you can.*

Ruma's office looks the same as it always has: Giant abstract painting of the sun on one wall, comfortable sofa and armchair, and a single digital photo frame on a shelf among various artifacts from Ruma's years of travel around the world. The frame displays all manner of photos, from gorgeous rainforest canopies to snapshots of concerts from Josiah's bar and club days. Pictures of her parents, Aunt Elle, and Uncle Clark, younger than she's ever known them, cascade across the display.

The screen fills with a child's face: Celeste's innocent green eyes pierce through the decades. The image zooms out to reveal the cloud of blonde hair encircling her face, and Lucinda has to turn away.

Ruma sits at her desk, staring in Lucinda's direction without seeming to see her. Her eyes are somehow both wild and exhausted. She looks like Lucinda feels, which is to say she could have lived a year in the last several days. She's got the look of someone who can't rest until she's finished something important, an assignment whose end is nowhere in sight.

Lucinda is about to sit across from her mother when Ruma stands abruptly, picks up her mobile, and holds out her hand for Lucinda's. She leaves both devices on the shelf, next to the photo frame, and Lucinda follows her out and up several floors to the rooftop deck.

There was a time when sitting in the black night air would feel invigorating. When the cool breeze filling her lungs would speak of adventure and possibilities.

Now, as she sits knee-to-knee with her mother in one of the few places private enough to have a confidential conversation, the weight of questions unasked and unanswered threatens to compress her into nothingness.

"Mom, what's going on?" she asks when her mother doesn't speak right away.

"An investigator came to see me this morning."

"And? You didn't drag me all the way to your office at eleven at night to tell me something you could have said over text."

Ruma looks around, lowers her voice despite their isolation. "And I'm concerned," she says. Lucinda waits, tapping her fingers. Why can't her mother just get to the point? "Have you talked to Martin?" Ruma asks.

"No," Lucinda says. "Not today."

"Well," says Ruma, "judging by the questions this man was asking me, he had already spoken with both Yvette Blair, the medical examiner, and Martin."

"Okay. But why are you so worried? The medical examiner was one of us, right? Didn't you two agree on a story? And I'm telling you, I don't think Martin will say anything. He came out and told me he didn't see a reason to get the rest of us involved."

Ruma presses her fingers to the bridge of her nose. "I just don't know if it's going to work," she says. "All the preparations and the contingency planning and the coaching, and I just don't know if any of it is going to matter in the long run. They've got her implant. We knew they would, and we used your algorithm to mask her health data, but something in the way he was questioning me made me nervous. Like he knows something's off."

Lucinda swallows. "My algorithm?" She created the program that overwrites implant data so hormonal fluctuations from menstruation, pregnancy, and childbirth don't trigger alerts in the health monitoring system. And her mother used it to cover up the fact that Celeste was giving birth when everything went wrong. "I—the algorithm wasn't intended for that kind of scenario."

"Bernie made some small adjustments," Ruma says, referring to her technical assistant. "To fit the…situation."

Lucinda's stomach sinks. Her algorithm was written to run passively in the background, making hormones look stable like they do for safeguarded women. She's not sure how it will hold up to close scrutiny, especially not knowing what adjustments Bernie made. Her mind immediately wanders through the code, identifying all the weaknesses that could be exploited. There are probably a hundred more she's not even considered.

Could the algorithm be used to find other women with the same program running on their implants? What if it is traced back to her? She pictures herself sitting in an interrogation room, or in a courtroom, expectant eyes boring into her. How would she explain her actions without exposing the society and endangering every person in it? And what's the penalty for tampering with government programming? Ten years in prison? Twenty? Maybe more, now that someone is dead.

If her mother notices her sudden panic, she doesn't mention it. Her face is clouded, her brow deeply creased.

"Did my name come up? Or anything else that would indicate where the investigation stands?" says Lucinda.

"No," Ruma says. "He just thanked me for talking to him and told me he'd be in touch if he needed anything else. He didn't offer any information, and I was trying not to sound too interested."

Lucinda takes a deep breath. "Okay," she says. "Everything is fine, Mom. It's a matter of course for premature deaths to be investigated, and he's probably just looking into it so he can say he performed his due diligence. Right?"

Ruma nods, but her eyes betray her doubt. "Yes. I'm sure you're right. Soon the case will be closed, and we all can move on."

The two women sit in silence. Lucinda searches Ruma's eyes for reassurance, but it's obvious that her mother is looking for the same from her. Neither is equipped to provide it. And when did it become Lucinda's job to assuage the fears of the entire Society, anyway?

Back in Ruma's office, Lucinda retrieves her mobile and starts for the door.

"I'm sending you the detective's contact card," Ruma says to her back. And then, after a pause, "It would look suspicious if I reached out. But if there's any way for you to…learn more…"

Lucinda stops in her tracks. She's no stranger to the network. She uses it to flash her masking protocol onto all the Sisters' implants with each new member or protocol update. But hacking into the Bureau's case monitoring system would be ten crazy steps beyond that. Surely that's not what her mother is suggesting. Ruma says nothing more, leaving the sentence for Lucinda to finish.

Ruma won't see the scowl that crosses Lucinda's face as she raises and then lowers her chin, acknowledging her mother's words without speaking any of her own.

She rides home in a fog, and it's not until she's in bed and halfway to sleep that she remembers to check her mother's message for the detective's contact card.

When she sees a familiar pair of dark, watery eyes staring back at her, she very much wishes she'd waited until morning.

"You look like shit," Adi says. She stands in the doorway of Lucinda's office. "How long has it been since you slept?"

Lucinda stares at Adi, trying in vain to come up with a clever response. "I feel that way too," she says instead, pressing on the puffy spaces under her eyes. "Is it that bad?"

"Yeah," Adi says, stepping in and putting an arm around Lucinda's shoulders. As Lucinda leans her head into her Sister's embrace, a memory that came to her last night surfaces once more. Shortly after Lucinda and Adi began working together, there was an awards banquet where Adi was recognized. Lucinda, alone and new at the organization, was seated at the same table with Adi's parents and a handful of other people.

She's had no reason to think about that evening for more than a decade, but now she can remember it clearly in her mind's eye. Older than her own parents, with a gentle warmth and an affinity for good wine, the couple was a delight to be around. Adi's father, Emeka, was a detective whose childhood in Nigeria had left him with a faint accent even all these years later. He spoke fondly of tending the animals on his family's farm—Lucinda could relate, having spent many springs and summers on her own grandparents' farm—and had the entire table cracking up at his retellings. Emeka's partner, Abigail, was his match in wit as well as demeanor. She ran an art shop downtown and could retell the detailed history of every piece she displayed.

After a glass or two of pinot, Lucinda surprised herself, casting aside her usual reserve and becoming more gregarious than she ever was around her own parents. Later, on the ride home, she would replay the conversation over and over. How deeply she pined for the loving mother, for the unremarkable childhood she imagined Adi's upbringing had provided.

When Adi joined them after receiving her award, it was obvious how perfectly her two parents had combined to create her. This had been by design, of course. Her parents, like all other parents, had sat together testing out different combinations of their genes on the wallscreen. Swipe right for one combination, left for another, and at the end you can see what your baby will be, before they're ever even created. Lucinda's parents had done this with her; Adi had even done it with Micah, who at the time of the banquet was still in the nursery womb awaiting her prescribed birthdate.

Serafina hadn't been born yet, but Lucinda knew she would be the first person in decades not to manipulate her child into existence. She also knew that one day, now that she'd recruited Adi to join the Society, Micah would have the choice to have her own child naturally, too. How would Emeka and Abigail feel if they knew their granddaughter wouldn't be safeguarded?

"You falling asleep on me?" asks Adi from above Lucinda's head.

Lucinda straightens and clears her throat. "Nope. I'm fine. How have you been doing?" This isn't the place to talk about their shared secrets around Celeste's death, but it wouldn't be right not to acknowledge the loss.

"I'm okay," Adi says. "It's hard, talking to Micah about it." She opens her mouth as if to say more but shakes her head instead. She doesn't return the question. She can probably see how Lucinda's handling things from the dark circles under her bloodshot eyes.

"Well, hey," Lucinda says. "If you ever want me to talk to her, I'll give it a shot. I love that kid. I want her to feel okay about things. As okay as anyone can feel right now, anyway."

"Thanks," Adi says and turns to leave. "By the way," Lucinda says, and Adi turns back. "How are your parents doing?"

Adi tilts her head. "Fine?" she says, "We went to a play together the other day, before…" She pauses, looking down at her hands. "Why do you ask?"

Adi must not know her father is investigating Celeste's death. Lucinda attempts a smile. "I was just re-membering that night at the awards banquet."

A faint smile crosses Adi's lips. "That was ages ago! What made you think of it just now?"

Lucinda shrugs. "I guess it just popped into my head. Sleep deprivation can do funny things."

After Adi leaves, Lucinda sits back in her seat and runs scenarios in her mind, as she's been doing since late last night. Best case: her algorithm fools the detective and Celeste's case is closed. Worst case: the investigation uncov-ers the holes in her software, exposes the real cause of Celeste's death, and results in the arrest—and after that, who knows—of every single member of the Garden Society. Their partners are arrested, and their children are taken and sterilized, and the situation of women in the world is no bet-ter off than it was a hundred years ago. Her entire life will have been for nothing. She swallows down the bile rising in her throat.

For the good of the many. It always made sense in the abstract. Evie's words guide us. Evie, the forebear who turned the Society from theory to action, a ghost but also an example of what it means to have a mission—something to live for beyond your own skin and bones.

But there's an asterisk in those words, isn't there? What it should really say is, *For the good of the many, we must sacrifice the few.* Celeste wasn't the first sacrifice. Maybe it was Serafina's unborn twin. Maybe it was someone else, somewhere else, that Lucinda never even heard about. They focus so much on the many that the few—the sacrifices—fade from existence.

Even in the best case, if the Society goes on the way Evie orchestrated it all those years ago, will these sacrifices even be remembered? The very language of their mantra ignores the inevitable losses along the way. Who will be the next Celeste?

No one. That has to be the answer. Lucinda needs to make sure something like this never happens again.

8

"ABUTO!" SAYS A VOICE AS EMEKA STEPS OUT OF THE elevator and onto the floor. Gina Rodriguez, one of the Bureau's newest analysts, rushes around the corner to greet him. Her eyes are ablaze with excitement. "I was just about to call you."

"Oh?" asks Emeka, barely making eye contact. He's spent the entire car ride trying to find a weakness in the Harlow case. He reviewed the conversations with both Dr. Das and Celeste Harlow's partner. He checked and re-checked the timeline of events against the medical examiner's report. He can't find a source for his unease, but that hasn't stopped it from building in his gut. The next place he can turn for answers will be the data from Ms. Harlow's implant.

Which he gave to Rodriguez for analysis yesterday. Suddenly he is much more interested in what Rodriguez has to say.

"Mmm-hmm," she says. She's grinning. Whatever she's got for him, she must find it very exciting. "I have something to show you. Follow me."

Rodriguez leads Emeka over to a conference room, where an image is projected onto the room's full-size wallscreen. Emeka looks at the legend. *Heart Rate, Blood Pressure, Respiration.*

"Check this out," says Rodriguez.

As Emeka watches, several lines of data populate from left to right, creating a jagged graph of the different health attributes over time. After the lines reach the end of the display, Emeka looks back to Rodriguez. "Okay," he says. "Am I supposed to know what to do with this?"

Rodriguez looks ready to jump out of her seat. She takes a deep breath and composes herself. "Detective Abuto. I believe you're acquainted with thirty-four-year-old Sasha Bain." He is, of course. She is one of the other junior analysts. "She's allowed us to use her health data for the last twenty-four hours as a point of comparison."

"Okay…" Emeka says. He's beginning to understand the point of this exercise. If only Rodriguez would get to it.

Rodriguez continues. "Notice the jumpy, jagged nature of the curves. Blood pressure, heart rate, respiration— there is an obvious trend, but the actual data points jump around like popcorn."

And, just like that, the feeling that's been nagging at him takes shape. Since this investigation started, each piece of it has seemed too—

"I added Celeste Harlow's data below," says Rodriguez. The chart shifts upward, and below it, another, similar chart appears—similar, that is, until all the lines in the lower chart bottom out. "Notice anything?" asks Rodriguez.

"Smooth," Emeka says, finishing the sentence he was thinking a moment ago. "It's too smooth. Too tidy."

Rodriguez nods thoughtfully, massaging one hand with the other as her eyes scan the graphs once again. "That's a good way to put it, I think. There's not as much scatter— not as much as you'd expect to find in a real, live human. At one point, Miss Sasha's heart rate was recorded at, like, a hundred, and then a minute later it was back down to seventy. And this is with a fully functioning, lifetime-guaranteed implant. There are no jumps like that in Ms. Harlow's data, not a single one. It's—as you said—just a little too smooth and tidy."

Emeka searches his mind for an explanation. "Celeste was on leave before she died. Is it possible she was just not taxing herself very much?" He knows the answer before he's finished the question.

Rodriguez sucks in a breath through her teeth. "I'm no doctor, but I would say that's pretty unlikely. I'm pretty sure that spike in Sasha's heart rate happened while she was eating a veggie burger."

Emeka chuckles. "I see. So, what's the explanation? Why does the Harlow data look like this?"

Rodriguez shakes her head. "I couldn't tell you, Detective," she says, but her hands are restless. She's got something more on her mind.

"What is it?"

She chuckles nervously. "It's nothing," she says, "Just…"

Emeka raises his eyebrows and waits.

"The implants are supposed to be tamper-proof."

"They are," Emeka says. The words are certain, but he feels anything but.

"Well," says Rodriguez, meeting Abuto's eyes. "What if they're not?"

Emeka's pulse quickens. The possibility crashes through his mind, upending a certainty he's always taken for granted. "It's impossible," he says.

"It's the only explanation I can think of," says Rodriguez.

She's right. But who would have tampered with her health monitoring data? And why? "Rodriguez, I need you to figure out how Ms. Harlow's health data was faked. We need to know who did it, how they did it, and what they were covering up."

Rodriguez's smile has become less eager, but she knows this is more than a suggestion. "Sure thing, Detective. I'm on it."

The pieces of the investigation swirl in his head as Emeka walks to his desk. Snippets of timeline that *mostly* match up; health data that is a little *too* tidy; clips from the interviews he's watched and re-watched in an effort to put a name to the unease both interviewees stirred up.

Someone felt it necessary to cover up the true cause of Ms. Harlow's death. Something was happening to her vital signs that someone didn't want to be uncovered. But what, and why? One thing is clear: Celeste Harlow didn't die of an aneurysm. And without an autopsy, it's going to be very difficult to determine the true cause of her death.

Cremation within twenty-four hours is routine, now that implants can be retained and reviewed. But the absence of Ms. Harlow's body, and whatever clues it might hold, is beginning to seem like an intentional barrier to his investigation.

Without the body, the only clues Detective Abuto is going to find are the ones he can glean from the people who knew Celeste Harlow. What clues should he be looking for? What could Dr. Ruma Das and Martin Granby possibly have to hide?

9

ELECTRONIC DINGS AND ZOOMS DRIFT UP FROM THE BACK seat. "Could you turn down your video game, sweetie?" Lucinda says. "It's hurting my head." The half-hour nap she took after work did little to clear her head, and while she should be excited to be meeting Aunt Elle and Uncle Clark for dinner at her favorite restaurant, she would rather curl up in a ball under a blanket on the balcony and stay there forever.

"Okay, Mama," Sera says, but it doesn't help. The headache is more from all the conflicting thoughts clashing together than from the game. And hunger, probably—she can't remember the last time she ate anything substantial. But when she tries thinking of her favorite seared scallops with balsamic glaze, rather than growling with hunger, her stomach roils with nausea.

Zavi takes her hand, rubbing the space between her thumb and index finger with his own thumb. He says nothing, doesn't need to. She relaxes her knotted-up shoulders and leans into him. He smells of spice and lavender, and she closes her eyes for a moment, breathing him in and trying to block out the rest of the world.

At the restaurant, the three of them navigate to the back corner table. Aunt Elle and Uncle Clark are already there, backs to the windows and the breathtaking nighttime view of the river and the city skyline.

"Aunt Elle! Uncle Clark!" calls Serafina, rushing ahead and pulling one parent behind her with each arm. The couple looks up from browsing the menu. As always, they look like they just finished a high-society photoshoot: Elle, face framed by a short blonde coif, wears a charcoal-colored dress with red heels; Clark is in his typical black business suit, today with an iridescent blue tie that matches his partner's eyes.

Lucinda smiles. Elle and Clark are her parents' closest friends—so close, she's called them *Aunt* and *Uncle* since she was old enough to talk. She used to feel the same exuberance as Sera, visiting them in their home upstate. She can almost smell the immaculate air of the woods behind their house, feel the mud of the riverbank between her toes. If she were to trace the river just out the window, she would eventually end up in that same spot where she spent so much time as a child. After, that is, passing through the shallows where she finally came to rest all those years ago.

Elle's voice, still touched by the South despite all her years up here, cuts through the memory. "Luci? Sweetie? You with us?"

Lucinda blinks and turns her eyes from the view, consuming Elle in an embrace before settling into the seat next to her. Clark reaches across the table and squeezes Lucinda's hand. "I heard about your friend, Celeste, kiddo," he says. "You doing okay?"

Lucinda swallows hard, and she can feel Zavi's hand on her knee. Serafina searches her mother's face. At least they're getting this part over with. That way Celeste's death won't be hanging over the conversation for the entire evening. She nods, swallowing down the sadness rising in her throat. "I guess so," she says. "I'll be okay." She looks at Sera. "We'll be okay."

Lucinda loves Elle and Clark, but she's always on high alert around them. Clark is the Director of the Population Science Bureau, the government department in charge of approving families' applications for expansion and making sure female infants are safeguarded. Lucinda is always afraid to slip up and say something that will give the whole Society away. Even more so, now that Serafina is old enough to understand but not quite old enough to always think before she speaks. Sera, though, just scoots closer to Elle and leans her head against Elle's shoulder.

Elle puts her arm around the little girl and squeezes. With the other hand, she taps her mobile and lifts it, running her eyes back and forth swiftly as she reads the screen. Another tap and her attention is back at the table. "Sorry," she says.

"Everything okay?" asks Clark.

"Mmm-hmm," says Elle. "Nathan just had a question that needed an answer." She turns back to Lucinda, ignoring Uncle Clark's raised eyebrow. Lucinda doesn't know who Nathan is, but Uncle Clark seems to have an opinion about him. "I was thinking just the other day, Luci," Elle says. "Do you remember the time you and Celeste took that art class, and then when you came over afterward, you took all Myles' guitar picks and made them into a mosaic?"

Lucinda chuckles. "Oh, yeah!" she says. She can still see Myles' face, twisted up in almost cartoonish rage when he saw his picks glued to the craft board. "Ooh, he was mad."

Elle and Clark's son is one of the only friends Lucinda grew up with who wasn't in the Garden Society with her. He was a few years older and probably saw her as a nuisance growing up, but she's always looked up to him and they grew closer in adulthood. "How are he and Peter doing these days? I owe them a visit."

Elle detaches once more—another tap, another twenty-second pause to read, followed by a furiously tapped reply—but Clark looks happy to answer. "They're great," he says. "We were there this past weekend, and we got to see the baby. She's starting to look less like an alien and more like a real person." He chuckles.

Lucinda smiles. She might not be a fan of the nursery wombs, but she'll admit there is a certain intrigue in being able to watch through the viewing window as the baby develops.

"Oooh, a baby girl!" squeals Serafina.

Lucinda raises her eyebrows. She'd always assumed Myles and Peter would choose to have a boy. Maybe because Uncle Clark always referred to a grand*son* whenever he referred to hypothetical future descendants.

"Mmm-hmm," says Clark. He doesn't seem disappointed. "They left everything else up to chance, but they chose a girl." During selection, parents theoretically have the freedom to select for any trait which could be made from combining their genes. Lucinda would have expected Myles to take more advantage of the process. After all, his dad's department wrote the book on reproduction and genetic selection.

"It'll be nice to have another little girl around," Elle says. "Aside from Sera, we haven't had one of those since you and your sisters were little."

The hair on the back of Lucinda's neck stands up. It's not a word typically heard outside the Garden. Due to limited natural resources families are allowed only one child, and it's been this way for generations. There are no sisters and brothers, no true aunts and uncles either. Lucinda was close with Astor and Celeste growing up, though, and she remembers their parents affectionately referring to them as sisters. Uncle Clark's expression doesn't change, and the pounding in her ears quiets.

Clark and Zavi get onto the topic of Zavi's work as an agricultural engineer, and soon they're talking about quotas and allotments and other things Lucinda tries her hardest to learn nothing about. Serafina tells Aunt Elle how her first year of school has gone so far, and Elle recounts more of her favorite stories of mischief from when Lucinda was that age.

By the time dessert is served, Lucinda's nerves have calmed. Despite her and Zavi's protests, Elle and Clark take care of the check. She'll always be a little girl in their eyes, and right now that doesn't bother her. It's nice to be taken care of for a change.

Before they part ways on the sidewalk, Elle wraps Lucinda in a warm embrace. "I know it's so hard right now," she says, holding Lucinda at arm's length as Zavi and Sera say their goodbyes to Clark. "But everything happens for a reason. I know you miss Celeste, but one day you'll realize how her loss helped you grow. It might not seem like it right now, but I really do believe that."

Unexpectedly, Lucinda bristles. Her muscles tense and she pulls away, turning her eyes to the pavement.

Elle's hand is warm on her shoulder. "I'm sorry, sweetie. I shouldn't have said that. It's too soon. I just wanted you to know, the hurt won't last forever."

Lucinda looks out over the water, watching a gull dive from the sky and settle on the water. "It sure feels like it will."

Serafina tugs at Lucinda's dress. "Mama, can we go for a walk on the river?"

Lucinda sighs, picking her up. "Oof," she says. Sera's gotten bigger since the last time Lucinda held her like this. "It's past your bedtime, little girl."

"I promise I'll go right to bed when we get home." Sera bats her eyes, tilting her head like that cartoon cat she likes to watch. "Promise, Mama."

Zavi catches her eye and shrugs. Why not? "Fine," Lucinda relents. "But right to bed."

"Pinky promise," says Serafina. She'll probably fall asleep in the car on the way home, anyway.

Lucinda walks along the river's edge, hand-in-hand with her daughter, watching the city's lights glint off the water. She turns Elle's words over in her mind. Elle seemed so certain there's a lesson to be learned from Celeste's death. It sounds like a different version of what Lucinda's been trying to convince herself, that Celeste was an acceptable sacrifice. It was a sacrifice, for sure. But was it acceptable? With each day that passes, Lucinda becomes less certain.

10

Emeka sits in one of the big yet surprisingly uncomfortable rolling chairs in the same conference room into which Rodriguez pulled him yesterday. Generic black-and-white photos span each of the side walls, and he's reviewing the Harlow case information on the screen at the front of the room. In a few minutes, Rodriguez will be joining him to deliver what she insists is *super big news*.

She must have figured out why Celeste Harlow's implant logs were tampered with, and hopefully she's also got an idea of who did it. Without those details, it's been impossible to make any headway. All the evidence he's gathered—the interview with the doctor, the partner's statement, the timeline—has served to corroborate the story he's been told. The implant must be the key.

But health monitoring implants and their firmware are designed to be impervious to tampering. In all his years as a detective, Emeka has never seen or even heard of log alteration. If Rodriguez has found that someone broke in and altered the raw data on Celeste Harlow's implant logs, Emeka and the entire Bureau will be in uncharted territory. He'll have a much bigger investigation on his hands than one woman's untimely death. Not to mention the fact that if logs have been altered once, they can be altered again. Or maybe they have been already. What if this has been going on for years and they're just realizing it now?

Rodriguez rushes into the room, breathing quickly and straightening her short, dark spikes with her hands. "Abuto. Sorry I'm late."

He didn't even realize she was late. The floor is only now beginning to stir for the day. "It's fine, Rodriguez. What's this super big news you're so excited about?"

Rodriguez straightens and fills her lungs. "Yes, of course. I just need to introduce you to some people first." She presses a button on her mobile and two faces are projected on the screen in the front of the room, replacing his case file. "Detective Abuto, I'd like to introduce you to Dr. Montissol and Ms. Golev." The women on the screen wave in turn. Greetings are exchanged all around before Emeka reverts his attention back to Rodriguez. "Dr. Montissol is a physician and Ms. Golev is a software engineer. They're both friends of my parents," she adds, a sheepish grin creeping onto her face. "Anyway, I asked them to review Celeste Harlow's health monitoring implant so we could try and figure out what happened with her data." Emeka raises his eyebrows, but before he can speak, Rodriguez interjects. "Don't worry, they both signed NDAs. And I've known them all my life. They're trustworthy."

"Well, okay, then," Emeka says, impressed. This analyst just started at the Bureau a few months ago, but she's certainly earning her place.

Rodriguez continues. "Ms. Golev? Want to start?"

"Good morning, everyone. Thank you for inviting me to talk with you this morning. Gina—I'm sorry, *Ms. Rodriguez"* —Rodriguez bows her head, flushing and hiding a wide smile— "suspected Ms. Harlow's health information was forged, and she asked me to take a look. Naturally, I was intrigued, especially given how tamper-proof the implants are supposed to be. Now, most of my work has been on computer systems. And in a computer system, when data are overwritten, a shadow of those data is left behind for a time. Particularly since the suspected overwrite was so recent, I reasoned I'd be able to find a substantial amount of the overwritten data using forensic data recovery techniques. And that is exactly what happened. Underneath the smoothed-out data Rodriguez showed, there was another set of data that was all but smooth." The image of Golev fades, and a chart appears in her place. "Here is a chart showing the raw data I found hiding beneath the mask."

Golev is silent for a moment, allowing the group to take in the information. In stark contrast to the graph Rodriguez showed yesterday, the heart rate measurements on this chart are all over the place. Emeka takes a deep breath. So, it's true. It's verified by an expert, and the evidence is right in front of him. Someone altered Ms. Harlow's health monitoring data. Someone has figured out how to tamper with a tamper-proof system. Once he's accepted the theory as reality, he tries to process the data aloud. "There is a spike in heart rate every couple of minutes, and then it goes back down."

On the screen, Golev nods. "After a while, everything normalizes. But then there is a sudden drop in blood pressure, accompanied by an increase in heart rate, before all of her vitals bottom out as she continues to bleed internally."

Emeka's brow furrows as he looks at the information. "Okay, so what does that tell us?"

"Miss Esther—I mean, Dr. Montissol?" says Rodriguez. "Want to take over?"

"Yes, of course," Montissol says. She straightens, adjusting her collar and greeting everyone once more. "When I received the unmasked data from Ms. Golev, the first thing I did was to look at the health information from the morning of Ms. Harlow's death—not only her vital signs, but other pieces of Ms. Harlow's health data that might suggest what was happening in her body at the time." It's Montissol's turn to bring up a chart. "I borrowed Ms. Rodriguez's idea of comparing an average woman's information side by side with Ms. Harlow's."

Rodriguez chuckles. "I'll be expecting a royalty check in the mail."

Montissol laughs along before returning to the chart. "Now, I dove deeply into a lot of Ms. Harlow's medical information. Most monitoring stats were just as we would expect. But certain ones stood out as remarkable, and those I will highlight. The first, represented in the chart, are the levels of the hormones progesterone and estrogen. In nature, these hormones function to modulate female fertility and to stimulate the development of secondary sex characteristics such as pubic hair and breasts. You may know that in primitive populations, these hormones were unregulated. About two hundred years ago, scientists developed a way to regulate these hormones artificially, and this technology has been a part of the safeguarding procedure female infants undergo. It's the ideal circumstance—to prevent eventual pregnancy and other…inconveniences, while still allowing for the development of those uniquely female characteristics.

"In an average woman today, the hormones are very evenly produced, and they circulate in a woman's body at predictable concentrations. Notice, though, the difference in

Ms. Harlow's graph. The concentration of progesterone in her blood was exceptionally high at the time of her death, and when I looked back, I saw that it had been rising for several months."

Celeste Harlow's number is easily a hundred times the average woman's. Emeka has no idea what this means. "But wouldn't her implant have alerted her and her doctor if her levels were that far out of range?" he says.

"That was my question as well," says Montissol. "Alerts for sex hormones were, in fact, turned off on Ms. Harlow's implant. It looks like they had been since the implant was placed."

"Is that a normal thing to do?" asks Emeka.

Montissol looks doubtful. "The alerts are there for a reason. I've never heard of anyone turning them off. I certainly have never done so."

"It's almost as if the person who set up her implant knew that her hormones would be out of whack but didn't want anyone to find out," says Rodriguez.

"Yes, it seemed that way to me, as well. Many people are unaware of this, since we don't really encounter naturally regulated hormones in women anymore, but before safeguarding, women used to have monthly cycles where their uterine lining would shed and menstrual matter—blood, mainly—would flow from their body for several days."

"Okay, is that really necessary?" Rodriguez says with a half-grin. She shifts in her seat.

"Only to say this," says Montissol. "During those monthly cycles, women would have alternating sharp increases in progesterone and estrogen production from the ovaries. I looked back at the last several years, and Celeste's history matches exactly this pattern."

"Okay. So somehow this woman was having, as you put it, monthly 'cycles', and nobody noticed?" Emeka chimes in.

"Can you imagine your partner hiding that from you?" says Rodriguez, raising one eyebrow.

No, he can't. "Are you telling me, Doctor, that Celeste Harlow did not have her safeguarding procedure when she was an infant? That she's been walking around—what word would you use? Non-safeguarded? Unaltered? Intact?—for her entire life, and her partner knew it?"

"That's what it looks like, Detective."

"But what does that have to do with her death?"

Dr. Montissol clears her throat, taking a sip of water and then replacing the glass off-screen. "Well, I worked with Ms. Harlow's data for a long time, and I found many curiosities," she says. "Allow me to bring up another chart."

Emeka takes a deep breath, stifling a half-mad chuckle. So much for his dream of closing this case quickly and getting back to his other investigations. His thoughts are racing, trying to connect the dots into a story that makes sense. They can't be suggesting what he thinks they are. He won't let himself believe the possibility until he hears them say it aloud.

"Ms. Harlow's hormone levels, combined with the fact that the alerts for these hormones were disabled, seemed to suggest something very specific happened to cause Celeste Harlow's death, and it had nothing to do with an aneurysm. Tell me, Detective," she continues. "Did Celeste have a child?"

Emeka's pulse quickens. "Yes," he says. This can't be real. "Yes, her daughter is tiny. Just a few days old."

A grim, humorless smile passes over Montissol's face. "Remember when I said that there had been a steady increase in Ms. Harlow's progesterone level over the last several months? Well, progesterone is the hormone responsible for maintaining pregnancy once an embryo forms. All signs so far pointed to a natural pregnancy, as outlandish as it seems. Once I began suspecting pregnancy, there was only one logical place to go next in the logs: oxytocin. Oxytocin is a neurotransmitter and hormone that is involved in the warm, fuzzy feelings we get from physical contact—hugging your partner or child, for example, or petting a fluffy animal. It circulates through our bodies all the time. But it's also really good at stimulating uterine contractions during labor."

Emeka looks over at Rodriguez. She is leaning forward in her chair, eyes wide, watching for Emeka's reaction. He hates to disappoint, but after being a detective for most of his life, he's learned to be unreadable. He can't help it.

When nobody speaks, Dr. Montissol brings up the chart that represents Celeste Harlow's oxytocin levels in comparison with an average woman's. Once more, her levels are nearly ten times higher.

The room is quiet. Emeka doesn't dare speak. If he does, this whole thing will become real. The others are silent as well, waiting for him to assemble the pieces they've each brought to the puzzle.

At last, Emeka takes a deep breath. "Okay," he says. His eyes dart back and forth as he mentally organizes all the information the two professionals have just presented. "Let me get this straight. Celeste Harlow did not have a safe-guarding procedure when she was an infant. Instead, she went through the last thirty-four years, intact or unaltered or whatever you want to call it, in complete secret. And no one knew because the implant data that would have signaled her condition has been overwritten and the alerts disabled."

"This is what I believe to be true, yes," says the doctor.

"And the day she died…" says Rodriguez.

"The day she died," says Emeka, "she was having a baby. She was having a baby naturally."

"That is my medical opinion," the doctor states.

"Fuck," says Rodriguez, sounding astonished, though she knew the conclusion before Emeka ever walked into the room. He couldn't have said it better himself.

Emeka's car slows to a stop in front of Martin Granby's apartment building, but his thoughts are darting in all directions.

What a senseless death. Why anyone would choose to give birth in such a primitive way is beyond him. The modern way is so much safer and more predictable; that's why it's mandated by law. And how could this woman have gone through an entire pregnancy without anyone being the wiser?

It is Dr. Das he's after, but he has decided to re-interview Martin first. The man is holding on by a thread. If Emeka pushes the right buttons, Martin will break down and be straight with him. That is, if he doesn't shut down completely. This one must be handled carefully.

Martin looks the same as he did last time Emeka was here, down to the white t-shirt and green lounge pants. The shave on his face is fresh, but it does nothing to hide the circles under his eyes; if anything, the smooth skin accentuates them. "Detective Abuto. I wasn't expecting to see you again," he says as he opens the door widely, gesturing for Emeka to enter. The place hasn't changed, except that Indian takeout containers have taken the place of Chinese ones on the dining table.

"I had a few follow-up questions that I wasn't able to answer on my own," says Emeka. "Shall we sit?"

"Sure," Martin says, gesturing to the counter where Emeka sat before.

"How's the baby doing?" asks Emeka, looking and listening for the baby but not detecting her presence.

"Anabel," Martin says. "She's doing good. She just had a bottle and went down for a nap."

Emeka can't help feeling relieved. It will be easier to talk without the distraction of a newborn between them. "Martin," he says, choosing familiarity over formality today, "you indicated last time I was here that you and Celeste had only been on leave for eight to ten weeks prior to the baby's arrival. Can you say more about that?"

Martin's shoulders tense, but he tries to pass it off as a shrug. "There's nothing much to say," he says. "We chose to leave more time to spend with the baby after she was born, instead of sitting around and being bored for three months before she came. People do that."

"People do," says Emeka, "but I'm sure you know it's pretty uncommon."

"Not much common about our lives these days, is there?" Martin asks, his voice taking on a cynical edge.

Emeka pulls back and changes direction. "Do you have support?" he asks. "Friends and family to help you out while you get used to being a single parent?"

"Sure," Martin says. "My parents have been by a few times, and a couple of Celeste's friends have dropped by with food and stuff. I keep telling them I can handle it, especially with the autochef and everything, but they insist on coming over." Martin shrugs.

"And which friends are these?" asks Emeka.

"Oh, her childhood friends. Lucinda and Astor mostly." Emeka lets the silence stretch between them. "I don't know—I guess I'm glad they come by. It's better than being cooped up all day with just the baby. It takes my mind off the fact that it was supposed to be the three of us." His face twitches, but no tears fall this time.

"I can only imagine how hard it is to be a single father with a newborn," Emeka says, patting the man's upper arm. "When my daughter was first born, it took the two of us plus another handful of friends and family just to get acclimated to life with a baby. That was quite a few years ago now," he says. "But childrearing hasn't gotten any easier, I'd wager."

Martin offers a weak smile.

Emeka sees an opening here and goes after it. "I'll bet when Celeste first became pregnant, you two were over the moon."

"Yeah," Martin says, a distant look in his eyes. "We—" His smile fades, and he meets Emeka's eyes. He grows quiet in a dark way that differs from the pained silence Emeka's become used to. "You know," he says plainly.

Emeka nods. "Yes, son, I know." Once again, he lets the silence expand until Martin can piece together what he wants to say.

"I knew it was a bad idea," Martin says, looking in Emeka's direction with empty eyes. "But I loved her so much and this was what she wanted. It's what she said she wanted, anyway. The way I saw it, she didn't have much of a choice."

Emeka sits patiently on the stool, leaning against its back and letting Martin take his time.

"Listen, I don't know much about it," Martin says. "All I knew was that she had some *thing* where she could have a baby the old way. And, like, that was expected of her."

"She didn't tell you how that came to be?"

"She always told me the less I knew, the better," Martin says with a shrug. "She loved it, being pregnant. She saw the monthly bleeding as a blessing, she said—a sign that she was fertile. *As nature intended*, she would always say."

"How long had you known about Celeste's…status?" asks Emeka.

"Oh, I mean—she told me before we got married. It explained a lot of her sex stuff, I guess. I didn't really know how I felt about it, but I loved her, and I wanted us to be together, so I said fine. Let's do it."

"What do you mean, if you don't mind me asking, about her 'sex stuff'?"

Martin swallows and looks at his feet, cheeks red. "I mean, it feels weird to talk about, but there were just times when she was ravenous and times when she didn't want anything to do with me. Later I figured out that she avoided me at times she could get pregnant, to make sure it didn't happen accidentally. I guess there used to be, like, pills that women took, and other things people could use. But you can't find that stuff anymore. So she had to know her cycles really well. Which made me pretty much an expert, too, I guess."

"And you were okay with this?"

"Well, I guess we could have asked the doctor to fix her so she didn't get pregnant accidentally…" His voice trails off. "*Fix* her. I always looked at it like that—like she was broken and needed to be fixed." He looks down at his hands, eyes welling for the first time since they began their conversation. "She'd always say, 'No, the *other* women are the ones who are broken, and they've got no right to take my choices away.'"

"'They'?"

Martin shrugs again. "The doctors, I guess? The government? I don't really know. Again, the less I knew, the better off I was." He spits out this last part, not bothering to conceal the bitterness. "Anyway, she wanted to do it the old way—the dangerous way, in my opinion—to carry the baby inside her and give birth naturally. But something went wrong. The baby came early. And she died." He refocuses his eyes once more on Emeka—eyes that are almost black and completely spent.

The detective steeples his fingertips in front of his face for a moment before replacing them in his lap. "What happened that night, Martin?" he asks, quietly.

"She started having pains—contractions—in the middle of the night. It was too early. She wasn't due for another couple of weeks. The baby came fast, and she seemed okay for a minute, but then when Celeste was holding her and getting ready to feed her for the first time, she kind of...passed out, I guess. I saw all the blood and knew there was no hope. She just never woke up."

"So you had this brand-new baby—"

"And a dead partner," Martin finishes.

"And the doctor contacted you, when she got the alert?"

"I guess she did, yeah. But I was so dazed, and I was trying to figure out what to do with the baby, and she was hungry, and we hadn't planned on doing this so soon. I called her back a little while later and she was on her way, but we all knew it was too late."

"Why didn't you make an emergency call?"

Martin looks around the room, and Emeka is thankful he isn't in a position to see the sofa where Celeste died. The immaculate, white sofa. "It all happened so fast. When I picked up to make the emergency call, I saw Dr. Das had tried to contact me, so I got in touch with her, and she was on her way. She said she would call them when she got here."

"Who else was here?" asks Emeka.

"What? Oh—just me and the baby and Celeste. And then Dr. Das, later."

"It seems like a curious choice of language, then," Emeka presses.

"What do you mean?" Martin asks, emotionless.

"Well, you said, 'we all knew it was too late.'"

Martin's brow furrows. "Did I? I must have misspoken. But no, just Celeste and Anabel and me, and then Dr. Das when she showed up."

Maybe he misspoke. Or maybe he's not telling the full truth. "Tell me about Dr. Das's role in all this," Emeka says.

Martin thinks for a moment. "She was our family doctor," he says. "Celeste had known her since—well, I guess, since she was born."

"And she was upset when she arrived to find Celeste had died during childbirth?"

"Oh, no. I mean yes, I guess she was probably upset. But she didn't know Celeste died during childbirth. Or if she did, she didn't say that to me. I had cleaned things up by the time she arrived. She told me she thought it was probably an—an aneurysm rupture, I think she called it?"

"Okay, Martin, I'm starting to get confused here," says Emeka. "Dr. Das was Celeste's physician since birth, correct?"

Martin nods.

"Okay, and you're familiar with the safeguarding procedure that female infants undergo?"

"I—I guess so," says Martin. "I've never really thought about it."

"Well," says Emeka, "Celeste was able to become pregnant because that procedure was not performed on her."

Martin stares at something just behind Emeka's head. "Okay. Okay, that makes sense."

"And Dr. Das would have been the physician responsible for performing this procedure. Or *not* performing the procedure, as it were."

Martin's eyes widen, just slightly. He turns his head to look down the hallway where the nursery must be, and then back to Emeka. "But we never told her that Celeste was pregnant. Or I didn't, anyway."

"She had to have known that it was an eventuality, though, right?"

"I guess so? I don't know, I can't tell you what she knew or not."

"Are you saying Celeste didn't receive medical care during her pregnancy?" asks Emeka.

"I mean, she had her implant which would measure all her vitals, and once the baby started moving, she took that as a sign that everything was moving along okay. She used to say that for most of human evolution, women would just get pregnant and have a baby and there was no monitoring or medical care, and—well, we wouldn't be here as a species if things didn't work, y'know? Besides, the rest of the animal kingdom does things this way." He looks back down at his lap. "It was stupid," he says. "I should have spoken up. I knew it was a bad idea."

"Mmm-hmm," says Emeka. "But you claim you and Dr. Das never discussed the pregnancy."

"No. Never."

It just doesn't seem plausible. "Why not?" Emeka asks.

"Huh? What do you mean?"

"Why wouldn't you tell Dr. Das, your family physician, of her medical condition and of the fact that she had bled to death minutes after giving birth? It seems like pertinent information for her to know, doesn't it?" He's past the point of gentleness. Martin is still hiding something. Maybe it has an impact on her cause of death or maybe it doesn't, but something in this story feels bigger than the surface-level scratching he's been able to accomplish thus far.

"She told me not to," he says simply. "She made me promise not to tell anyone about her…condition, and I told her I wouldn't. Even when we found out she was pregnant, I suggested going to see Dr. Das for a checkup, and she refused. She didn't want to pull the doctor into her illegal situation. And so I didn't pull her in afterward, either." He pauses for a moment. "Now, after this—" He opens his hands, palms up, and makes a circular gesture toward Emeka "—I realize maybe she was already in. But I didn't know that then, and I chose to keep Celeste's secret. The last thing I wanted was for her to be found out after she died." He stops, his mouth twitching. After a moment, he adds, much more quietly, "I didn't want *that* to be the headline that people associated with her name."

Something is off about Martin's story. Emeka will have to keep digging, and he's not going to get any further here. He stands to leave, shaking Martin's hand. On his way out, he finds his eyes drifting back toward that white sofa. "By the way," he says, making it sound like an afterthought. "Those friends of your partner's. Know where I can find them?"

The door to Dr. Das's home opens just as Emeka is about to knock on it. The doctor nearly bumps into him as she exits the apartment, looking down to button her coat. "Oh!" she gasps. "Sorry. I was just on my way out." When she sees it's Emeka, she straightens. "Oh! Detective…Abuto, is it?"

"Yes, Doctor. May I come in?"

She offers Emeka a smile that somehow conveys both regret and condescension. "I'd be happy to talk, if you'll just make an appointment at my office. Now, if you'll excuse me, I'm late to meet my daughter for dinner." She tries to brush past, but he blocks her way.

"I actually have some questions that cannot wait," he says.

She looks up into his face and stands motionless for a moment before presumably deciding he has given her an order and not a request. "Very well. Come in." She reopens the front door and gestures for him to enter first. The home echoes her office in many respects: the sparseness and intentionality of the decoration; the warm comfort; even the pleasing smells, though here they're of Eastern cuisine rather than essential oils. She pulls out a chair at the dining table. "Please," she says. "Sit."

"Babe?" a man's voice asks from somewhere Emeka can't see, and a second later a lean, pale man with brown, curly hair and blue eyes rounds the corner, dressed in an oversized t-shirt and gray sweatpants. "I thought you were meeting Lucinda," he says, then pauses when he registers Emeka, who was halfway to being seated but stands once more in greeting. "Oh. Hello."

"Lucinda?" Emeka asks. Wasn't that one of the names Martin Granby gave him?

"Our daughter," says Ruma before turning to her partner. "Josiah, this is Detective Abuto. He just had a few questions. We shouldn't be long." Josiah approaches the dining table and extends a hand. It's another unsatisfying handshake, and Emeka resists a chuckle. He, Adi, and Abigail have an inside joke about the importance of a firm handshake. Obviously, this couple has never had the same conversation.

"Okay, then," says Josiah. His eyes lock with hers, asking an unspoken question, and she gives him a slight nod. He wraps an arm around her waist and kisses her cheek. "Say goodbye before you leave, okay?"

She smiles, eyes tired. "Sure, sweetheart."

Josiah disappears back down the hallway. A door slides closed, and muffled guitar music begins to play.

"My partner is a musician," Dr. Das says with a smile. "We actually met at a club where he was performing—long, long ago."

"Doctor—" Emeka begins.

"Ruma, please."

"Dr. Das," he reinforces. "As you gathered, I am here following up on the Celeste Harlow case."

The woman's golden eyes remain crystal clear and expressionless. He's seen those eyes before. He has a sudden memory of the first time he visited Martin. Dr. Das wasn't there. But the woman from the elevator had these same eyes. Eyes which now stare into him, a silent challenge.

He accepts. "Celeste Harlow did not die from a ruptured aneurysm."

Dr. Das straightens up. "Why on earth would you think that? No autopsy was performed, and there is virtually no other explanation for her death."

"Except that there is, once we shift our frame of reference a bit," says Emeka. "And, let me tell you, my frame of reference has shifted quite a bit since we last spoke."

"Well, I'd be very interested to hear what you think she died from, then." Her tone until now has been a mix of condescension and defiance—a surprising combination considering her deference and eagerness to help at their first meeting—but he can see panic creeping in. She folds her hands in front of her and raises her shoulders once more. She has to know what's coming.

Emeka has memorized his case notes. He's organized all the data that were shared by Montissol and Golev, and he's confident he knows what happened to Celeste Harlow. He even practiced the specifics on the way here, speaking them directly into the form he just submitted to the Medical Board. "Martin Granby says Celeste died during childbirth," he says. Pauses. Watches her reaction to the blow. Her face remains impassive. Too impassive for this news to be a surprise.

Her voice low, she leans forward to address Emeka. "Childbirth? That's ridiculous. How would that even be possible?"

He lowers his voice to match hers, mirroring her posture. "Well, Dr. Das, I think you know how it would be possible, but let's start from the beginning. Shall we?" She swallows. Glances to her right, in the direction where her partner Josiah went. Emeka continues. "I'm no doctor, so please feel free to correct me if I've mistaken any of the details. In order for a person to become pregnant, an egg cell must become fertilized by a sperm cell and implant into the wall of the uterus. So far so good?"

"Yes, but I'm still—" she attempts to interrupt.

"Don't worry. You'll see it soon if you don't already." He says, though he's sure she knows exactly what he's getting at. "In order for a healthy pregnancy to be maintained, the hormone progesterone is secreted by the woman's body and later by the placenta. Over the eight months before her death, Celeste Harlow's progesterone levels climbed to roughly ten times the levels in an average woman. The average woman, of course, being a woman who is incapable of becoming pregnant." Another pause. Another swallow, another glance. She really does not want her partner to come out here. "At the end of pregnancy, a rise in the neurotransmitter hormone oxytocin causes contractions in the uterus, which lead to the baby's birth. During the hour before her death, Ms. Harlow's oxytocin level was similarly elevated—about nine times that of an average—nonpregnant—woman."

Dr. Das sits, listens, says nothing. Her face shows a stone-cold resolve. But her eyes, increasingly more bloodshot, reveal the true gamut of emotions through which she's racing. Her brown skin looks just a shade paler, the dark circles under her eyes deepening before him. And he's not even to the good part yet.

"I'd say her contractions were about two minutes apart," he says, "based on her heart rate during the hour or so before she died." He watches Dr. Das's face carefully. He's not supposed to know what Ms. Harlow's actual heart rate was during the hour before she died, but he suspects she

knew the forged logs were for naught when he started rat-
tling off levels of hormones that were supposed to be hidden.
"And Martin says she died just minutes after the baby—
Anabel, right?—was born. What would you presume to be
the cause of death of a woman who loses her entire blood
volume within minutes of giving birth? Assuming, of course,
it were possible for a woman to become pregnant and main-
tain a healthy pregnancy?"

At first, he thinks she hasn't heard the question. Or
is she just stalling to make it look like she's thinking? When
it seems like she'll never respond, she opens her mouth.
"Well," she begins, that honey-molasses voice of hers barely
above a whisper, "Considering everything you've told me,
I'd assume there was a placental abruption—a tearing of the
placenta away from the wall of the uterus. That can cause
heavy bleeding and premature birth."

"When was the baby due, again?"

"Pardon?"

"When were Celeste and Martin expecting their
baby?"

"Oh, I can't be sure of the exact date without checking my files," she says.

"It's interesting, then, that you mention premature
birth."

"Well," she says, understanding his question, "the
baby only weighed about two-point-seven kilos, which is a
bit lower than a full-term newborn typically weighs. Assuming she was born naturally, as you're saying, the low birth
weight—combined with the mother's sudden death—suggests a premature birth."

"It sounds as if you'd rather not acknowledge that she was, in fact, born naturally."

Dr. Das sits back in her chair and folds her arms. As she does, his overlay detects a familiar bright flash in her left hand. It's only there for a fraction of a second, but that's long enough to throw him temporarily off-kilter.

"Okay, well, let's continue, then," he says when she doesn't speak, focusing his mind back on the data in front of him. "We talked about what happens from conception forward, but what we haven't discussed is what happens before conception. Ovulation happens, right? That's when the egg is released from the ovary so that it can be fertilized? And this happens every single month from the age of...twelve or so, all the way up until the woman becomes pregnant. And each month that a woman doesn't become pregnant, she has a...menstrual cycle, is it? The lining of the uterus sheds and is expelled from the body. Is that all correct?"

"According to my medical training, yes. Anyway, I don't see—"

Emeka continues. "And there are hormonal fluctuations which accompany this cyclical event in a woman's body—fluctuations which Celeste Harlow's data mirrors. Her sex hormone alerts were disabled at the time of implant configuration, though, so one wouldn't have noticed these fluctuations unless one had been looking for them." He pauses. She remains silent, staring straight into his eyes. "In order for an egg to be released, a woman needs to be fertile, wouldn't you say? An egg could not be released and fertilized in the body of a woman who underwent the safeguarding procedure which is mandatory for every newborn girl. Right?"

Dr. Das becomes still as a statue. If she was cautiously alert before, now she's a prey animal, petrified in place as the predator gets ever closer. It's as if, until now, she didn't believe he had the knowledge or understanding to view her as ultimately responsible for Celeste Harlow's death.

He's never minded too much being underestimated, though. It's actually made his job easier over time. "Dr. Das, Celeste Harlow was entrusted into your care shortly after her birth to receive her health monitoring implant and undergo her safeguarding procedure. What did you do on that day?"

"Detective, that was nearly thirty-five years ago. I couldn't possibly—"

"I'll tell you, then, if you're having trouble remembering. You brought that baby in for her procedure, and you gave her the implant, and—against the express written wishes of her parents, and against the law, you did *not* perform the safeguard procedure. Dr. Das, you might not have been present at Ms. Harlow's death, but I'm sure the Council Attorney would agree that you are responsible."

Dr. Das swallows and says nothing.

"Tell me, Dr. Das, have you seen Anabel for her procedure yet?"

She shakes her head, a slight movement, but does not dare speak.

"I suggest, then, that you advise Mr. Granby to find another family physician. Your license to practice is suspended pending investigation."

Her jaw drops, then rises again.

"You'll have confirmation of the suspension and next steps waiting in your inbox," Emeka says as he stands.

"Do me a favor, Doctor. Don't leave town anytime soon." Dr. Das remains seated, and he moves to leave. "I'll be in touch," he calls over his shoulder as he steps through the door and it closes behind him.

11

LUCINDA IS EATING LUNCH IN THE FIRST-FLOOR CAFÉ AT THE office when her mobile lights up: *Incoming call from Elle Vincent Baker*. A smile sneaks across her face as she answers.

"Aunt Elle!" she says. Her colleagues turn in her direction, peering at her from the other tables. "Sorry," she mouths, cheeks flushing as she sinks into the chair. She lowers her voice. "Aunt Elle, what a pleasant surprise." It's typical for weeks to pass between hearing from Elle. It hasn't even been two full days since they had dinner together.

Elle smiles. "Hi, Luci, sweetheart, how are you holding up?"

Lucinda sighs. In many ways, she is closer to Elle than she is to her own mother. Elle used to take her for ice cream after swim meets, or when she and Astor had a fight. It was Elle who offered advice when things with Zavi began to get serious. Yet, just like everyone else, she has to stay at arm's length.

She wants to weep and tell Aunt Elle how she can't erase from her mind the image of Celeste's green eyes rolling back into her head, and how she sees the red-black pool spreading across the floor every time she closes her eyes. Instead, she says, "I miss her, but I'm doing okay." Her voice doesn't even crack.

"It's going to take some time," Elle says. "I know she'd never tell you this, but I think your mother is having a hard time, too."

Lucinda nearly chokes on her drink. "My mother?" she asks, laughing. "I think you've got the wrong woman."

Elle doesn't laugh along. "Your father was just over," she says, "and he's worried about her. He said, as Celeste's doctor, she feels responsible for her death. Apparently, last night, a detective came to the house to ask her about it. After he left, she went up to the roof alone and didn't come back until after midnight. Dad said she seemed really rattled."

Lucinda's heart begins to pound. So that's why her mother abruptly canceled their dinner date. What happened during that conversation? Last time she saw her mother, the detective—Adi's father—had already been to see Ruma once and she was concerned the coverup hadn't been successful. The fraud they've committed will ruin them if it's discovered.

But she certainly can't tell Aunt Elle any of that.

"From what she told me," Lucinda says carefully, "The Bureau investigates all premature deaths. Sounded like they just wanted to know what alerts came through from Celeste's implant. Make sure the system is working as it should, you know. See if there's anything the implant missed." Sounds plausible. She shrugs. "I don't know what the detective talked to her about last night, but once the case is closed, I think she'll start getting back to normal. I think we all will. As normal as we can be," she adds, looking down at the table and pushing her plate away, "with Celeste gone."

"Just, do me a favor and keep an eye on her," Elle says. "I know she seems solid as stone on the outside, but she's feeling this loss the same as you. Maybe more."

Doubtful, but there's no point in arguing. "Of course, Aunt Elle. Sometimes I forget she has feelings at all." She means it as a joke, but it comes out flat and serious.

"Of course she does, Luci," says Elle. "She just doesn't have the luxury of being able to wear them on her sleeve." Lucinda suppresses a scoff. Sounds familiar. All her life, Lucinda has had to meter every interaction—every smile and frown, every word she says—because someone is always watching.

Unlike Ruma, though, Lucinda has learned the art of subtlety. She can show warmth and compassion to her loved ones even as she keeps from them secrets better left untold. She loves and praises even as she teaches and demands. She's never had to turn off her affections in order to perform her duties, as it seems her mother has done. Or at least, that's what she's done with Lucinda.

"Oh! Did you get the invitation for the baby naming?" asks Elle.

"Hmm?" asks Lucinda, confused.

"Myles and Peter. They sent out invitations for the baby naming. Did you know they're having her on my birthday?" Elle's voice bubbles with excitement about the new addition to their family.

"Oh, yeah. I mean, no, I haven't seen the invitation yet, but I've also been kind of buried with everything else going on. That's quite an honor. I'm excited for them. And for you, Grand—"

Elle cuts her off. "Uh-uh," she says. "No grand-anything, please. I decided to have her call me 'GiGi.'"

"That sounds familiar." Lucinda reaches back a life-time. "Wasn't that your grandmother's name?"

Elle chuckles. "Well, it wasn't her name, but it's what I called her. Maybe she had trouble coming to terms with the other *G* word, too. You met her once, when you were just a little girl. Do you remember?"

A flash of gray hair, close-cropped just like Aunt Elle's, appears in her mind. A warm smile, framed with little lines, and a tiny glass building full of hydrangeas and azal-eas, orchids and roses. The smell inside was one of earth and green leaves and natural perfume. A smell that, even as a young girl, she recognized from only one other place. She inhales, here in the cafe, and can almost smell it once more.

"She was nice," Lucinda says, wistful.

"She taught me everything," Elle says, and she can hear the smile in her aunt's voice. "So, while Myles and Peter honor me with a granddaughter born on my birthday, I can honor her by keeping her name alive."

What a sweet gesture, Lucinda thinks, and immedi-ately feels guilty that this kind of thing would never occur to her. Nor would it occur to Ruma, though, she realizes, and then she doesn't feel so bad. She wonders if, decades on, Serafina will be moved to honor her mother, her grand-mother, the women who came before her. Hopefully Lucinda's approach has differed from her mother's enough that such a thing would cross Serafina's mind.

"Forward me the invite," Lucinda says. "I'll be there." Too many moments go by before she says, "And I'll go check in on my mom later today."

12

THIRTY-FOUR. THIS MAKES 34 TIMES EMEKA HAS SEEN THIS photogram. The petals of the purple flower open and rest on the soft brown skin of the girl's palm.

He's become accustomed to wearing his overlay passively in the last few days. At first, like at the medical examiner's office, he left it on unintentionally. But once he started paying attention to the photograms, he saw them everywhere. Slowly and patiently, he began observing at every opportunity, catching glimpses on the street and in restaurants and trying to piece together the image that was being projected.

Today, as he searched this uptown convenience store for some fruit to complement the sandwich he'd already ordered, he saw his chance. A young woman, no older than sixteen with twists of pink hair pointing in all directions, was reaching into one of the food delivery compartments. When she opened her hand, the photogram appeared.

"Pardon me, Miss," he said as she placed the wrapped food into her bag.

She jumped, startled. After looking him over, though—gray hair and leathery skin covered in a business suit and shiny shoes—she turned in his direction and smiled up at him. "Yes?" she asked.

"I was wondering if you'd mind showing me your photogram," he said.

Now, here they are, the young girl's palm opening and closing in midair. With each new unfurling of her fingers, the flower does the same—like a time-lapse photograph of a flower blooming in the morning light.

Suddenly, his mind wanders back to the woman who stood outside the elevator when he first went to question Martin Granby. The woman he's now nearly certain is Lucinda, lifelong friend of Celeste Harlow and, most likely, Dr. Ruma Das's daughter. The same woman he met ages ago when he and Abigail went to that awards banquet for Adi. She was standing just like this, staring at her open palm. Emeka hadn't been wearing his overlay at the time. If he had, would he have seen the same iridescent flower?

"If you don't mind me asking," he says, "where did you get it?"

"Oh—uh—it's a, kind of like a club, I guess, that I belong to," she says, sounding as if she's deciding on each word as she utters it. "Me and my mom. It's, uh, like a gardening club. My mom always says gardening is, like, a lost art."

"Oh? Interesting. Are there a lot of members? In this club?" He sounds like he's interrogating her. He pulls back his eagerness a little, softening his tone. "I just ask because I've never noticed this photogram before and, suddenly, I seem to be seeing them everywhere."

"Oh. Well, yeah, I mean, I guess. We just go there and, like, tend the gardens and stuff. We don't really talk too much." She abruptly takes her mobile out of her jeans pocket with the flower-hand and makes a few taps on it. If she's trying to be subtle, she's failing. "Sorry, I just need to…" She doesn't finish her sentence before turning away and walking out of the store, nose buried in her mobile, leaving Emeka more suspicious and puzzled than he was before.

There's something to these photograms, he'd put money on it. They have popped up at every turn during this investigation, just like this Lucinda woman. Hopefully his next interview will help him figure out what that connection might be.

If there was ever a question that Celeste's friend, Dr. Das's daughter, and the woman Emeka met all those years ago at Adi's award banquet, were the same Lucinda, seeing her once more has erased all doubt. She is taller and leaner than her mother, but with the same ochre skin and golden eyes. Even her voice, while not low like her mother's, has the same musical cadence.

In most other aspects, though, Lucinda and Dr. Das appear to differ. Lucinda is striking, but her style is simple: long-sleeved tunic over charcoal-colored leggings, no makeup, hair piled haphazardly atop her head.

Like her, the apartment is decorated in grayscale, apart from a few pieces of colorful art popping out on the walls and some plants sitting on otherwise sparse shelves. While the space borders on sterile, Lucinda could not have been more inviting when Emeka arrived and re-introduced himself. "Nice to see you again," Lucinda says. "It's been ages. I put some coffee on when I saw you were coming up. How do you take yours?"

"Oh. No coffee for me, thanks," he says. This is a new experience for him, questioning someone he's met before outside of work, and he doesn't want to get too comfortable. Besides, it's after five in the afternoon. Drinking coffee now would be a prescription for insomnia.

"Well, then," she says, smiling. "More for me."

She retrieves one of the two cups from the delivery compartment in the autochef and gestures for Emeka to follow her to the living room, where a pewter-colored loveseat makes a perfect corner with a matching sofa and built-in chaise. She sits on the chaise, and he takes a seat on the loveseat facing her.

"So, what brings you here this late in the day?" she asks as she settles into her seat. "No rest for the wicked? Isn't that the saying?"

Emeka offers a faint smile. "I just had some questions about your friend, Celeste," he says. "By the way, I am very sorry for your loss."

Lucinda dips her head and swallows. "Thank you," she says quietly. "Of course, I'm happy to help in any way I can, but I have to say I'm surprised you're here. I thought Celeste's case would be closed by now. And I'm not sure how I could help your investigation anyway."

Emeka would have expected the case to be closed by now, too. But is there an impatience in Lucinda's tone? He recalls Dr. Das saying something very similar when he interviewed her. "There are still some unanswered questions," he says. "I'm sure you understand."

Lucinda nods, and for a moment, she looks very tired. "Of course," she says. "How can I help?"

"Your mother is Dr. Ruma Das, correct?" Emeka asks.

"Yes," she says, but it sounds more like a question. She brings up her mug, cupped in both hands, for a sip. The tiredness has faded, and her golden eyes are alert.

"She was Celeste's family physician, correct?"

"Yes."

"And she was present the morning of Celeste's death?"

"I'm sure you know my mother can't share anything with me about her patients," Lucinda says. "All I know is what the medical examiner's report says."

"When was the last time you saw or spoke with your mother?" Emeka asks. How much does she know about what her mother's been up to? And is Lucinda herself involved?

The woman shrugs. "We were supposed to meet last night, but she asked for a rain check. Said something had come up." The same placid look remains on her face. Too placid. "Why are you asking about my mother? Didn't you come to ask about Celeste?"

"Indeed," Emeka replies. "I just want to make sure I understand how everyone is connected. You'd known Celeste for a long time, right?"

"Yeah," Lucinda says, looking down into her steaming cup. "Since we were babies," she says. "I can't even remember ever meeting her. She was always just…there."

"Your parents must have been close friends, then, too?"

Lucinda nods but doesn't look up. "Sure."

"There were a few of you, right?" Emeka says, recalling the other women Martin mentioned. "You and Celeste, and—was it Astor?"

Lucinda's eyes flick up to his at the mention of her friend's name. Fear flashes behind her stony expression. "Yeah," she says. Her voice is quiet but level. "Them and Myles. All our moms were really close when we were little. We grew up like siblings."

"Lucinda, do you recall anything out of the ordinary about Celeste as you were growing up? Any…strange behavior?"

"Strange behavior?" she asks, looking confused. "No, none that I can think of. What do you mean?"

"Just—anything out of the ordinary? Particularly in her early teens?" Surely Celeste would have confided in just one friend when she began having her monthly cycles. And Lucinda was the most likely candidate.

Lucinda's eyes look around as if, hidden on the walls, she'll find the information he's requested. She shrugs. "Nope," she says. Then she adds, with a nostalgic grin, "Her teenage drama was no different from the rest of ours."

Emeka smiles. He was relieved when Adi left her teen drama behind, but now Micah is edging into that territory. "Right. Do you recall when Celeste told you that she and Martin were planning to have their baby?"

"Sure," she responds.

"And did you notice anything out of the ordinary throughout those nine months?"

"Not that I can think of," she says. Her voice has a hollowed-out sound to it. Maybe the grief is getting to her. Or maybe she's hiding something.

"Did you visit Martin and Celeste during that time? See the baby in the incubator?"

Lucinda shrugs. "I guess," she says. "I mean, I'm sure I went to visit them at some point, but I don't spend a lot of time watching babies incubate."

"I see," says Emeka. "Do you have a child? I don't remember you having one when we last met, but that was years ago."

Lucinda takes a sip of her coffee. "I do. A daughter. Serafina. She's six." She looks as if she's about to say something else but stops herself. "Anyway, her birth seems like ancient history by now and I wouldn't have been much help to Celeste other than to be excited with her."

Emeka looks around the apartment. All the art is abstract except for a small framed photo of Lucinda's parents and one large canvas, a gorgeous black-and-white rendition of Lucinda with a man and a little girl who must be her partner and daughter. His eyes are drawn from the canvas to the floating shelves next to it, where a collection of plants sits.

"Your plants are beautiful," Emeka says, leaving the couch and moving toward the varied pots. "What kind are they?" It's an unnecessary question; though she can't know it, Emeka's overlay has been activated the entire time he's been in here. With a glance, he can see any information about the plants he wishes—down to the level of moisture in the soil and details about the flowering stage.

She unfolds herself from the sofa and joins him at the plant stand. She rests her thumb and forefinger on either side of a thick, firm vertical leaf and traces its vein down to the soil. "This one is Sansevieria." Next, she points to a burst of pink flowers so perfect it seems impossible they're real. "An orchid. And a peace lily," she says, gesturing to the last plant, which has more delicate leaves than the first one and more realistic-looking flowers than the second. "Good fortune, feminine strength, and peace." Turns out he didn't need his overlay for this part; her succinct descriptions are on the mark.

"You seem to know a lot about plants," he says. He thinks of the garden club the girl from the convenience store described. The girl with the flowering blossom photogram in her palm. What are the chances Lucinda is hiding one of those photograms right now? He glances again at her hands, but her arms are crossed in front of her now, left hand tucked in behind her right elbow.

She stares at the orchid. "I guess I do," she says thoughtfully.

"Where'd you learn?" he asks.

She pauses for a moment. "I've always been interested in gardening, I guess," she says. "I always considered it kind of a lost art, you know? We have these massive agricultural greenhouses that automate and control everything, from how much water the plants get to how and when they're pollinated. It's amazing what our technology can do, don't get me wrong—my partner is an agricultural engineer, and he never lets me forget it—but there is something more…intimate about preparing the ground, planting and tending the seed with your own two hands."

Emeka's eyes are demanding to see those two hands. He didn't realize until now how attuned he's become to the photograms, or how practiced Lucinda is at keeping her palms out of sight.

A thought occurs to him. A flimsy one, maybe, but it's worth a try. "I saw a flower once, and I wonder if you could tell me what it might be," he says. "I want to get one for my partner, but I just can't figure out what to ask for. The petals are pointy at the ends, and they face up, toward the sky? As if the flower grew inside a bowl." He holds out his hands together, fingertips cupped upward to represent the petals He studies Lucinda's face.

She swallows. Her eyes dart around the room and her hands search for pockets her long top doesn't have. She clears her throat. "That sounds like a lotus flower," she says cautiously. "Where did you see one of those? They've been endangered for years. I've never seen one in real life."

"You know, it's been so long, I don't remember," he answers. "Maybe it was an advertisement somewhere. Lotus flower," he repeats. "Thanks for the lead. I'll have to look them up."

"Certainly," she responds, slowly moving back to her seat on the sofa. "But you'll have to settle for a painting. It's illegal to own the flowers themselves."

"Too bad," he says. "Did Celeste enjoy gardening, as well?" he asks as he sits. "Is that one of the things you did together?"

"Sure," she responds, her gaze narrowing. That hollow tone has crept back into her voice. "I guess you could say that."

When she offers no further explanation, he asks, "Lucinda, how did you first find out about Celeste's death?"

Her eyes cloud over. "Martin called me the morning she died."

"Where were you when you received his call?"

She looks down at the coffee, once again warming her hands and acting as a shield between her and the detective as she sits, with her feet curled up underneath her and one elbow on the arm of the sofa. "Here," she says. "Right here, on this sofa, actually. My partner, Zavi, and I were having coffee and talking. Our daughter wasn't up yet."

"You must have been devastated," says Emeka. "What did you do?"

She shrugs. "I went over to help Martin with the baby. I was worried he wouldn't be able to cope."

"Speaking of the baby," Emeka says.

Lucinda shifts a bit, placing her coffee on the low table and sitting with one foot on the floor and the other ankle crossed over her knee. Her hands are folded in her lap. Either she's used to hiding her hands, or she knows what Emeka's looking for. Or both. "Sweet little girl," she says, smiling wistfully. "I'm assuming you've met her?"

"I have," Emeka says. "Tiny little thing, isn't she?"

Lucinda shrugs. Do her eyes narrow, just a bit? Or is that his imagination? "She's a newborn. Newborns are tiny. She reminds me of when Serafina was little."

"When did you meet Anabel for the first time?" asks Emeka.

Lucinda pauses before responding. "That day, I guess—after Celeste died."

"Doesn't that seem a little strange?"

"What do you mean?" she asks, golden eyes wide and impossibly earnest.

"What I mean is that parents usually invite close family and friends over to meet the baby on the day of the birth—in fact, the party is usually planned months before the baby is born. And being one of Celeste's closest friends, I would have assumed you'd be first on the guest list. Martin said Anabel was born on Friday, and Celeste died on Saturday morning. Wouldn't you have expected to be invited to visit your closest friend the day her daughter was born?"

"Celeste and Martin's decisions are their business," Lucinda says, in a tone that straddles the line between indifference and defiance. "They are—were—both very private, reserved people. There's no law that says parents have to have a big party when their baby is born. If they wanted to keep that special moment to themselves, it would have been their prerogative. In fact, Zavi and I did the same thing."

Did the same thing. Well, that could mean a whole handful of things. What truth hides behind those words? Emeka allows the silence to fill the space for several seconds. It creeps up to the highest corners of the ceilings and down into the baseboards. Still, Lucinda sits, stoic, coffee cooling and still mostly full on the table, as if she's got all the time in the world and nothing to hide. "Where'd you say you were when you found out about Celeste's death?" he eventually asks.

"Here," she says. "With my partner."

"And that was at what time?"

"I don't know. In the morning."

He could reveal his hand right now. He could tell Lucinda everything he knows about the morning of Celeste Harlow's death and watch as her cheeks twitch and her eyes avert and her arms cross and she sinks deeper into the corner of her gray sofa. In his younger, less-disciplined years, he probably would have done so, just to watch her crumble as he backed her into a corner.

In the end, though, he will learn more from holding these particular cards close to his chest for a moment or two longer than he will by jumping into gotcha mode. Something is going on here, and it's bigger than a rogue doctor experimenting on one patient. He needs to poke around more and find the edges of the case. Otherwise, the true story might become even more slippery.

"Thank you for your time," he says, as he rises from his seat. "If you think of anything else I should know, please contact me."

Lucinda stands, cupping her drink with both hands once more. "I will be sure and do that," she replies. Her smile is tight, forced. Much different from the genuine, warm one she offered him when he arrived. "Thank you for coming, Detective Abuto." She extends her hand and squeezes his firmly. "Please be sure to reach out if you need anything else."

Lucinda opens the door for him to leave and closes it behind him as he steps out. The afternoon light shines through either side of the crack under the door, interrupted by her shadow as she stands on the other side. Emeka stays in the corridor for several minutes, organizing his thoughts and clearing his schedule for this afternoon, and never once does she move.

13

Lucinda tries Martin again. She hasn't been able to contact him in two days. She tried stopping by his apartment after work today, but nobody answered when she rang at the building's main door. Her call goes unanswered. She even reached out to Holly, Celeste's mother, but she and Martin haven't spoken since the day Celeste died.

She reviews her messages to him over the past 48 hours, each more urgent than the last. She sends another. *Martin, please respond. I'm worried about you.*

And she is concerned for his safety. But, just as urgently, she needs to know what Martin has told the detective. Abuto seemed to know more than he directly said, and there are only so many places he could have gotten that information. Maybe that's why Martin is missing. What if he spilled everything he knew and then took Anabel somewhere so he wouldn't have to face Lucinda again? Lucinda's mind races. What would Ruma do?

"Shit," she says, looking at the clock. She almost forgot her promise to Aunt Elle that she would go check on her mother.

All she wants is to curl up in bed, to escape from the world, if only for a few hours. But instead, when Zavi gets home with Serafina, she asks him to take care of dinner, throws on an oversized black zip-up sweatshirt, and boards a car to her parents' place. Might as well get it over with. The sooner she's satisfied her mother is okay, the sooner she can collapse into bed and, hopefully, a blissful black sleep with the horror of Celeste's death receding ever farther away.

The car seems even more soundless than usual today, and she realizes it's because she's silenced notifications. There's no greeting as she gets situated, no prompt to turn on music or adjust the climate control. The navigation system knows from her summons where she's headed, and so there's no need for her to interact with even the technology. At first, she welcomes the quiet, but soon the noise in her head rises to fill the void.

Her grief at the loss of Celeste, she realizes with a twinge of sadness, is now an afterthought. Her mind is just as conflicted as it was a week ago, but now instead of weighing her guilt and responsibility against the unpredictability of Celeste's death, she is running herself into exhaustion thinking about all the evidence the detective might be gathering at this very moment. Does he know about the masking algorithm? About the real reason for Celeste's death? About her mother's role, or her own? Will he trace all this back to the Society? And will he realize that his flesh and blood is connected to this case in a way that is far too close for comfort? How can she get ahead of all this so she can prepare her Sisters for what might be coming?

The questions swirl around in her head, but no answers follow. She is in a helpless limbo and all she can do is wait and see.

"*FUCK!*" she yells to herself as she slams a fist down on the dashboard.

"Is everything okay, Lucinda?" asks the emotionless voice of the car, no doubt breaking through her silence settings for safety reasons.

"It's fine," she snaps back. "Can we drive around the block before parking?"

"Certainly, Lucinda," the car answers, and through the right-side window, she watches her parents' building glide past. She needs to get her thinking straight before going up to talk with her mother. Dad will surely pick up on her twisted and roiling emotions if she doesn't get her breathing leveled out. And she's in no mood to make up explanations today.

"Play one of my dad's songs," she says aloud, and the car's speakers begin playing an acoustic, folky tune from her childhood. *Lullaby*, he called it. Written for her when she was too young to remember. She sits back against the seat, resting her head and closing her eyes, singing along with her father's voice as she has countless times. The song ends, and with her hands on her knees, she breathes deeply and exhales one long "*aum.*" She hasn't meditated much as an adult, but as a kid, she used to try so hard. She would walk in on her mother sitting motionless, mind clear and body still, and sit down next to her. She'd cross her legs, arrange her hands on her knees, and attempt to quiet her mind. "It will bring you peace," her mother would say, "but you have to bring the quiet." She never could quite bring the quiet.

Her mother still sits morning and night, breath shallow and mind blank, in front of that huge sun canvas in her office. When was the last time Lucinda even tried?

Nonetheless, the *aum* returns to her now, through all her inner turmoil, and the vibrations in her chest bring her awareness—just for a moment—into the center of her self rather than to the racing, frantic thoughts.

She keeps her eyes closed until the car finally parks itself in front of her childhood home, once again silent as if waiting for Lucinda to act.

She takes a deep breath, then opens her eyes and takes stock of her emotions. Still a chaotic jumble, but a little quieter now.

Lucinda slides over to exit the car next to the curb. She is closing the door and turning toward the building when she hears a woman's voice. While the sound is faint, it's most certainly one of distress. And it's coming from very high up. She looks up in the light of dusk and, impossibly, sees a form—a human form—falling through the air.

It must only take a few seconds for the form (the *person*) to reach the ground, but in those few seconds, Lucinda lives a lifetime or more. Her mind cannot reconcile what it's seeing. It can't be a person falling from the sky. But it is. It must be a dream. But it doesn't feel like a dream. She is too paralyzed and perplexed to call out. A buzz creeps into her ears, slowly becoming the only sound she registers.

Her every instinct calls on her to intervene in some way, but there's nothing she can do that will change the outcome. Stepping in between this doomed person and the ground would certainly mean death for her as well. Her stomach sinks past her shoes and deep, deep into the cement below her feet. She is going to watch this person die without being able to do anything to stop it. She would turn, avert her eyes, but she can't. It's more than the human curiosity that brings the other bystanders to the scene, eyes wide and mouths agape with painfully audible gasps. Because as the falling figure (*person*) gets closer, she sees something familiar.

And then, with a flap of bright pink and gold fabric—a long, flowing skirt Lucinda's seen a thousand times before—the buzzing inside her head comes to a crescendo and then ends abruptly. Now, the only sound left is her own screaming, which doesn't stop until her voice gives out.

Shiny leather shoes approach.

The man from the picture, the man from the elevator, the man from the awards banquet. The man who, an hour ago, was in her apartment asking questions that made her increasingly nervous.

He is there, and his kind arms gently lift her from the ground, and his kind hands turn her away from the scene in front of her, and his kind voice tells her to let it all out as she heaves and sobs and pukes and all the tears and snot and regurgitated food swirl down into the gutter, and he keeps her from going down there with it.

And her father is there, through the revolving door, and his face turns into something she doesn't recognize, and he is on the ground next to Ruma before he looks in Lucinda's direction, and she reaches her arms out like Serafina would do if she had fallen here on the pavement, and instead of going to her he bends over the grotesque twist of fabric and long black braids that used to be Mama, and she can't blame him because she can't move either, and he reaches out with dumb fingers searching for a part of Ruma that's not broken, and he cradles her hand between both of his own, and Lucinda looks on from the side, from above, from below, and they're both wailing, and people have gathered, and sirens come closer, and no one can move, and it's like a still photo except it's real life, but it can't be real life, because this didn't just happen, it couldn't have.

A click-click-clicking, black high heels, and then Aunt Elle is bent down beside her, and Elle's arms are around her, and there is a sadness in her eyes that makes something inside Lucinda crack, and she collapses into her aunt's arms and doesn't know how she'll ever get up again.

People in uniforms arrive. They quietly close off the area and send away the onlookers. They attempt to do the same with Josiah, but it is a losing battle until Elle steps in. Leaving Lucinda kneeling on the sidewalk with her face in her hands, she pulls him up by the shoulders and turns him away from the gruesome scene. Arm wrapped around his back, she walks him back to the revolving door.

From the back he looks almost normal, his curly hair pulled back in the same bun it had been in before he was a widower. In that moment, Lucinda feels the loss of her mother not for herself, but for her father, who always deserved better than the half-truths her mother gave him but was never the wiser. Will he ever know, now that Ruma's not here to tell him? Maybe not. Maybe it's better that way.

The detective has backed away, but he hasn't left. His hand is up to his ear and his mouth is moving, but if he's talking Lucinda can't hear him. What is he doing here, anyway? It can't be a coincidence.

A few feet away, Lucinda sees an object, black and solid and shining in the glare from the streetlights above. She looks around at the emergency personnel. They are focused on tasks Lucinda would rather not consider. She reaches forward, stretching her arm out in the space between her and her mother, and retrieves the tiny mass of plastic and metal. Overlay glasses, light and smooth in the palm of her hand. Her mother's; they have to be. Glancing around once more, she carefully folds the device and shoves it into her sweatshirt pocket before sitting back on her heels, willing the detective to keep his distance.

She doesn't realize she's shivering until Elle is back at her side, saying, "Let's get you inside, sweetie, warm you up."

"I came to talk to her," Lucinda says, steadying herself on her feet. "I just came to check on her, like you said. I just came to make sure she was okay…" The sobs come back, wracking her body as they pass through the revolving door and Lucinda sees her father, presumably just as Elle left him, standing in front of the elevators as the doors open and close, staring but not seeing.

"I know, honey. I came to check on her, too," says Elle, hugging Lucinda close. "We were just too late."

14

EMEKA STEPS INTO THE STIFF, IMMACULATE OFFICE OF THE Director of Population Science. "Director Baker, thank you so much for meeting with me this morning despite the unfortunate news." Emeka had seen a lot of crime scenes, but the image of Dr. Ruma Das falling to her death has been a hard one to shake.

"Of course, sir." Clark Baker looks to be in his 60s, with a sandy crew cut and impeccable posture. Military, maybe. Baker gestures to a light-skinned Black man about Baker's age who stands next to a stiff-looking armchair. "And this is our medical director, Doctor Nathan Mackenzie. His team is responsible for implant and safeguarding protocols." Mackenzie and Baker don't make eye contact. These two must work together frequently—it seems their jobs are closely connected—but the air between them is cool enough to give Emeka a chill.

The three exchange greetings and Emeka takes the other stiff armchair, facing Baker at his desk. He scheduled this meeting before the death of Ms. Harlow's doctor. He realized while preparing, though, there is a connection between Clark Baker and Dr. Das. A coincidence, maybe. But what are the chances of this particular coincidence?

"Mr. Baker, I read that your partner went to school with Dr. Das?"

Baker clears his throat. "Yes, she did. They were always close friends. Her partner, Josiah, and I as well." He clears his throat again, but his gaze is steady. "Elle was actually on her way to visit Ruma when she—when it happened. She just couldn't get to her in time." He lowers his eyes.

"I'm so sorry for your loss," says Emeka. He must have said this phrase thousands of times during his career, but he genuinely means it each time.

"It's just so hard to believe she would resort to such extreme measures over something she couldn't possibly have controlled," says Baker.

Couldn't have controlled. If Baker actually believes this, Emeka is about to shatter his image of a longtime friend. He never delights in this kind of thing, but there's no way around it. After a pause, Emeka begins gently. "I know this is a difficult time for you and your family, and I want to thank you again for meeting with me. Would you mind if I direct your attention to the purpose of our meeting?"

"Of course," Baker says, his eyes clearing. Beside Emeka, Mackenzie nods.

"All right," says Emeka. "I'd like to present some of the information I've uncovered while investigating Celeste Harlow's death—shocking information, frankly. Shortly you'll see why the Population Science Department would be interested in the untimely death of a young woman in the first place." He pauses. "And I'm afraid it concerns your friend, Ruma Das."

Emeka reviews the details of the case. He shows the same graphs Rodriguez and Montissol showed him, aware of how incredulous the men's faces are becoming. He doesn't intend for it to be sensational, but the truth is so outlandish he can hardly help it.

"The implant logs were tampered with?" Mackenzie interjects at one point, leaning forward in his seat. "That's impossible."

"Yes," Emeka says, "that's what we thought, too. But the real data is right here."

"But why?" asks Baker slowly. "Did someone kill her and want it to look like an accident? Or maybe there was something chronically wrong with her that someone didn't want people finding out about?"

"*How?*" Mackenzie says. "The implants have been engineered to gather and transmit data. It would take someone intimately familiar with the device's design to be able to modify the logs."

"We need to look more into it," Emeka begins, looking at Mackenzie, "so we can figure out who forged the logs and how, so we can prevent it from happening again. As you said, though, it would have had to be someone who is pretty familiar with the way the system is designed, someone who knew about Ms. Harlow's death before even the authorities, because the logs were falsified before she arrived at the coroner's office." Or at least before Emeka got there and retrieved the implant. He thinks back to that first flash of bright purple in Dr. Blair's hand at the medical examiner's office. Was she involved in this coverup? "As far as the question of *why*," he continues, turning to face Baker, "well, I think we have an answer to that part." The men wait for him to continue. "The logs showed that Ms. Harlow was pregnant." Baker's mouth opens and then closes. Mackenzie can't even muster that; the blood that used to be in his face seems to have pooled elsewhere. "Thirty-eight weeks pregnant, to be exact, which, as you know, is a bit early for a baby to be born. The baby survived, but, of course, Ms. Harlow did not. According to Dr. Das, and another doctor who consulted on the case, the likely cause of death was a placental abruption. Ms. Harlow died during childbirth."

It's Baker's turn to be indignant. "That's not possible, though," he says. Safeguarding guarantees against that kind of thing. There's no way she could have been pregnant."

"It would seem as though there is," Emeka says. "Logs reaching as far back as her teenage years confirm her hormone levels were naturally developed, rather than the carefully metered synthetic ones present in safeguarded women. The safeguarding procedure was never performed on Celeste Harlow. And it's no coincidence that her family physician—since birth—was—"

"Ruma," says Clark Baker. The room is washed in silence. A cloud passes over the sun, momentarily darkening the light coming in through the windows.

"She didn't safeguard Celeste," says Mackenzie after a moment, voice barely above a whisper. His shoulders slump as he sits back in his seat, eyes staring but unfocused.

Baker steeples his hands around his nose and inhales deeply. "That's not a thing. How is that a thing? You can't just *not* do the procedure. Why would she do something like that?"

"That's a question I've been pondering myself," Emeka says. "That, along with the question of how likely it is that Celeste Harlow is the one and only woman in the entire world who walked around unaltered for her entire life without anyone knowing."

"So, to summarize, at least one doctor falsified at least one patient's safeguarding procedure," Baker says. "And, separately, at least one patient's health monitoring logs were falsified to hide this fact."

"That's the shape of it," Emeka says.

Mackenzie chimes in. "And wait—you said Ruma admitted to knowing Celeste was pregnant, admitted to the cause of death?"

"In a roundabout way, yes."

"And then she committed suicide because—what? Because she felt responsible for the woman dying?"

"You know," says Baker, looking thoughtful, "Josiah came to visit us yesterday morning because he was concerned about Ruma. He did mention something about Ruma feeling guilty for Celeste's death. That's the whole reason Elle was over at their building last night."

"Anything I say would be speculation," he admits, "but that would fit with the story that seems to be coming together."

"How certain are you of all of this?" asks Mackenzie. "The forgery, the falsified procedures, Ms. Harlow's pregnancy and cause of death?"

"Certain."

The gravity of the situation settles over everyone at once. After several silent moments, Mackenzie shakes his head and rubs his temples. "I've never heard of anything like this before," he says.

"Me either. Looks like we have some work to do," says Baker, looking Mackenzie in the eye for the first time.

"Yes," agrees Emeka. "Our offices will need to work together to figure out how this happened and who is responsible. And if anyone else is involved," he adds, leveling his eyes toward Baker.

Baker's eyes widen. "You mean to suggest there could be others?"

"We can't rule it out," says Emeka.

The mood is grim when the meeting finally ends, and Mackenzie's eyes are troubled as he stands to leave Baker's office just behind Emeka. Mackenzie and Emeka leave Baker standing, hands atop his desk and a look of disbelief on his face.

In the elevator, Mackenzie taps on his mobile. "Will you be attending the memorial for Dr. Das?" asks Emeka.

Mackenzie is distracted, eyes fixed on the screen. "Just a second," he says. After a moment he focuses on Emeka and answers. "Sorry, just organizing my thoughts about how to go about looking into this…issue. Yeah, I'll be at the memorial."

"Were you and Dr. Das close as well?" Emeka asks.

"Huh?" Mackenzie responds, attention back on his screen.

"You were in the same class in medical school with her. I thought maybe you two knew each other."

"Oh, well. Thirty years ago, we knew each other," Mackenzie says. "I was never close with Ruma the way Ellie was, but our paths did cross from time to time."

The elevator comes to a smooth stop at the ground floor. "Thanks for your time, Doctor," says Emeka. "Take care." He thinks about offering condolences, but Mackenzie seems much more concerned about the conversation they've just had than about the death of Ruma Das.

Mackenzie's eyes once again need to shift their focus from the screen so he can respond to Emeka. "Thanks, Detective," he says. "We'll be in touch." Mackenzie steps out of the elevator but stands just a few feet away, focused once more on whatever information he is reviewing on his mobile. People, dressed in business suits and in varying stages of engagement with their mobiles themselves, walk past him on all sides, taking little notice other than to avoid running into him. But the doctor remains, still as a statue, in the middle of it all, brow furrowed in concentration, oblivious to the activity around him.

He's still standing there when Emeka walks through the doors and into the overcast day.

15

RIVULETS RUN DOWN THE WINDOW, SMEARING THE VIEW from Lucinda's childhood. As a girl she used to imagine soaring like a bird among the buildings and above the streets, swooping down into a tree for a rest before gliding down over the river. The river is still there, in the distance, but when she tries to imagine flying through the air all she can see is the billowing fabric that used to be her mother.

The door behind her opens, and she jumps. It's just Aunt Elle. "You scared me half to death," Lucinda says, clutching her chest.

"I'm sorry, honey," Elle says, joining Lucinda at the window. "I thought I'd find you in here."

Lucinda looks around her father's music room, adapted from her childhood bedroom when she moved out. Even in the dim overcast, she can see the mural on the wall next to the closet—a meadow full of wildflowers representing every color of the rainbow under a blue sky dotted with wispy white clouds. Her parents stenciled out the mural, and helped her paint it, when she was only, what? Eight or nine, probably. It must have taken months, stealing snippets of time here and there between homework and music lessons and cooking and gardening, before they made the last brushstroke. She sat at the foot of her bed that day, one parent on each side, arms around each other, pride shining from all their faces. They had finally completed this thing of beauty, and they had done it together. The air was so thick with love, she can see it now. If only she could reach out and grab it.

Tucked away in the mural, hidden in a little pond at the very edge of the landscape, sits one purple blossom—the same one she carries in her left hand wherever she goes. As she focuses on that one flower, the warm haze of love surrounding her eight-year-old self and her happy family turns dark. As if shot from a cannon, she moves through decades of deception, past all the forks in the road where they could have gone back but kept pressing forward, and then she's back here. Not in her childhood bedroom but in her father's music studio, with no mother and no clue what to do next. Images from Anabel's nursery flash in her mind, a hauntingly similar work of art that will never be complete.

"Luci?" Elle is saying.

"What? Yeah," she mumbles, shaking her head in a futile attempt to lift the fog. "I'm fine," she says, though she's not sure Elle asked how she was doing, and anyway it's a lie.

"Oh, sweetie," Elle says. "This has got to be so awful for you."

Lucinda can't bring herself to say anything, doesn't know what she'd say if she could. She stares instead at the door over Elle's shoulder.

"Mind if I just sit with you for a while?" her aunt asks. "Until you're ready to go back in there with everyone else?"

Everyone else is all the friends and colleagues and family members who have come to pay their final respects to Ruma, represented now only by a framed photograph and a potted peace lily, placed in the middle of the family room.

Lucinda doesn't want to be in the room with them, and she's assigned Zavi to cover for her while she clears her mind in here. She gestures for Elle to sit down on a piano bench, hesitant to speak for fear of letting escape the emotions it's taken her days to rein back in. She is an overfilled balloon, and even too deep of an inhale would cause her to burst.

And so they sit. Elle picks out a horrendous tune on the piano, and Lucinda picks up her father's guitar and makes an equally terrible attempt at playing one of his catchier songs. They laugh at themselves and each other, and for a moment a little light creeps into the blackness.

"What I'm about to tell you," says Elle, "is cliché, and I know it. But I want you to know that it's also true, and I wouldn't say it if it weren't." Lucinda is silent, and Elle goes on. "The best way you can honor your mother, and be sure her death wasn't in vain, is to keep going. The world won't stop for your grief, and your life can't stop either. The things you and your mother did together, don't forget about those things—those will be what keeps her memory alive, even if her body is gone."

"What *things?*" Lucinda asks, too numb to sound bitter.

Elle gestures to the wall. "Like this—the painting, the cooking. The gardening." Elle pauses here, her blue eyes meeting Lucinda's. "All you learned from your mother—through them, she will live on. And as Serafina gets older, you can teach her everything her grandmother would have taught her, and your mother will live on in her as well. Not just as some DNA code, but as the living memory of a person who was very, very important to the world."

Very important to the world. Lucinda considers the words, disapproving of their weight. All these years she's spent walking the line between resenting her mother and following her without question, and even now she can't figure out on which side she'll fall.

"I'd like to be alone," she says, throat tight. Her eyes drift past her aunt and the mural and the instruments and the ghost of her childhood bed, finally landing back on the rain-streaked window. She imagines a pink and gold bird flying, floating, falling.

Maybe Elle says something as she walks to the door, or maybe she leaves as quietly as she came in. Lucinda doesn't register anything at all until Zavi comes in, wraps her in his arms, and whispers into her hair, "Let's go home."

Lucinda collapses into the car, no longer able to hold herself up.

"Astor was there, at the beginning," says Zavi as they close the doors and the car begins moving. "She said you two need to talk. She didn't stick around long."

"I'll bet," Lucinda mumbles, staring out the window at the damp streets.

Zavi looks over in her direction, raising an eyebrow. "Still not seeing eye to eye?"

She shakes her head. Is the pang of guilt that swells in her chest because she's losing Astor? Or because she can't seem to care?

Zavi's hand rests on Lucinda's knee. He says nothing and she's thankful. At this point, any noise might send her over the edge. In the silence Lucinda leans back against the seat, breathing deeply and attempting to quiet her mind. Sleep has been distant and fleeting lately. Maybe it wouldn't be such a bad thing if she rested for a moment. She closes her eyes.

A loud chime sounds from her mobile. *Urgent message, source unknown.*

She suppresses a groan. Not now. It's probably another condolence message from a distant friend or colleague; they've slowed but haven't stopped completely. She'll listen later, after she's had a chance to clear her head. For now, she'll rest her eyes until they get home.

In the elevator, she stands in broken silence, Zavi's hand entwined in her own. The few minutes of rest have done nothing to dampen the cacophony of memories, dreams, and faces thrumming in her mind.

"Tea?" Zavi asks when they reach their floor.

Lucinda's affirmative response has barely passed her lips when she stops cold. "Astor," she says flatly. "What are you doing here?"

Astor is sitting in the hallway, knees up to her chest, hands hanging around her ankles. Her mobile sits on the floor next to her. Her half-shaved hair is pulled back into a neat, tight French braid. Astor stands. "We need to talk," she says, throwing a sideways glance at Zavi and then refocusing on Lucinda. "Alone."

Zavi raises his eyebrows. "Right. Three cups of tea, then," he says, disappearing into the apartment and leaving the two women standing in the hallway.

The door latches behind him and Astor takes another step forward, close enough for Lucinda to smell the tinge of gin. "Lucinda, you need to get out."

"Get out?" Lucinda asks. "What do you mean, 'get out'?"

"The Garden," Astor says, her voice low but urgent. "I'm worried about you. I don't think you're safe."

Lucinda glances around the deserted corridor. "Astor, we've been over this. What happened to Celeste—"

"I'm not talking about what happened to Celeste," she says, her tone insistent. "I'm talking about what could happen to you."

"Me?" she asks. "Astor. I already had my baby. Many others have too, without incident. And things will only get easier as we add more members."

"Lucinda, I'm not talking about babies!" Astor whisper-shouts. "Listen to me. There's an investigation going on." There is real fear in Astor's eyes. But the investigation is old news to Lucinda.

"Yeah, I know," Lucinda says. "The detective questioned my mother. Martin, too. It's a requirement. No big deal, right? As long as everyone sticks with the official story—"

"That's what I'm trying to tell you, Lucinda. I'm pretty sure the official story is blown."

The blood drains from Lucinda's face. There is still no one around, but she grabs Astor's wrist, anyway. The hallway is not the place for this kind of conversation. "Come here," she says, opening the apartment door. She leads Astor past the kitchen, where Zavi and Serafina are still talking with the babysitter, and to the sliding balcony door. She leaves her overlay glasses on top of a bookshelf and motions for Astor to do the same.

Lucinda stands under the heat lamp, hugging herself against the cold mist. "Why do you think the story is blown?" she demands.

"The less you know, the better," Astor says, "but I have a feeling this investigator guy found something on Celeste's implant that proved the coroner's report wrong."

Oh, no. The hair on the back of Lucinda's neck stands on end. The only way he would have seen something on the implant is by breaking the mask. "Are you sure? Or is this just a conspiracy theory you put together after a few drinks and decided to run with?"

"Fuck you. I'm sure, Lucinda. I think he was onto your mother. In fact, I am pretty sure he was on his way to arrest her when she died. And I don't know how long the rest of you have before they find out about the whole operation. It's—"

"*Us*," Lucinda says, turning toward Astor and pulling back her windblown hair with an elastic band. Astor stares at her. "You said 'the rest of *you*.'"

"*Us*, sure, whatever," Astor says. "Are you even listening? I'm telling you that you are in danger. Serafina—even Zavi—might be, too. You need to do something to protect yourself." She pauses as if weighing her next words, then looks Lucinda squarely in the eyes. "Lucinda, I love you. I don't want you to end up like your mother."

"My mother?" Lucinda says, incredulous. "My mother was battling her own demons, Astor. She felt guilty for Celeste's death, and to tell you the truth, I don't blame her."

Astor tightens her jacket around her body and moves closer to Lucinda and the heat lamp. She looks at Lucinda, her stony eyes warming for the first time in a long time. "Sister, I'm sure all that's true. But I don't think your mother killed herself."

For a moment Lucinda can't speak. Of course Ruma killed herself. Lucinda saw the whole thing. *Saw it from the ground*, says a voice inside her. *Saw the end*. How does she know what happened before she stepped out of the car? "My father, though," she says. "She told my dad she felt responsible for Celeste's death."

Astor takes another step closer. "We all feel responsible for Celeste's death," she says. "But your mother had to know something like this would happen eventually. She was the one most prepared to deal with it. Why would she be the one to break under pressure?"

"She was the head of the Family," Lucinda says, her voice tiny. "If she hadn't recruited Holly, Celeste would have been safeguarded and she never would have gotten pregnant. She was more responsible than anyone, and she couldn't get over the guilt." That's what happened. What else could it have been?

Astor shakes her head in vehement denial. "I know it's easier to believe that," she says. "But I don't think it's true."

"Why not?" Lucinda demands, breaking away and putting space between the two of them. As if more air will buffer her against the twinge of uncertainty Astor's words are giving her.

"Lucinda, your mother was a part of the Society from the very beginning. She knew things no one else could have known. Don't you think it's awfully convenient, just as a detective is coming around and asking questions, that she, the top capital-M-Mother, comes up dead?"

"So, you think she was, what? Assassinated?" Lucinda demands, her voice rising. "That's impossible." Isn't it?

"Quiet!" hisses Astor, despite the howl of the wind. "I think, yeah, I think either someone killed her because they didn't want the Bureau finding out all the Garden's dirty secrets, or I think she sacrificed herself in the name of plausible deniability, hoping the investigator would close the case without looking any further. Either way, I think the Garden is front and center in her death."

"No," Lucinda says. Her mother's choices were her own. "No, that's not what happened." Maybe her mother intended to protect the Society when she jumped off that building. But someone killing her? Ruma was their leader. Who would want her out of the picture?

"For fuck's sake, Lucinda!" Now, Astor's voice is the one that's rising. "How many times do you need it to sock you in the face before you understand? Not everyone is as altruistic and pure-intentioned and as naïvely committed as you! Don't you realize that yet? 'For the good of the many.' How many times have we sung their mantra back to them over the years? Enough times that we've all forgotten the part we don't say. The part that says it's okay to sacrifice one. One of our Sisters, one of our Mothers. Who gave them permission to sacrifice your mother, or Celeste? Who gave them permission to sacrifice me or you? Because you know damn good and well, if it came down to sacrificing one of us to further their self-righteous cause, they'd axe us in a heartbeat." Astor's fists have clenched as she's spoken, and with this last assertion, she raises a hand and frees one finger, slicing it across her own throat.

Lucinda's mouth opens and then closes. She can think of nothing to say in rebuttal. There is no *they* in the Garden, especially with Ruma gone. What Astor is saying is ridiculous. She has been building animosity toward the Garden for ages, and with this conspiracy theory, she's finally gone off the deep end.

The Garden Society has nursed these two and their Sisters since birth, feeding them with knowledge that has disappeared from mainstream society and giving them the tools to start taking back what was taken from them so long ago. If she wasn't so exhausted, she would be fascinated by how differently they both incorporated that knowledge, how they channeled their autonomy in such different directions.

Astor looks to Lucinda, waiting for her to say something, but grief has depleted her emotional reserve. She doesn't have the energy to do what she always does, talking Astor down from her paranoia and trying to convince her of what Lucinda's known all along: The Garden is here to protect them, to remind the world they deserve the right to make their own decisions about their bodies. After years of being the voice of reason, she just can't do it today.

"Think about it, Lucinda," Astor says at last. "You'll see it makes sense. You should get out while you can, and you should take anyone you care about."

Lucinda reaches for the door handle. She can't take any more of this. "I've got a responsibility," she says. "And I'll be at the next meeting, supporting my Sisters, because I'm not going to turn my back on the Society that raised me."

Astor looks away. "Well, then I guess you'll have a front-row seat on the sinking ship."

Lucinda shakes her head bitterly. There's no reasoning with Astor when she gets like this. "I guess I will," she says. "Now, if you'll excuse me, I need to go inside. I can't listen to any more of this. In case you've forgotten, I watched my mother die at my feet. What I need right now is a cup of tea and a long sleep—not to listen to some unhinged rant about the Society's dark underbelly."

Astor's face softens. "Shit, Lucinda," she says. "I got carried away. I should have been more sensitive. I'm so sorry about your mom." She reaches out to touch Lucinda's arm.

Lucinda jerks away. "Probably should have led with that," she responds as she walks away from her oldest friend. "You can let yourself out."

As much as Lucinda tries to shut them out, Astor's words linger long after she leaves. As she rolls restlessly in bed, trying in vain to sleep, she can't help wondering what Astor knows about the investigation that she doesn't—and what that might mean for the Garden and her Sisters?

Lucinda wakes with a pool of dread in her stomach.

Despite her mind's restlessness, her body couldn't keep going and sleep claimed her shortly after Astor left. Her tea still sits, cold and half-drunk, on her bedside table.

As soon as the light hits her eyes, her brain is back in overdrive, demanding to know what the detective has learned and how she can protect herself and her Sisters from being exposed. If he knows Celeste's reported cause of death was a lie, does he know how she really died? If he knows she was pregnant, he can surely trace her fertility back to Ruma.

But Ruma is gone now. Maybe, as Astor suggested, the investigation will end there. Or will he keep pushing, sensing there's more to the story than one fertile woman and her doctor, both of whom now happen to be dead? *I don't think your mother killed herself*, Astor's voice echoes in her mind. But who else would have done it?

Tap-tap-tap-tap-tap. Someone's at the door.

Sera's scrambling footsteps race past Lucinda's bedroom, and Zavi calls from the living room for her to wait. Lucinda can't tell who makes it first, but the door opens with a swish.

Zavi's voice drifts into the bedroom, along with another man's, and then Sera's feet once more, growing louder as she skips down the hall. "Mama, a very tall guy wants to talk to you!"

Abuto. Her heart rate doubles as she flips off the covers with shaking hands. "Tell him I'll be right there," she says. She dresses in the master bath before pulling a brush through her hair and splashing warm water on her face. She recalls Adi standing at her office door. *You look like shit.* "Sure do," Lucinda mutters. She doesn't bother trying to hide the bags under her eyes or her swollen cheeks.

"Lucinda," says the detective as she enters the living room. His eyes convey only a guarded compassion. She imagines he's had a lot of practice at revealing only what he wants people to know. The apartment is silent apart from the whirring of the autochef. Zavi must have set breakfast to cook and taken Sera out to shop for their trip to see his parents.

"Good morning," she says, uncertain how to proceed. This is the man with whom she shared several bottles of wine a lifetime ago, the man who picked her up off the ground when her mother died in front of her eyes. But he's also the man whose investigation might now be pointing at her. In which capacity is he here today?

"I'm very sorry about your mother," says the detective, and the softness of his features seems genuine. But she gets the feeling he's not here simply to offer condolences.

"Do you mind if I sit?" he asks, gesturing in the direction of the living room.

"Go ahead," Lucinda says, and they both assume the seats they took last time they met. Lucinda curls her legs up underneath her.

"I've just been to see your father."

Lucinda stays silent, mind flashing back to last night's conversation with Astor. Is he investigating Ruma's death? If so, he must think there's something to investigate.

"Your father expressed some concern for your mother's mental state," he continues. "Was that a concern you shared?"

"Yes," Lucinda says. "We were all concerned about her."

"It seems as though she was feeling some guilt following Ms. Harlow's death," Abuto says, clasping his hands together on his lap.

"That's what I understand," Lucinda says. "She died before I could talk with her about it directly."

"Any idea why that might be?"

Lucinda's arms are crossed over her chest. She uncrosses them and repositions herself in her seat. "I'm no doctor, but I know my mother took her work seriously. I suspect she feels a responsibility to all her patients," says Lucinda. "And Celeste was so young. I think she just wished she could have done something to prevent it."

"And when you say you were *all* concerned, you mean…?"

"My father and me, and my Aunt Elle." Emeka raises an eyebrow. "My mother's close friend," she says. "They've known each other — they knew each other — since college. I've always called her my aunt."

"I see," says the detective, his expression unchanging. "And your mother never talked to you about this guilt she was feeling?"

Her mind flicks back to that evening on the balcony. "Not specifically, no," she says after a moment.

"But you discussed it with your father and with … Elle?"

Lucinda's eyes wander beyond detective Abuto, to the framed photo that hangs on the wall behind him. In it, her parents gaze at each other with a love so pure Lucinda never fully understood it. "Not with my father," she says. So many secrets. "Elle called me in the afternoon on the day she…" she swallows, then finishes. "On the day my mother died. She said my father had come to her that morning, concerned about my mom. I told her I'd check in. I figured she just needed to talk it out. None of us ever expected…" her voice trails off again and she looks back at Abuto. "I was on my way to check in on her," she says. "Five minutes earlier, and maybe I could have stopped her." It's not the first time she's thought this. The idea has dominated the constant stream of *What if*s running through her mind. Her eyes fill, and a tear falls from each, but the sobs don't feel imminent, which is an improvement over yesterday.

The apartment door opens, and Serafina bursts through past Zavi's outstretched fingertips. She runs to Lucinda and wraps her arms around her, leaving a wet imprint on Lucinda's top. "Daddy took me to the pool!" she says before jumping back down and bounding into the kitchen, leaving a trail of droplets behind her. "He says after my bath, we're going shopping!"

"She sure has lots of energy," says the detective.

"More than we can handle sometimes," says Zavi, chuckling.

Abuto looks wistful. "I remember when Micah was that age," he says. "Heck, it seems like yesterday that *Adi* was that age. You blink and they're grown."

Serafina rushes back to Lucinda, eyes wide. "He knows Micah!" she says in a whisper that can be heard across the room. "And Adi!"

Lucinda raises her eyebrows to Zavi and gestures with her head toward the hallway. Serafina should know not to talk about the Garden. But Lucinda can't take the chance she'll say something by mistake. "Always so excited," she says to Abuto.

"Come on, little one," says Zavi, wrapping up the little girl and hauling her off. Soon the sound of water running into the bathtub drifts in from the hall.

The detective leans forward with his elbows on his knees. "Lucinda, can you think of anyone who would want to harm your mother?"

Her spine straightens. "No," she says. It comes out almost defiant, and she softens her tone. "Why would anyone want to hurt her?"

Abuto doesn't speak for several moments, as if considering what to say next. Or maybe he's giving her time to reconsider. She waits him out.

"Is it possible someone else shared your mother's concerns? Might someone else have thought responsibility for Celeste's death rested on her shoulders?" he asks.

Martin's face flashes in her mind. How long has it been since she heard from him? "I don't— I'm not—" Lucinda stammers before she recovers. No. Hurt as he is, Martin would never kill somebody. "Celeste's death couldn't have been prevented," she says. "It was a freak thing that just—that just *happens* sometimes. Why would anyone hold my mom responsible?"

Once again, Abuto doesn't answer right away. Does he know as much as Astor thinks he does? Maybe he knows more. "Are you aware of your mother being involved in any illegal or underground activities?"

Looks like she didn't have to wonder for long. Lucinda focuses once more on the photograph behind the detective. She tries to channel her father. How would someone who knew nothing of the Garden Society, of Celeste's status, answer this question? "Of course not," she says, with what she hopes is convincing indignation. "What do you mean, illegal activities? She was a doctor and a mom and a partner. Just an average woman. What illegal activities would she be involved in?"

Emeka nods but doesn't answer. "So, you can't think of anyone who might want your mother out of the way, or who might want to silence her for any reason?"

"No!" Lucinda says, possibly a little too forcefully. "Detective Abuto, my mother jumped off that building. She had a lapse of judgment, or an episode, or whatever you want to call it, and she thought things were too much for her to handle. Everyone who knew her loved her. No one would have done this to her. I'm sure of it."

Is she, though? Suicide was the only possibility she had considered until last night. But first Astor's suspicions and now Abuto's line of questioning have her wondering how certain she can be. And what about the detective? Does he believe Ruma was murdered, or are these the same questions he always asks?

She doesn't know how she's going to figure it all out, but one thing is for certain. Abuto is a good detective who is going to follow any thread of information until it has unspooled completely. And if she is going to keep herself and her Sisters safe, she's going to need to tie up every loose end he could possibly find.

"Hello? Micah?" Lucinda says as she knocks on Adi and Micah's front door.

Lucinda had scarcely closed the door behind the detective when her mobile chimed with the call. "I need you," said Micah. "My mom's not home, and I need you." Lucinda was getting ready to make a cup of tea and clear her mind out on the balcony. Now, she's rushed across town at the behest of a twelve-year-old girl.

Micah cracks the door, then rushes Lucinda inside and slams and locks the door behind her. Her dark eyes are troubled, her voice high-pitched when she finally speaks. She is terrified. "Lucinda," Micah says, and then throws her arms around her Sister.

Lucinda's mind races, fearing what could be the problem. After the last few days, it could be anything. "Micah? What is it?" she says as the two sit on Micah's bed. "Is everything okay? Is your mother alright? Has someone threatened you?"

"Lucinda. I got it." Micah's frantic voice says. She looks straight at Lucinda, an appeal for help rather than an announcement.

"Got what?" Lucinda asks, though her heart is slowing as it begins to dawn on her what Micah is talking about.

"I got my period," is Micah's hushed response.

"Micah, that's wonderful news!" says Lucinda. She can't help gushing despite her Sister's obvious panic. Micah was so disappointed she couldn't attend Celeste's birth. Of course, that turned out to be for the best. But now, Micah will finally have the opportunity to see a birth, and surely the next one will go as planned.

"You should have told me! I would have brought the photogram cartridge. I'll run back home and get it so you can finally get your flower."

Micah shifts on her bed. There's something she's not saying.

"What's up, kiddo?"

When Micah speaks, her voice is barely more than a whisper. "I'm scared," she says.

For a moment Lucinda is lost for words. The only thing she remembers feeling when she was in Micah's situation was excitement. She had been eager for her body to begin resembling the picture of the fertile, maturing woman her mother taught her she'd be one day. She didn't expect any of her Sisters to feel differently. Especially not Micah.

"Scared?" says Lucinda. "Micah, are you worried you don't know what to do? That people will know? You don't need to worry about that. You're well prepared. We've been talking about this for years, remember? Do you have supplies like we talked about?" Because safeguarded women don't have periods, Garden members have had to be creative over the years. The girls are taught what items they can use, how to use them, and to never be anywhere without them. "You should keep them in your backpack or your handbag to be sure you're never—"

"Lucinda, stop!" Micah says. "It's not that. I've got all the supplies I need." She looks to the side and bites her lower lip.

"What is it, then?" Lucinda says. Her voice is quiet, tender. Motherly, really. She may call this child *Sister,* but Micah is practically her daughter. For the first time, she imagines having this conversation with Serafina.

Micah pauses to swipe at her eyes. She sniffs. "I just…I just don't want to end up like Celeste."

Lucinda looks into Micah's eyes. There is a line for this—one which she should be delivering with a soothing blend of comfort and logic. She should be reminding Micah that nature knows what it's doing, and that in almost every single case, births go off without a hitch. Babies and mothers survive and go on to live happy, healthy lives. She should be pulling out the clichés, comparing what happened to Celeste to being struck by lightning or eaten by a shark or killed in a plane crash. Any other day, she would.

But not today.

She was there when Celeste died.

She watched her Sister bleed to death with no recourse but to hold her hand and say her name and cry until the tears ran out.

She's watched Martin and Anabel try to cope with a loss that should have never happened.

She watched her mother pay the ultimate price. Whether from the torture in her mind or because someone feared what she would do if she were allowed to live, she would never have died if Celeste were still alive.

With so many people suffering from just one unexpected death, *the good of the many* has lost some of its luster. A hollow feeling in the pit of Lucinda's stomach asks if she's been mistaken all this time.

Well, if she has, then now is the time to get it right. Lucinda stands from the bed and reaches out her hand. "Micah, listen to me. I promise, I am going to make sure that doesn't happen. To you or anyone else."

Micah looks up. "Really?" she says, eyes glistening. She's just a child. Lucinda remembers spending time with Adi when Micah was a baby, holding her as she grew bigger and more alert. Her eyes were always wide and calm, quietly observing. She had no way of knowing what was in store for her. Even now, she can't possibly understand the ambiguity of the world she's been brought up in. Yet, even in all her confusion, she trusts Lucinda.

Lucinda swallows and squeezes Micah's hand. "Yes, really." She will protect her Sisters. She just needs to figure out how.

16

LUCINDA IS LYING. OR SHE IS IN DENIAL. OR BOTH. BUT after leaving her apartment, Emeka didn't have time to decide which before an incoming message interrupted his thoughts.

From: Gina Rodriguez. But wait. There's more.

Last time she was this enthusiastic, her lead on the health monitoring logs broke open the case. He didn't need any convincing to direct his car toward the Bureau office to see what she had for him.

"Okay, Rodriguez, let's see what you got," he says, rounding the corner past his desk to find the young analyst sitting at her cube.

"I got to thinking last night," says Rodriguez. "The health logs were forged, right?" Rodriguez continues without waiting for Emeka to respond. "And if the health logs were forged, then who's to say something else wasn't forged?"

Emeka looks around for a chair and takes one from another cube. He moves it next to Rodriguez and sits. "The only other thing the implant monitors is location, though," he says, and before he's even finished the sentence, he recalls the image of a pristine white couch.

Martin's voice. *"I saw all the blood and knew there was no hope."*

"She wasn't at home when she died," Emeka says. Seems so obvious now.

"No," says Rodriguez. "No, she was not."

"Okay, then where did she die?"

Rodriguez gestures toward her computer screen, and Emeka looks over her shoulder. "Apparently, here," she says, indicating a flashing yellow dot. Though her eyes don't move from the screen, she must sense his raised eyebrows. "Don't worry, the warrant already came through."

As Emeka watches on, Rodriguez zooms out to show the distance between where Celeste died and her apartment, where her partner says she died. "That's a long way," says Emeka. "What is this place?"

Rodriguez highlights the yellow dot, and a box appears on the screen with location details.

"Public Greenhouse?" Emeka mumbles.

Flowers. Plants. The *lost art* of gardening. Come to think of it, it's been ages since Emeka has thought this much about the act of plant cultivation. Yet it seems everyone connected with this case has had something to do with plants. Gardens.

Purple lotus blossom photograms.

Emeka stands. "Thanks for this, Rodriguez. Anything else for me?"

"Nope," she says. "That's it for now."

"Well, it's more than helpful," Emeka says. "I'm going to look into this more. But for now, I've got a date with a twelve-year-old." He winks at Rodriguez, who smiles. Rodriguez has always been partial to Micah—the youngster has taken to Rodriguez the few times Emeka's brought her into the office. Micah is fascinated with numbers and, while most children would complain about being *so bored* if they'd been forced to go to work with their grandfather, she usually disappears as soon as they walk in the door and spends most of her day with Rodriguez and the rest of the analysts.

Rodriguez raises an eyebrow. "Oh? What's on the agenda today?"

"The arcade," Emeka says, feigning excitement. "My favorite."

"Maybe I should go instead," Rodriguez says with a chuckle. "I love arcades."

"If only," says Emeka, grinning. "I might not love the arcade, but I do love my granddaughter, and I don't mind taking her if that makes her happy."

Rodriguez gives a little two-finger salute. "Well, say hi to Micah for me, and let her know I'll put in a good word with the higher-ups when she's ready to come work for us."

Emeka laughs heartily. "Oh, I sure will," he says.

He passes his cubicle on his way out, and he feels his desk calling to him. He even goes so far as to walk in and pull out his rolling chair. If he sits down to work, though, he'll get lost in it. Hours will go by, and he will swim up out of the maze of data and timelines and interview videos, and he'll have missed picking up Micah. This case has been blurring his boundaries, pushing him to work in the evenings and on the weekends like he never would have done before. But his time with his granddaughter is special, and work will not get in the way of that.

And so, even though it's a bit early, rather than sitting at his desk with the temptation of work pulling at him to sit down, he simply straightens its contents, pushes in his chair, and walks away.

"Abuto!" the Director calls when he passes her office. He pauses reluctantly in front of her door, hoping whatever she has to say is quick.

"Araleus," he says. "I was just on my way out."

"I've seen your logs, Abuto. You've been hard at work," the Director responds.

"Lots to do," he says. "I take it you saw my brief from yesterday."

"Mmm," says Araleus. "I did, but that's not why I wanted to talk to you. I know you'll handle the case. Or ask for backup if you need it."

Emeka chuckles. Backup. Part of the thrill of these complex cases is working through the twists and turns all on his own. It's like those jigsaw puzzles Micah does—she won't accept even an ounce of help, and if anyone tries, she breaks it apart and starts over.

"I just wanted to remind you about the gala," Araleus says, stretching out the last word.

The gala. In all the unexpected tumult of the week, he forgot about the silly gala and the silly speech he's supposed to give. "Yep," he says. "The girls gave me some good ideas after we spoke." *Talk about what made you want to be a detective*, Micah said when he told her about the speech. It was a simple idea, obvious perhaps, but it called to mind those missing girls back home—girls who might have stayed missing if he'd minded his own business as the local police warned him to do.

"Mmm-hmm," Araleus says. "So, you'll be ready to give the speech?"

"Sure. How long do I have, again?"

"For as long as you can offer something useful to the audience," she says. "Try and cap it at twenty minutes, though, okay? We need time for awards."

Emeka laughs. "You think this old man can talk for twenty minutes? I am flattered by your confidence. And I promise I'll have something ready."

Araleus seems satisfied by the time Emeka excuses himself to pick up Micah, though he still hasn't got a clue what he plans to talk about. Maybe the girls can give him some more help when they get back from the arcade. He's sure going to need it.

"Hi, Daddy," Adi says, smiling widely as she opens the door to the apartment. "Micah will be right out."

Emeka follows Adi into the apartment, standing just inside the door.

"Mama said you were at work?" Adi asks.

"Unfortunately, yes," says Emeka. "I can't get into it."

"I know, I know," says Adi with a grin. "Ongoing investigation and all that."

A door clicks open in the hallway and Micah comes out, "Hey, Papa," she says, but her smile doesn't approach her eyes.

"There's my girl," says Emeka, smiling despite his granddaughter's obvious mood. "Ready to go?"

"Yeah, I'm ready," she says, forcing her smile wider. She's making an effort, at least. "Where are we going?"

"Now, sweets," her grandfather says, wagging a finger in her direction. "You know the first rule of Fun Time With Papa."

She rolls her eyes, but a grin swells in her cheeks. "No questions asked," she says, doing her best imitation of his voice.

"That's right," he says, in his best Papa voice. "You'll find out when we get there. Now, why don't you tell me how that school play is going." He puts an arm around his granddaughter, steering her out of the apartment and waving goodbye to Adi as the door closes.

He will not let his thoughts drift back to the investigation. This greenhouse, and what might have happened there, stays at the office. At least until after he's dropped Micah back off at home. The case will still be there tomorrow. It's a mantra he often offers to the newer detectives, encouragement to take care of their personal and family needs before their professional ones so they don't burn out. As enticing as it might be to try and unravel the thread he's been following back and forth for the last week, his time with his granddaughter is more important.

Micah spends the entire car ride telling Emeka about the play, and her character, and the other kids in the drama club, who are pretty nice, she guesses, and all the lines she has to memorize, and how the kids are building their own set. It would be easy for him to get distracted, to let his mind wander. But, as much as he knows that the play she was in at the age of twelve will eventually be a mere comma in the book of her life, today it is her entire life, and so he immerses himself in the conversation.

She chatters, absently rubbing one palm with the other thumb, and he listens intently, commiserating and interjecting from time to time. It has taken years and years of practice, but as he's worked to become a good investigator, a good partner, and a good parent, he's realized the key to all three is to be an exceptionally good listener.

The car pulls to a stop on a side street choked with projection awnings. Restaurants, department stores, candy shops, and jewelry stores all advertise their wares in all directions. Micah looks toward the rotating projection of a very realistic-looking ice-cream cone, a hopeful glimmer in her eye. But instead of into one of the shops, Emeka leads her to a building whose sign is a simple icon—a yellow circle with a wedge cut out to look like a mouth. "Oh, sweet," says Micah. "Thanks, Papa." The only hint of excitement is the smile that tugs up the corners of her lips. He smiles to himself. Adi thought herself too cool once, too. But the wide and unself-conscious smile she gave him when he arrived to pick up Micah is proof: Their essential selves are still in there, and they always come back through eventually.

"Of course, sweets," he replies. "Now—do you want to eat first, or play first?"

"Let's play," she says with a grin, leading the way to the podium. "Can we get headsets?"

"Sure," Emeka says, and she doesn't even have to beg. They could use their own overlay glasses to play, but these headsets are more immersive and have enhanced gaming features. If he's going to subject himself to the arcade, he might as well enjoy it.

Micah settles her headset over her ears as Emeka pays for the rentals and an hour of game play. Micah is running toward the gaming floor before he can even get himself situated. "Come on, Papa! Let's go!" she shouts, pulling him by the elbow.

The gaming floor is an assault on all Emeka's senses. The noise of the arcade's energetic ambient music fills his headphones. The sound of yelling children and teenagers, and the occasional adult, filters in, muted but not completely blocked by the ear coverings. The room is just a shade above black, but bright photograms shine all around. They would be invisible to the naked eye but shine iridescent and animated in front of his overlay.

Micah settles in front of her favorite game, one where players have to pop CGI bubbles floating in the air. "Play against me," she says.

If Micah isn't too cool to have fun here, Emeka might as well give in to the experience. He stands on the platform next to her and waits for the game to begin. He's bashful at first, but as he pops more and more bubbles and watches their scores leapfrog each other, he becomes less self-conscious and more competitive. "You forgot I had a height advantage!" he calls over her giggles, reaching upward with an outstretched finger.

They're both laughing and moving this way and that, trying to pop the bubbles before they float out of reach, when Emeka glimpses something familiar and bright purple on Micah's side of the game field. Her hand opens and closes so frequently as she catches the imaginary bubbles, he can't get a clear look at it. But that doesn't matter. He knows what it is.

Emeka's play slows, his mind suddenly stuck on a new puzzle.

Micah ends up beating him handily, but if she's noticed his distraction, it doesn't show.

Questions swirl through his head for the rest of the visit, and his emotions swing from curiosity to anger to disappointment, though he can't pinpoint exactly why. Micah has the purple lotus photogram. Does Adi have one, too? She is friends with Lucinda, after all, and while he's never managed to glimpse one of these animated tattoos on Lucinda, he'd be willing to bet she has one.

Over dinner, Emeka recalls once more the girl from the convenience store. A gardening club. The Public Greenhouse. Where Celeste Harlow died. And this photogram seems to connect everything. But how?

"You okay, Papa?" Micah asks as she slurps down the last of her spaghetti.

"What? Oh, yes, sweets, I'm fine," he says.

"You haven't eaten anything," she says, gesturing to his untouched plate of veal piccata.

Emeka takes a deep breath. He can't talk to Micah about this. Not now. Not here. Not at all, actually, because she is a family member, and he is in the middle of an active investigation in which she might very well be a subject. The realization settles in his stomach like a ball of lead. "You know, kiddo," he says with a weak smile, "I don't feel too well, all of a sudden." He gestures at the cacophony around them. "Must be all this."

He takes his food to go. Maybe he'll find his appetite after he gets some answers.

Back at Adi and Micah's apartment, Emeka sends Micah up with apologies. Usually, he'd come in and have a sit with Adi, talking until long past Micah's bedtime. But with more pieces of the Harlow case swimming around in his mind, he's going to have to do some work before he can talk with either of them again.

Reluctantly, he directs the car toward the office for the second time today. Without the loud distraction of the arcade, his mind is free to get going. Before he's even pulled out onto the main street, he knows what he needs to do.

Emeka feels a guilty relief as he steps out of the elevator onto the deserted office floor. Best to be alone as he works things out. At his desk, he finds the message Rodriguez sent to him with the coordinates of the greenhouse where Celeste Harlow apparently died. He enters them, along with the date and time of Celeste's death, into the Bureau's tracking system.

He expected more than just Celeste's beacon to appear. At the very least, Martin must have been with his partner as she gave birth to their child. Still, when the logs finish loading, he does a double take. A red badge appears next to the flashing dot, a stark number 5 displayed in the center.

His finger hovers over the badge for a moment. With a deep breath, he taps the number and expands the display. Slowly, he reads each name, careful not to let his eyes stray farther down the list.

Celeste Harlow
Martin Granby
Lucinda Conroy Das
Astor Flynn

He reads the next name, then bows his head and massages his forehead with his fingertips. On some level, he expected to find this.

But now that he knows for sure, what is he supposed to do?

17

LUCINDA HAS BEEN WAITING TO SPEAK WITH ADI ALONE ALL day. Adi was home when Lucinda returned with the photogram cartridge for Micah, but before she had a chance to tell Adi about the investigation—and that Adi's father is in charge—Lucinda received a reply to a message she forgot she'd even sent.

Through the haze in her mind, Lucinda recalls her mother saying her technical assistant, Bernie, modified Lucinda's masking protocol. She also has a vague memory of messaging Bernie, hoping to get ahead of the Bureau and figure out what they might uncover if they found the mask. Now she's sitting on the same rooftop deck where she last met her mother, but this time Bernie is describing what Ruma asked her to do. Her conversation with Adi will have to wait.

"She asked me to modify the algorithm you were already using to cover hormonal shifts. The mask would need to simulate the vital signs of an average, healthy 34-year-old woman who died suddenly from an aneurysm rupture, and it had to be done quickly." Bernie's voice is flat, expressionless. Was she this impassive that morning, knowing a woman had just died? Knowing she was helping cover up the death? "I flashed Celeste's implant as soon as I was finished with the mods," Bernie says. "I added a location mask at the last minute, so it would look like she never left her apartment."

Another mask. The data mask has always been a flimsy cover, but Lucinda's more keenly aware of it than ever, now that the data are being handled by the Bureau. Her cheeks flush with fury at nobody but herself. She should have created something more intricate. She knew a mask wouldn't stand up to hard scrutiny, but it never needed to until now. She never expected anyone to look that closely. But she should have.

No, she thinks. Stop. None of this would have been necessary in the first place if not for the Society and its illegal activity. Celeste would still be alive, and she and Bernie wouldn't be talking about a computer program created to cover up someone's death. She's got a right to be furious, all right. But not with herself. She shakes her head. She's starting to sound like Astor. But she's also not wrong.

"I know it wasn't ideal," says Bernie. "It was just the best I could throw together on such short notice. Your mother wanted to be sure the implant was removed and her body cremated before the authorities arrived."

"It's fine, Bernie. I'm surprised you even had time to do that," says Lucinda. It's not Bernie's fault all this happened; she was doing her best to protect the Society. To protect Ruma. "You couldn't have had more than an hour or two."

"Oh, no, your mother contacted me at maybe two, three in the morning," Bernie replies. "She told me to rush, but I ended up having several hours to work before she called me again and told me to flash it." The silence stretches as Lucinda looks backward, seeing the time as clearly in her mind now as she did that morning. *2:53 a.m.* "Still not enough time to fully reprogram the implant," continues

Bernie, "especially from a distance. But—wait, did I say something wrong?"

Lucinda's lips have tightened, along with her shoulders. Fire courses through her veins. "Are you sure?" she asks, taking great care to unclench her teeth. "About the time. Are you positive?"

Bernie's brows wrinkle with concern. "Yes, I'm positive. Why? What's wrong?"

She was gone before you ever arrived.

Lucinda's fists tighten. "She knew. My mother knew Celeste was going to die that morning." And still, she did nothing. Instead, she stayed far, far away, leaving Lucinda and her Sisters to watch.

Lucinda is riding home from her mother's office, still stewing over her conversation with Bernie, when the notification comes through. At first the quiet alert doesn't register, but soon it's grating on her eardrums, and she remembers the urgent message she dismissed yesterday. With Astor's visit and her utter exhaustion, she completely forgot about it. And today has presented even more to worry about.

She blows out her breath. Might as well get it over with. As she pulls up the message on her overlay glasses, she realizes her face is still wrinkled into a scowl. She's always felt an undercurrent of irritation with her mother, but it's been years since she felt this deep and flowing anger.

How dare she. How dare she leave Celeste to die, just as she left Lucinda to drown all those years ago. Instead of going to help Celeste, instead of trying to save her, she called

Bernie for help covering up her death. Before it had even happened.

These girls, Lucinda's Sisters, even Lucinda herself—Ruma didn't care about them at all. She was so invested in protecting the Society. Did she forget she was supposed to be their nurturer, their leader, their Mother? Was the Garden's mythical aim so important to her that she forgot to care about the real people inside it? It must have been more important than her self-preservation, because she allowed it to—

An image appears on her overlay, interrupting the torrent of thoughts. For a moment, she is disoriented. She expected a message of condolence from one of her friends, but this is something different.

Briefly, the familiar lotus opens and settles in front of her eyes, then fades as a figure appears in silhouette. "Lucinda." The voice is masked, just as the source of the message has been. "The time has come for you to take over for your mother as the Garden Society's Lead Gardener. I regret the circumstances, but I trust you will be what the Society needs as we heal from the loss of our Sister."

The voice goes on to give details for some sort of training call, where she will learn what exactly the job of Lead Gardener entails. All the things Lucinda will now be required to do, though she never agreed to anything at all. By the time Evie—by now, she's sure it's Evie speaking— ends the message, Lucinda's heart is pounding and her ears are ringing. "I'm truly sorry for the loss of your mother, Luci," says the voice just before disconnecting. "Without her, none of our work would have been possible."

Lucinda is staring at her mobile when the car finally stops in front of her building. Her thumb hovers over the display, alternately reaching for and recoiling from Astor's contact entry. Ordinarily, Astor would be the first person she'd call after something like this, but though she wishes she could confide in someone, Lucinda isn't ready to forgive Astor's intrusion after her mother's memorial.

What would she say to Astor if she did call? "Now that my mother's dead, I'm taking her place in the Society, so please try to be supportive despite your moral misgivings"? She can imagine Astor's response.

No, she is on her own with this, at least until she's had time to decide what's next for the Society. To figure out how she's going to keep her promise to Micah and protect their Sisters.

Lucinda puts her mobile away and heads up to the apartment, empty until tomorrow, when Zavi and Serafina come back from their trip. Left to her thoughts, she paces the floor as her thoughts dart between a lifetime's worth of conversations.

She was around Serafina's age when she understood she was different from other girls, the day her mother explained to Lucinda and her Sisters the true purpose of the Garden Society.

Conversations she's had with Astor over the years come back to her. Looking at them all together, she realizes how much less guarded—and more insistent—Astor has become over time.

Astor's argument has merit. Lucinda has been reluctant to admit it, but Celeste's death has illuminated the flaws in the Society's methods, well-intentioned as they might have once been. What seemed like an abstract and distant threat as they were growing up has now become more real than they could have grasped as little girls.

Their Sister is dead. If her true cause of death comes out, the safety of Society members everywhere will be threatened. Women could be arrested, their children taken away. They, and their intact daughters, could be forced to undergo safeguarding, and who knows what else? Lucinda shudders to imagine what might happen to natural-born children if they are discovered. And the government might not be the only threat to their safety.

Lucinda sits at the dining table with her overlay on, absently opening and closing her hand, watching through unfocused eyes as the flower inside it blossoms again and again. The message from Evie plays on loop in her head, and with each reiteration, her chest fills a little more. With resentment. Regret. But also, opportunity.

Of course it falls to her now. It's embarrassingly obvious in retrospect. She's been elevated all her life as the First Daughter, the other girls waiting for her to make a move before they dared to act or speak. She always wanted to see herself as equal to the others. But she's known better all along, hasn't she?

That day, at the river. The day she learned she could count on no one, not even her mother, to save and protect her. That was the beginning. And she now sees this message from Evie for what it is: the culmination, premature though it may be, of decades of grooming. The First Daughter becomes the first natural Mother in the Garden Society.

You are the future of the Society, Ruma said last time they were all together.

Ready or not, the future is here.

18

EMEKA SITS BACK IN HIS OFFICE CHAIR AND PUSHES OUT A breath. On the screen in front of him is the same map he worked with yesterday. He's assigned colors to each person of interest, and he's watched them—and many others, colored a generic yellow—enter and leave the greenhouse as he's dragged the time slider back and forth through hours, weeks, months. It's hypnotic, watching the various dots come and go over time. He must have gone right to left and back again a hundred times.

There is green for Celeste Harlow, who seems not to have moved from that location for over two months—since the beginning of that parental leave Martin told him about. Martin in blue. He did leave the area from time to time, but for the most part, he was right there with his partner. Purple for Lucinda Conroy Das, who came and went somewhat regularly, at least once a month, and much more frequently in the days leading up to Celeste's death.

Orange for Dr. Ruma Das. Black for Astor Flynn. Red for Adi. Once a month, the dots all come together at the greenhouse and then disperse. Once a month, they're all in the same place, along with too many yellow dots to count. Each of them, a potential member of this club, which Emeka is now certain is involved in the death of Celeste Harlow.

This club in which his daughter and granddaughter seem to be members.

Emeka can't sit at his desk any longer. He saves the data to the cloud so he can look at it later. His heart is in his stomach as the elevator descends. As the car brings him through the latticework of downtown streets, he tries to explain to himself why his daughter was present at Celeste Harlow's death. Why his granddaughter has the strange photogram tattoo he'd never noticed on anyone before this investigation began. What they've been up to right under his nose, and for how long.

19

WE NEED TO TALK.

Lucinda stares at Astor's message as she sits at their customary back-corner table on the empty second floor of Bel's. Astor and Adi will be here any minute. She doesn't know what to expect. Is Astor ready to call a truce? Is Lucinda? She's not sure if Astor is right about the Society having dark motives, but even if they did, does it matter as much now that she's going to be in charge? She can change the motives. But first, she's got to figure out a way to protect her Sisters from the immediate threat of this investigation.

Astor slides in across from Lucinda without bothering to announce herself or even offer a greeting. Lucinda looks over at her, but Astor is staring straight down at the table, punching her drink order into her mobile.

"We are fucked," says Astor, before Lucinda can think of what to say. Her voice is flat, her face without expression.

Her pulse quickens. How much trouble are they in? Visions of her Sisters in handcuffs, being led away from the outstretched hands and cries of their children and partners, swim in her mind. How many lives are in her hands? She swallows and says, "Let's talk about it when Adi gets here." Her words are slow and deliberate, spoken through numb lips. Her entire body is telling her to run, but she's got nowhere to go. It's up to her to figure out what to do next, and hopefully Astor and Adi can help.

Astor's eyes flick up to Lucinda's. She didn't tell Astor she was inviting Adi, but Astor has to understand. She nods once and averts her eyes to the delivery compartment, as if her drink will come faster if she just stares hard enough.

The atmosphere doesn't get any less uncomfortable when Adi seats herself on the stool next to Astor. Even though Adi's been in their Family for more than a decade, she and Astor are not particularly close. Astor has never had a surplus of trust, least of all for strangers. And Astor seems to still see Adi as a stranger. What's more, Lucinda doesn't think she's imagining the tinge of jealousy she feels from Astor whenever Adi's name is mentioned. It's as if Lucinda having recruited Adi somehow undermined the relationship she and Astor have had all their lives.

The women speak without making eye contact. Astor shares what she's been able to overhear by staying close to her colleagues in the Council Attorney's Office, and Lucinda recounts her conversation with the detective. Adi listens and tries to assemble all the details together, pieces in a giant puzzle that is yet to be complete. Their voices stay low, their heads close together. Their overlay glasses and mobiles are put away and the music is loud enough, hopefully, to drown out their words. Their bodies remain so motionless it would take a moment for someone to realize they were here.

Nor would anyone notice Lucinda's steadily climbing heart rate, the wildness creeping into her eyes. Her panic rises with every new piece of information Astor shares. How will they ever get out of this mess?

By the time all the information has been spoken, there is a spent atmosphere at the table. Adi didn't know Celeste's death was being investigated, much less that her father was in charge. Lucinda watched her Sister's face sink as she and Astor spoke, and her guilt added to the emotions churning in her gut.

"So, my father knows Celeste died having her baby," Adi says.

"Almost certainly, yes," says Astor. "Like I said, I haven't been able to catch all the details, but it sounds like he knows Celeste didn't die from an aneurysm."

Lucinda's turn. "And he knows she wasn't at home when she died."

"Yeah," says Astor. "I heard they got a warrant for something to do with a location mask. What's the first thing you would do with a location mask if you were in their shoes?"

Lucinda swallows, but the lump in her throat remains. "Break it," she and Adi both say at once. "They could do that in five minutes," Lucinda adds. Her voice comes back to her empty and toneless, as if she's talking into a vacuum.

"Okay, let's assume he knows *how* she died and *where* she died," Adi says. "What else does he know?"

Astor shrugs. "I can't ask any questions without people getting suspicious. But I'm sure he's going to find out soon enough that the rest of us were with her."

"What makes you so sure?" asks Adi.

Astor levels her gaze at Adi. "What's the second thing you would do, after you knew where she died?"

Adi massages her temples. Takes a drink. Swallows. Massages her temples once more. "I'd scan the location to see who else was there." Adi locks eyes with Lucinda, and the look of betrayal is unmistakable. "Does my dad know about me?" she asks. Her eyes are shining, her voice small. "Does he know about Micah?"

Lucinda forces herself to look at Adi, though shame compels her eyes to focus anywhere else. If it wasn't for her, Adi wouldn't be in this situation. Her eyes blur until she must blink out the tears. "I'm sorry," she says. Her voice is barely above a whisper, but that's all she can muster.

Astor clears her throat. "Even if he doesn't know it yet, it's only a matter of time—and I'm talking days, maybe even hours—before he knows about a lot more than just you. What do you think he will do with that information?"

The table is silent for an uncomfortably long time. "I honestly don't know," says Adi, sniffing and wiping at her nose with a napkin.

"Would he arrest you?" Astor presses. "Turn in your friends?"

"With my father, it's always been right or wrong," Adi says. "One or the other." She looks at Lucinda once again. "That's why it was so important he could never find out about…about all *this*."

"I'm sorry, Adi," Lucinda says once more. "It's my fault, I messed everything up. If I'd just been able to do something for Celeste, we wouldn't even–"

"Shut your mouth right now," says Astor. Her tone is harsh, but her face softens as she continues. "Lucinda, none of this is on you. This is what I've been trying to tell you. You didn't choose this for yourself. It was chosen for you. You've been brainwashed into thinking the Society is your responsibility, but it's not. Just like it's not your fault Celeste is dead."

Lucinda's heart nearly stops. Her skin is on fire, and her body can't figure out whether it wants to laugh, cry, or scream. She can do none of them here, at any rate. So she sits, and Astor's words sit with her. This is the first time since Celeste's death that anyone has said them.

It's not my fault? At first, her mind poses it as a question. Soon, though, it's a statement, loud and clear. *It's not my fault.* It's not. Lucinda could never have saved Celeste, because Ruma let her die. It was never Lucinda's fault. Yet her mother still let her bear the guilt.

As Lucinda grapples with this new perspective, she remembers the message from Evie. Astor is wrong about one thing.

"Actually," she says, "As of now, I am responsible. Evie sent me a message yesterday. I'm to take my mother's place as the Society's Lead Gardener."

Both Astor and Adi's eyes look ready to pop right out of their heads. "Evie?" they both say in unison.

"Mmm-hmm," says Lucinda. "At least, that's who I'm assuming it was. She's going to call me with more details tonight."

"Tell her no," says Astor.

Lucinda blinks. "What?"

"Tell. Her. No." Astor speaks through clenched teeth. "You do not have to do what she says. You do not have to be who they want you to be."

"But what about the others?" asks Lucinda.

"The others can figure it out. Lucinda, listen to me. I know you feel indebted to them—to us. But you didn't choose to be the icon. This is your opportunity to choose for yourself. You can show the rest of them that they can choose, too."

Now Lucinda is certain she wants to scream. "Choose? Now we're back to this again?" She struggles to keep her voice down, to keep her hands from becoming animated. Adi looks on, mouth slightly open as if she has something to say, but she makes no move to interject. "How many times have we talked about this? The Society exists because women have been denied the right to choose for generations! Where's the choice, when baby girls are sterilized as soon as they're born? Where's the choice, when we have these bodies which are perfectly designed to create new life, and they aren't allowed to do it?"

Astor's nostrils flare and her palms press down on the table. She inhales deeply through her nose, and her words come out like a growl. "Have you not been listening all this time?" she asks. "I thought with this investigation threatening to take us all down, you'd be ready to listen to me and give up the delusion that the Society is good for anything besides keeping us locked up. It might have been created with good intentions, but those are long gone. Evie, whoever she is, is most certainly more concerned with saving her own ass than she is with women's rights."

"What?" asks Lucinda. "How do you know?"

"Lucinda. I love you, but you are so damn naïve sometimes. If this woman cares so much, where is she? What do you think she's going to do when the whole Society is unraveled? You think she's going to come running" — Astor holds out her hands, wrists touching— "saying, 'Take me instead, it was all my fault'? Why do you think it's just her *words* that guide us?" Astor looks at Lucinda. Her eyes are earnest, brimming with tears. "Your mother was her puppet for years, Lucinda. And she died because of it. Don't let her do that to you, too."

Lucinda slumps in her chair. A sudden wave of exhaustion sweeps over her. What's her next move? And does it even matter? Whether she takes over or renounces Evie and everything to do with the Society, Detective Abuto will still find out the truth and come after them. Ruma might be gone, but there are plenty of unaltered Sisters, and he's sure to find every last one of them eventually. Including—and especially—Lucinda and Serafina.

Lucinda shakes her head. "I can't do it," she says. "I can't turn my back on my Sisters. I've got to find a way to keep them safe."

Adi, who has watched Astor and Lucinda go back and forth all this time, straightens up. Lucinda and Astor both look up to see her dark eyes glistening. She is still afraid, but clarity has creeped into her eyes. "Lucinda, I think there might be a way to keep them safe," she says. "But I don't see how you do it without offering yourself."

20

EMEKA STANDS IN FRONT OF A BUILDING HE CAN'T remember ever seeing before, even though it sits right in the middle of everything. "Public Greenhouse," the stone etching proclaims. Carvings with blossoms and leaves frame the words, the only delicate touch he can see among the cold, hard lines of glass, concrete, and steel.

He activates his overlay almost unconsciously, and there it is. There *they* are, two purple lotus blossoms, one at each end of the curling floral frame. More evidence the photogram is somehow connected with this building. But how? And what does all this have to do with his family?

He passes through the glass sliding doors into a humid, green oasis. The air inside smells both clean and earthy. The ceiling stretches high overhead, but lights installed in the walls bathe the enormous space with more light than Emeka's ever seen in this urban landscape.

Other than the fact of its existence, though, the greenhouse seems unremarkable. There are plots of green and brown and various floral colors, tall and short, with paths carved between them. A handful of people are here, alone or in pairs or trios. None of them are saying much. He sees no hint of the photogram, and not for a lack of looking. It's hard to imagine the space being full, but those yellow dots on his screen were unmistakable, and they come here to congregate regularly.

Celeste Harlow's location data says she stayed in this building for weeks, and so there must be more to the building than this. In the huge chamber, it's difficult to see the edges of the space. In the center stands a clear glass column, hung with thick steel cables. An elevator.

As he moves toward it, an oversized portrait above the keypad comes into clearer relief. A Black woman, middle-aged, with smoothed hair and a shrewd smile. She wears elaborate jewelry of braided floss and beads, and her clothing flows around her. "Annette Gordon," reads the placard below. "First Administrator of the Public Garden Conservancy." Annette Gordon. He's never heard of her. The date on the photo is from before he was born. Yet there's something familiar in that face, those caramel eyes.

Inside the elevator, there are three buttons: *LL*, *M*, and *UL*. A glance upward reveals the mezzanine balcony, circling the space and connected to the elevator with a glass catwalk. It's probably quite a nice view, but Emeka's not here to enjoy the flora. He presses the *LL* button first. Nothing happens. He tries *UL*. Still nothing.

He presses each of them again, to no avail, before noticing the scanner next to the panel. He holds up his mobile to the reader, and a red LED appears. He holds up his wrist, where his implant is located. Another red light. Whose credentials might make the light turn green?

And what secrets is this elevator keeping?

21

LUCINDA SITS IN THE DARK SILENCE OF THE BALCONY, LEGS crossed, spine straight, draped in a heavy blanket that keeps her just warm enough to ward off the shivers. As she waits for the incoming call on the private line, she doodles on a sheet of paper, drawing a climbing vine around the notes she's written in advance of her call with Evie.

This is her first opportunity—possibly her only opportunity—to talk in person with the leader she and her Sisters have followed all their lives. And she's about to tell that leader it's time for a change.

Lucinda has a plan for the call. She has questions. Ideas. She is about to take charge of the Society, after all.

The call comes right on time. Without introduction, the masked voice on the other end begins talking, outlining the work her mother did for the Society—the work which will now fall to Lucinda. Within moments, Lucinda is sick to her stomach. Evie is not interested in saving the Sisters. She doesn't want to take the Society into the future. If anything, she wants to push them farther into the shadows, delving deeper into the other side of the law. And she expects Lucinda to facilitate it.

Lucinda doesn't find an opening to interject before Evie goes on to outline what she knows about Detective Abuto's investigation. None of what she says comes as a surprise to Lucinda. What surprises her is that Evie knows any of it.

"Who told you all this?" Lucinda asks.

"I have sources, same as you," Evie says without elaboration. "Lucinda, we need to stop this investigation before it goes any further. This detective's daughter and granddaughter are your Sisters. If stopping him means using those two as leverage, then that's what we'll need to do."

"Leverage?" Lucinda squeaks out after a moment, stunned at Evie's directness. "What kind of leverage?"

Evie continues without so much as a pause. "Everyone has a price," she says. "You'd be amazed what some people will do to avoid harm coming to their loved ones."

"Harm? You want to hurt them?" Lucinda cannot hide her incredulity.

"Want to? No, I don't *want* to hurt them. But if it comes down to it, we need to be prepared to do what's necessary," says Evie. "This is bigger than just those two. The Society's work isn't done, and we must protect it. Otherwise, everything we've worked for will have been wasted. If the Society is discovered, you can bet you and all your Sisters will all be exposed as well."

But not Evie, a voice whispers in the back of Lucinda's mind. When will the Society's work be done? And what is the end goal, anyway?

Lucinda tries to imagine herself standing in her mother's place in front of the Society. She'll hold out her hand and they'll hold out theirs, and they'll all say the words together.

And then what? Situations will keep coming, and Sisters will keep hiding, or living in fear, or even dying. How many people need to die for their sacrifices to outweigh whatever good the Society hopes to do? And is the Society really willing to threaten lives to protect itself?

But what does Evie have to lose? Ruma might have been the only person in the world who knew her true identity, and she's dead now. She communicates through private channels, never revealing her true face or voice. She can threaten detectives from afar, using Lucinda as a proxy, without ever endangering herself. Why would she ever agree to change anything about the way the Society was run?

Minutes ago, Lucinda was convinced she needed to accept that Detective Abuto would discover the details about the Society and find a way to work with him. Evie is suggesting something exactly the opposite, and far more sinister. Astor and her mother speak so loudly in her mind, it's hard for her to concentrate on what Evie is saying.

You don't have to be who they want you to be. This is your opportunity to choose for yourself.

You are the voice of the new generation.

"Evie?" Lucinda says. She intends to say something profound, something of value. She intends to take a stand. But when Evie speaks again, the hair on the back of her neck stands up.

"Yes, Luci?" says the masked voice on the other end of the line.

The world swims in front of Lucinda's eyes for a moment. She clears her throat. Swallows. "I won't let my Sisters down," she says. It's the one commitment she can make that doesn't make her want to curl up in despair.

An hour after the call disconnects, Lucinda is still sitting unmoved on the sofa, blanket pulled tight around her shoulders. The last of the lights in the apartment were extinguished long ago, bathing the balcony in pitch black. As Lucinda's eyes dart back and forth, she notices details in the darkness she's never picked up on in all the hours she's spent out here. A chip in the painting on the rail here, a discolored circle on the table there. It's as if she can see clearly for the first time.

Luci. Only one person in her entire life has ever called her by that name. Not her mother or her father, not even her partner. Only Aunt Elle. Elle Vincent Baker. Elle Vincent, as she was back when she met Lucinda's mother, before she married Uncle Clark.

E.V. Evie.

Aunt Elle has been in charge all along. It was Aunt Elle who convinced Annette Gordon, the Society's founder, there needed to be a change.

Aunt Elle who just suggested Lucinda use her Sisters as bargaining chips to extort Detective Abuto into not exposing the Society.

How dare she? How dare she exploit Lucinda and her Sisters, treating them as expendable commodities rather than human beings with families and their own free will? Lucinda was foolish to believe the Society wanted anything other than another Ruma to run things as they'd been run for decades before.

For a moment she feels embarrassed at her naïveté, but that feeling quickly gives way to rage. Lucinda isn't Ruma. She's not content to sit back and stay the course, watching her Sisters die because a group of misguided women started something they didn't know how to finish.

Lucinda is the First Daughter. Honored by the Mothers, revered by the Sisters. If she wants to change things, nobody's going to stop her.

22

ADI'S OLD BEDROOM IS DARK SAVE FOR THE MONITOR Emeka's just powered up. He sits at the desk where she used to write computer programs and work out page-long math problems, running his fingertips over the various band, movie, and character stickers that piled up over the years.

"I thought you were finished with work," says Abigail from behind him. Her hands settle on Emeka's shoulders, her chin resting atop his head.

He breathes deeply, taking in Abigail's familiar scent. "I know, sweets. I'm sorry. I just can't get my mind to quiet down. Every time I think I'm getting close to figuring this out, Something happens that sends me in a completely new direction. Did you know I spent the afternoon at a greenhouse?" he says, turning up to look at her.

"Greenhouse? Why on earth?"

"Mm-hmm. Not too far from the gallery, matter of fact."

Recognition flashes on Abigail's face. "Oh, yes," she says. "I pass that building when I go to the Indian restaurant for lunch. The wide one with the flowers over the entry door?"

"That's the one." Emeka studies his partner's face for a moment. Abigail has never mentioned the greenhouse. But, then again, neither has Adi or Micah. And it seems Ruma Das's partner, Josiah, didn't know what she'd been up to, either. Could Abigail—

"I've always wondered what it's like in there," she says. Relief washes over him. Her words are earnest, he can tell, and he's ashamed of his momentary suspicion.

"It's quiet," he says. "Peaceful. Beautiful, really." If you don't know what happened there, he thinks.

"Maybe I'll take my lunch there some time," Abigail says, turning to leave. "Come to bed soon, okay?"

"Okay, sweets," Emeka says. She pads out of the room, and he turns back to his monitor. The words *Annette Gordon* are typed into the search bar, and the cursor blinks after her name, beckoning him to press enter. *Herein lie the answers you seek*, it calls to him.

"Well, let's see it," he mumbles.

Advertisements fill the screen. *Find a lost friend or relative!* reads one. *Annette Gordon's background report is just a click away!* reads another. Dozens of Annette Gordons appear, all still living, none the one in the portrait at the greenhouse.

Garden he adds to the end of the search term. And this time, he finds what he is looking for. A handful of images appear before his eyes. Annette Gordon speaking at a conference, hands outstretched and inviting. Annette Gordon giving an interview, staring into the host's eyes with a striking calmness and acuity.

Annette Gordon, standing next to a podium, heavily pregnant. The caption reads, "Last Natural Birth Closes One Chapter of Human Evolution and Opens Another." Emeka blinks. The damn cursor was right.

"I knew I wanted to have my baby naturally, the way nature intended," Annette explained in the attached interview transcript. "I've always felt so fortunate that my body was built to bring new life into the world. As soon as I heard the law might change, I knew it was time."

Annette was not only the last woman to give birth naturally, but she was a vocal opponent of Ordinance 4.14, which prohibited natural childbirth and made the safeguarding of infant girls mandatory. She led protests on the steps of the Council in the weeks leading up to the vote. After the law was approved unanimously with only one abstention, Annette took an abrupt step back from advocacy, shifting focus to public greenhouses.

In the same legislative session in which 4.14 was approved, Ordinance 8.6 was also approved. This law requires municipalities to set aside spaces for public greenhouses and resources for naturalist education. The law was authored by Delia North, who then appointed Annette Gordon to oversee the design and construction of the greenhouses. Delia North, who happened to be the only Council member who abstained from the 4.14 vote.

Emeka's head swims. This handful of new facts is related to the Harlow case somehow. But how could two women who supported primitive childbirth a hundred years ago be connected to the death of a woman during childbirth today?

He rubs his temples. His eyes need a break, and so does his mind. Tomorrow he'll be back in the office, and he can run this new information by Rodriguez and see if she has any ideas. She's been indispensable since this case started. She's bound to have some insight. He'll have to be careful what information he allows her to see, though. He doesn't want anyone knowing about Adi and Micah's involvement until he knows more about what exactly they're involved in.

After quite some time in bed, Emeka drifts into an uneasy sleep. His dreams swirl with dots of all colors, sliding back and forth on a grid of crisscrossing streets, and that pair of caramel eyes, which he still can't quite place.

23

LUCINDA'S EYES ARE FILLED WITH TEARS BEFORE HER father even answers the door.

He says nothing at first. Instead, he pulls her through the doorway and into his arms, letting the sobs wrack her body and fill the apartment as the door swings closed behind them.

She calms enough to catch her breath, and they sit on the living room sofa. Her father doesn't rush her. He probably thinks she's grieving for Ruma. And she is. But a more profound pain sits just below the surface, a pain that's been stewing since the very first time her mother uttered the words, "You must promise never to tell your father."

She arrived unannounced. If she'd contacted her father ahead of time, she would have either backed out or broken down. On the ride over, she battled all the oppositional banter in her head. Her mother's voice, telling her she was breaking not only her trust but that of all the women she'd promised to protect as First Daughter. Her own voice, asserting the best way to stay safe was to keep the secrets they'd held so closely for so many years.

But then there was Adi's voice. *You can't save the Society without risking yourself.* If it wasn't for that one, she might have turned in the opposite direction and avoided this interaction altogether.

"Daddy," she says at last, hugging a throw pillow to her chest and pulling her sleek hair back from her eyes. "I have something to tell you."

No amount of rehearsal could have prepared Lucinda for the pain that shone in her father's eyes as he learned his partner had been keeping such a tremendous secret from him. She weeps as she speaks, and a dozen times she must resist the urge to close her eyes, to shut down, to leave and pretend none of this ever happened.

But it did happen. It is happening right now, and her father deserves to know before the entirety of his partner's life blows up in front of the world.

"It's going to come out, Daddy," she says. "Soon. There's no other way to protect them."

"Lucinda," he begins, but doesn't finish. His lips form a tight line as he looks down at his daughter's feet.

"I don't want to drag her through the mud, Dad, but her name's going to come up. I'll control the message as much as possible, which is why I'm trying to be proactive about it. But it won't take long for people to connect the dots. I just need you to understand that we don't have another choice. If we can find a way to work together with this detective and with the government, we may have half a chance both to protect the women of the Society and create the future I think Mom was trying to build."

At first, she's uncertain if her father has heard her. After a moment, though, he looks up. His blue eyes pierce through a tangled mess of curls and into the depths of her heart. "I'm sorry, Daddy," she says, tears filling her eyes for the hundredth time since she stepped through the threshold of her childhood home. "I wish I could have told you sooner."

Josiah reaches for her and, for the second time today, she collapses into her father's embrace. "It's okay, sweetheart," he says. "It wasn't your fault."

And those words release her like nothing else ever could.

24

EMEKA IS GETTING HIS SCHEDULE FOR THE DAY SET UP WHEN Rodriguez appears in his cubicle. "Abuto," she says. "You'll never guess what happened."

"Rodriguez," he says. "Do you ever sleep?" He is half-joking, but she does look like the long hours have gotten the best of her. Despite her neat dress, her makeup looks a day old and her eyes are bloodshot.

"The hits just keep on coming," she says. "I wanted to get this info to you last night, but it was really late."

Just his luck. Someone finally respects work-life boundaries and he's the one blurring them by working all night. "Okay, sit," he says to Rodriguez. "What's this all about?"

Rodriguez takes an excited breath as she takes a seat in the corner of Emeka's cube. "Okay, this is crazy. So, I had drinks with a friend last night."

Emeka waits for her to go on.

"We'd been meaning to get together for a long time, but things get busy, you know, with life and everything. He's got a partner, and a little kid, and anyway it's probably better that it took this long because—" She must have finally noticed Emeka's searing look because she takes another breath and continues. "Right, right. Getting to the point. My friend—Dylan's his name—he works for the Department of Population Science."

Population Science. The department responsible for enforcing population control measures. Measures such as safeguarding. Emeka straightens. Now he's listening.

"Mmm-hmm," she says, acknowledging his attention. "He was working as a compliance associate, until recently. He was reassigned last week."

"Reassigned?" Emeka asks. If he was reassigned before Celeste Harlow even died, how is he relevant to this case?

"Reassigned," she repeats. "Just after making a report to the medical director—a Doctor Mackenzie, I think his name was?"

"Mackenzie," Emeka repeats. "Yes, that's right. I met with him last week." Nathan Mackenzie was distracted during their meeting, particularly after Emeka shared the details of Harlow's death with him and Baker. Last Emeka saw him, he was standing in the middle of the foyer in the Population Science building, eyes glued to his mobile. "Report?" Emeka asks. "What was this report about?"

"Seems one of his local associates had found a teenage girl with unusual health data. Parents said the girl was safeguarded, but health monitoring data showed fluctuations just like we saw in the Harlow woman. Parents wouldn't allow the associate to question the kid, so they referred it up to Dylan. He did a little digging, and it turns out this girl wasn't the only one."

"Who are these girls? Where?"

"Well, that's the problem. When Dylan was reassigned, his access to his old region's data disappeared. He remembered a few of their names, but he hasn't been able to get back into the system."

"Hmm," says Emeka. "I bet we can find a way around that, don't you think, Rodriguez?"

Her eyes brighten. "I think you're right," she says. "He described the search query he applied to his region. It shouldn't be hard to use the same query for the entire population."

"What was he searching for?" Emeka asks.

"Oh, easy," says Rodriguez. "He just searched for girls and women whose sex hormone alerts were switched off. Says he found a pretty long list of them, all ages from birth to about thirty."

How deceptively simple. "Makes sense," says Emeka. "That one toggle is what tipped us off to the coverup of Celeste Harlow's data in the first place."

"Seems like that's not the only coverup going on here," says Rodriguez, standing. "I'll get started on the query," she says. "Depending on how many hits we get, it might take some time."

Emeka looks up at the analyst as she turns toward her desk. "I'd like first look if you don't mind," he says. "I want to see how this fits into the work I did this weekend. Maybe it will help us complete part of the picture."

"Sure thing," she says before disappearing around the corner.

His request isn't an odd one, and Rodriguez didn't seem suspicious of it. The lead investigator is usually the first to look at any data uncovered in the course of the investigation. But he can't help worrying. The possibility of his daughter and granddaughter's names appearing on that list is a little extra motivation to keep it to himself for the time being.

At any rate, there's no list yet. He's stuck waiting for now, and so he diverts his attention to the rest of this story. This Dylan fellow—he somehow stumbled upon a cluster of women and girls who hadn't undergone safeguarding as infants. Is it possible this discovery is unrelated to the Harlow case? What about the fact that he was reassigned just after coming forward with this story?

And there's Mackenzie. He's the one who reassigned Dylan. Once again, Emeka recalls the distraction in Mackenzie's eyes. Those clear, light-brown eyes the color of caramel.

The same eyes shining out from Annette Gordon's portrait.

Emeka is suddenly alert, aware of the blood racing through his veins. He adjusts himself in his seat, faces his monitor head-on, and picks up where he left off last night.

Annette Gordon's life was uneventful following the birth of her daughter and her appointment to the Public Garden Conservancy. If anything, there is a shortage of records about her life, considering she was a public figure. Emeka can only find one picture of her that isn't a portrait. In the low-resolution photo, she stands in front of a group of women and children who are all seated around a plot of soil. Her mouth is open and their gazes upturned, as if she is teaching them or making a speech.

Other than that, it seems the Conservancy faded into the background along with Gordon as she raised her daughter. The next mention Emeka can find of Gordon in the press is her obituary, dated decades later. Her involvement in the Conservancy is mentioned as a footnote, as well as the fact that stewardship was transferred to her daughter. Most striking to Emeka, though, is a sentence which he could have easily glossed over had he not been seeking it. *Annette is survived by her loving daughter, Sonequa (m. Natalie Mackenzie) as well as her grandson, Nathan, a medical student who thought the world of his Nana.*

Nathan. A few taps on the screen confirm the obituary is referring to Dr. Nathan Mackenzie. The man who appears to be responsible for burying a report about intact women, who became distracted and troubled as soon as he discovered Celeste Harlow died during childbirth.

Or, maybe that is, as soon as he discovered Emeka *knew* Celeste Harlow died during childbirth.

The more Emeka learns the more questions he has. It's a familiar pattern, one he's seen countless times over the years. At some point, the information will all come together and point in the same direction. He senses that point in this investigation approaching quickly.

"Excuse me, Detective?" says a voice a few feet away.

Standing in the entry to Emeka's cube is a middle-aged woman with a buzz cut and a small diamond stud in each ear. Her eyes are red-rimmed but she stands solid and square. "Yes, may I help you?" he says, standing.

"They told me I'd find you here," she says. "I'm here to turn myself in."

25

THE RIDE OUT OF THE CITY FEELS LONGER THAN IT EVER HAS before. Aunt Elle and Uncle Clark were like a second set of parents to Lucinda growing up, and she spent some of her favorite times at their home. The trip has always been filled with a sense of childlike anticipation, a comfortable contentment she only ever felt here and at her grandparents' farm.

Today, her fingernails dig into her palms as she tries to drown out the shouts in her mind and settle on a single train of thought. Attempting to focus, futile though it may be, is the only useful thing Lucinda can think of to do with the time.

It's obvious. It should have occurred to her before. Her mother and Aunt Elle were friends for decades. How many times has she heard stories of gregarious Elle dragging Ruma's nose out of the books, imagined her aunt carrying her mother on butterfly wings out of her comfort zone and dropping her into a game of volleyball or onto a river cruise boat? She could recite verbatim the story of how the two met Josiah and Clark at the same club, on the same night, and how thereafter nothing could come between the four of them.

Except that wasn't entirely true, was it? Ruma had made space in her life for a secret she couldn't share even with Josiah, and the only person who could have convinced her to do that was the one person in her life who predated him. And then there was Uncle Clark. There's no way he could know about the Society. What would he do if he knew his partner and their close friend were heading up an under-ground organization that directly undermined his own Population Science Bureau?

The secrets have driven a wedge between them all. But she doesn't have to stand by and accept it anymore.

By the time the car deposits her at Elle and Clark's doorstep, a calm determination has settled over her. This will be the end, and it will be the beginning.

It's dreary out. A damp chill hangs in the air, and Lucinda crosses her arms over her chest as she approaches the house. She tries the door before ringing the bell, though she's certain it will be locked. This far out of town, home security is non-negotiable.

Through the glass, she watches her aunt approach the door looking just as she always does. Simple black dress, flawless makeup, short, blonde hair carefully styled. Rage wells up in Lucinda's chest. How can Elle be so put-together, when Lucinda doesn't remember changing clothes since the day she watched her mother fall to her death?

She looks down at herself just before Elle reaches the door, realizing the feeling isn't entirely misplaced. Each morning, she's continued pulling on the same black sweat-shirt she was wearing that day. Maybe it's because she can't spare the mental energy to find another, or maybe because the article provides her some strange sense of comfort. Prob-ably a little of both. Pulling it more tightly around her, she feels something in the pocket, the small bulge that's become so familiar over the last several days she hasn't given it much thought.

The door opens and, for the first time, she can see through Aunt Elle's warm smile to the truth behind her eyes. "Lucinda! What brings you all the—"

"It's you," says Lucinda.

Elle was reaching out to hug Lucinda, but she stops mid-reach. Her fake smile fades.

"It's you," she repeats. "You're the only one who ever calls me Luci. It's been you the whole time."

"Let's go for a walk," Elle says. She removes a small wicker basket from the table next to the door. Elle removes her overlay glasses and places them inside. Lucinda does the same, and Elle eyes the mobile in Lucinda's hand. After a moment's hesitation, Lucinda places her mobile alongside the other electronics.

She fumbles inside her sweatshirt's pocket, finding a button and pressing it. Hoping it will turn out to be unnecessary. Hoping, also, that the battery inside her mother's glasses has some juice left in it yet.

They approach the wooded area adjacent to the property, passing by the greenhouse. Gigi's greenhouse, once teeming with lush foliage, now sits in disrepair without her to care for it. Maybe this was the first Garden. Lucinda wonders if Elle and Ruma held the first Society meetings here. "Why didn't you ever tell me?" Lucinda asks. She means to sound angry, but the threatening tears make her sound weak. Like a little kid.

"Too risky," says Elle. "When the Garden was entrusted to me, we determined my involvement would never be revealed to anybody who didn't absolutely have to know. Your mother and I agreed on this before she ever got involved, and that promise extended to you and your father. I let my guard down last night, and I shouldn't have. It was a mistake. But now you know, and we can't take that back."

"Who else knows?" asks Lucinda.

Elle's eyes are icy. "Now? Nobody."

"My mother was the only one?" Lucinda says. "None of the other Mothers ever knew who they were serving?"

Elle shakes her head. "Nobody knew *me*. But Evie was never a real person, anyway. She was a guiding hand, an eye in the sky. I came up with the plan, sure. But as far as the Mothers were concerned, they were following Ruma. And the Daughters, well, honey, they were following you."

Lucinda swallows. She's known it all along, of course. But hearing it aloud from the mastermind of the whole operation makes it somehow more concrete.

"That's why it's so important for you to continue the Society in your mother's absence. To stop the investigation and protect everything your mother and I have worked our whole lives for."

Anger wells up inside Lucinda. She stops walking and faces her aunt. Lucinda has been taller than Elle since adolescence, but she still feels tiny standing in Elle's confident air. "You said yourself," she says, "that the Garden wasn't yours anymore. My mother worked her whole life for this, not you. My mother sacrificed her relationships with me and my father, not you. My mother suffered the pain and guilt her involvement caused, not you. My mother died for this," she says, raising her voice and wiping at her nose, which drips in the chilly air. "Not you. You got to sit back and watch your plan unfold without lifting a finger to make it happen." Her eyes well up once more, this time with rage. "I can't believe all this time, you were the puppet master."

But what's not to believe? Elle and Ruma were friends, sure, but wasn't there always a lopsided nature to their friendship? Elle was always the one convincing, Ruma deferring. Ruma would have done anything for Elle.

Elle's demeanor remains cool as she looks back at Lucinda. Her eyes shine in contrast to the gray all around them. She turns and begins walking again, and Lucinda follows her. A roar creeps into her ears as they walk deeper into the woods. "Your mother died," she says without looking at her, "because she was too weak to handle her responsibilities. She was unpredictable, and that made her a liability. You are stronger than your mother was. You were raised to lead us, Lucinda, from the day you were born. We taught you independence, commitment, responsibility. You have such strong relationships with your Sisters because of the way we built the Garden. You feel a responsibility toward them because their safety has always depended on your teaching them what they needed to know, guiding them even in the absence of a clear path. They look to you because we designed it that way."

They emerge from a wall of trees, and the roar surrounds them now as they look down upon the river. A sea of memories swims in Lucinda's mind. As she looks around, some pieces settle into place. "That day," she says, staring across the rushing water. "When I fell in. You told her to leave me."

Elle stands, unmoving, in her periphery. "We both knew you could make it home," she says. "But it took some convincing for your mother to let you prove it."

"I was just a little kid!" Lucinda says, turning to face Elle once more.

"A little kid who needed to grow up quickly," says Elle. "You were born for something bigger, and you needed the confidence you could do it. I won't apologize for it, and if your mother were here, she wouldn't either."

"Oh, no," Lucinda says. "Of course she wouldn't. Not if you told her not to. And when Celeste died. You knew, didn't you? My mother had given up on her before anyone else even knew something was wrong." Fury and regret mingle in her veins. "All this time I blamed my mother. I thought she stayed away because she was protecting herself. It was you she was protecting all along."

"There was nothing anyone could do for Celeste," Elle says. "We both agreed that protecting the rest of you should be your mother's priority. Arranging for the pickup so Celeste's place of death wouldn't be found. Masking her health data so it wouldn't raise any red flags."

"You both seemed to agree on a lot of things," says Lucinda, not even trying to hide her bitterness. "What else did you convince her to do? Was it you who made her believe she was responsible for Celeste's death? Or was that my mother, finally coming to her senses after following you like a sheep for her entire life?"

Elle's chuckle is without mirth. "Oh, please, Lucinda," she says. "You don't give your mother enough credit. She was a grown woman. Nobody ever forced her to do anything. No one else can be blamed for decisions she made of her own free will. Everything she did was to protect the Society and give you and your Sisters the best chance possible."

Lucinda scoffs, rolling her eyes to the gray sky and smoothing a hand over her hair, now damp with mist from the sky above and the churning water below. "Well, she didn't do a very good job at that, either. You know the Bureau is about to descend on the Society like a pack of wolves, right? Whatever she had Bernie do, it didn't work the way they expected it to."

"Your mother is dead, and Bernie is in custody," says Elle, unblinking. "I'd say you're pretty well protected."

"Custody?" asks Lucinda. "What?" This is news to her. Bernie wasn't in custody when they spoke, barely two days ago.

"Oh, yes," Elle says with feigned gravity. "You didn't know? She admitted to helping your mother cover up Celeste's death. She turned herself in to that detective and agreed to show the Bureau how she modified the data for Celeste. *Just* Celeste," repeats Elle, raising her eyebrows.

Lucinda stares at Elle, eyes wide, as the significance of what she's just said sets in. "So, you're saying Bernie sacrificed herself for the rest of us? And you knew about it? You let it happen? No. What am I saying? You *forced* her to do it." But if the Bureau buys the story Elle—*Evie*—forced Bernie to tell, maybe they won't look any further. Maybe they won't seek out other Sisters or search the location of Celeste's actual death. They won't find the trail of lies that will lead them to Lucinda's feet. And to Evie's.

If it works, it will be genius.

If it works, Lucinda won't have to offer herself up as tribute, and the Society can continue as they always have. As furious as she is, Lucinda starts to second-guess her plan.

"What is it with you, Lucinda? You act like grown adults don't know how to make their own decisions. What do you think 'for the good of the many' means? This thing is bigger than Bernie, and your mother, and even you."

Images of Celeste's lifeless face, her mother's broken body on the pavement, wash away any hesitation she felt. "Bigger than Celeste, too, huh?" she spits. "Working for the good of the many doesn't mean the individuals stop mattering. When will it be enough? When will the individual losses be too many to keep justifying their sacrifices? You've been away for too long. Celeste, Bernie, my mother. These women are not pieces in some life-sized chess game. You're playing with real people here. Don't you understand that?"

"Of course I know these are real people," says Elle. "But that's part of the reason I'm abstracted from the Society. It's easier for me to make the right decisions for the group when I'm not bogged down by individual relationships. Sometimes we have to put those things aside when we have a bigger goal in mind."

"And what goal is that?" Lucinda asks. "In all my years doing your dirty work, no one has ever answered that question. What's next, *Evie*? Do we just keep hiding in the shadows, hoping we don't get caught or die? Or is there a point to all this?"

Elle sighs, turning away from Lucinda and walking upstream. "There's still a lot you don't know, Luci," she says.

Despite Lucinda's indignation, she follows. "So, tell me."

"There's a plan," says Elle. "But it's a longer game than I think you realize. We have to be certain everything is in place before we move forward. New legislation is written.

Speeches have been drafted. Negotiations have been prepared. But if we don't have the votes, if we don't have the
right people on our side, it will all be for nothing. This has
been in process for years—decades—and we've got one
shot."

Lucinda pauses as she takes in what Elle just said.
She's always known there were Sisters in strategic positions
in the government, just like she was encouraged to go into
programming to help with the technology side of things. But
she never knew such a deliberate plan was in development.
For a second time she wonders if she should just give it time
and let the plan play out.

And then she remembers Astor's visit the night of her
mother's memorial, the urgency in her eyes as they sat across
from each other at Bel's. Abuto's investigation is circling the
Society, and if they've broken the location mask it won't be
long before there's nowhere to turn.

"No," Lucinda says. "It can't wait that long."

"It has to," says Elle. "Otherwise, we risk the lives
and the families of everyone involved in the Society. And
I'm not willing to do that."

"We need to act now," Lucinda insists. "Do you really think the investigators at the Bureau haven't looked into
the location data?" she asks. "Bernie or no Bernie, if they
haven't yet, it's only a matter of time before they do. One
thing will lead to another, and the entire Society is going to
be split wide open. We need to get ahead of it while we still
can. *If* we still can."

This time, Elle is the one to stop walking. "If they
had broken the location data, they would have questioned

you about it—or one of the others who were there that night."

"How do you know they haven't? How do you know Astor's not on the phone at this very moment with the Council Attorney's Office, telling them everything she knows? How can you know Detective Abuto hasn't convinced Adi or Micah to talk?" The mist is turning to rain; Lucinda slides the damp layer from her forehead with one hand.

"The same way I knew your mother had become unreliable," says Elle. "There are still a lot of things you don't know about how the Garden works, about how it's continued to work for all these years. Trust me, it benefits everyone for the Bureau to believe Ruma was the problem." Elle says this with a cold indifference, as if she's forgotten she's talking about Lucinda's mother. "The deeper they dig, the more they'll uncover—and a lot of otherwise upstanding citizens in the Bureau and other government offices will be exposed. They're not equipped to answer all the questions that come up as a result, especially as public as it will become. Better to believe Ruma went rogue and did a little experiment on one of her patients a few decades ago. And when that experiment turned out to have dire consequences, she blamed herself and couldn't handle the guilt."

"You seem more than willing to stake the rest of us on that assumption," says Lucinda. "But I don't see you rushing to put yourself out there. What do you suppose Uncle Clark would have to say if he knew about your little side project?"

For the first time, Elle falters. Her eyes darken. Her mouth falls open; she snaps it closed. It's only a flash, but

Lucinda has found a sensitive spot. "There is no reason to get Clark involved," she says. Her lips barely move.

Lucinda shrugs. "I don't know, maybe there is. Maybe he deserves to know the truth about who he's been married to for the last forty years. Does Myles know?" Elle's eyes dart around. "Of course not," Lucinda says with an empty smile. "He's having a girl, right? Honoring you with her birthday? Will he name her after you, too? Are you going to convince him to raise her in the Society? Will you shut her off from the rest of the kids her age, so she can only socialize with girls who share the same secret? Will she be the new Evie when she gets old enough, like you want me to be the new Ruma?" Elle's eyes search the rocky ground as if it will provide her with an answer. "What if she never gets that chance? What if she's discovered and revealed for what she is, now that the authorities know about the masking?"

"The protocol will improve before that becomes an issue," Elle interjects.

My protocol. "No, it won't," says Lucinda. "Not if no one develops it. And even if she goes through her entire life undetected, what will happen when she eventually does get pregnant? What if she's one of the one percent of women who has complications that kill her? She can't very well be your poster child if she's dead, can she?"

"That won't happen," Elle says, more of a growl than a statement. "Things will improve."

"How?" Lucinda demands. "How will things improve if we keep hiding? If, to the lawmakers and doctors, we don't officially exist?"

"We won't always be hiding," says Elle, straightening up. "Once we have the votes, we will also have a plan in place. Trained professionals to help people through pregnancy. Medical care for those who need it. Prenatal care like we used to have before the nursery wombs took over. But we won't get any of that if we try and push this through before the world is ready to listen to our story."

Lucinda sighs. Elle's got an answer for everything. But her answers are always some version of, *Wait. Not yet.* "Who gets to decide when the world is ready?"

Elle stares at her in defiant silence. Ruma's low, syrupy voice sounds in Lucinda's ears, as clear as if she were standing alongside them. *You are the voice of the new generation. It's time for another change.*

Lucinda's eyes clear, her voice goes quiet and steady. "What happened with Annette Gordon?"

"What do you mean, what happened with her?"

"I mean, my mother told my Family she had to be convinced when it was time to change the focus of the Society. To move from education to action. She said you spoke for the new generation."

Recognition fills Elle's eyes. "That was different," she says.

"Was it?" asks Lucinda. "She needed someone to convince her it was time to move forward, and you were the one to do that. You took a risky move. One that Annette wouldn't have taken on her own. And you said it was for the good of the many. The Society is different now, and your choices threaten the well-being of the women you say you want to protect. You said my mother wanted to give us the best chance possible. But what chance do we have at a full life if we're living in constant fear of being discovered? And once the authorities do discover us—and it's only a matter of time until they do—what kind of life are my Sisters and our Daughters going to have?"

Elle's hair has succumbed to the rain; so has her makeup. She looks smaller at this moment than Lucinda has ever seen her. "No," she says, her voice choked. She clears her throat. "That won't happen. The situation has been controlled."

"And if Bernie talks?"

"Bernie has dedicated her life to the Society. She has nothing else. She knows better than to talk."

"And if they find the location data and use it to ferret out the other Sisters?"

"Then we'll find another way to explain it. Or we'll disappear. We have the resources to make that happen."

"You seem pretty convinced," says Lucinda. "But I'm not willing to wait. There's too much at stake. My Sisters are my responsibility, and I'm not going to let them get caught up in your little game of chicken."

Elle looks up at the overcast sky for a moment and then back to Lucinda, her eyes flaring through the raindrops. "So, what are you saying?"

"I'm saying that we are going to do things my way from now on. You can give your blessing or not, but you'd better be prepared for what comes next. We need to get ahead of the authorities, instead of trying to sweep up behind them. We're safe for now, but it might only be moments until they find something we can't explain away. Anyway, you said yourself, they look up to me. None of them even know who you are." She pauses, looking into those blue eyes she's looked up to through the best and worst times of her life. Eyes that were behind her complete manipulation for three decades. Eyes that persuaded her mother to go against her instincts, over and over again. Eyes that still think they are untouchable. She steels her voice. "And if you try to fight us, I will tell Uncle Clark and Detective Abuto everything."

She watches for a flicker in her aunt's eyes, waits for her to protest. Instead, the older woman merely bends toward the ground, picking off some stray leaves and strands of grass that have accumulated around her lower legs as they've walked.

"No," Elle's voice drifts upward, but she doesn't raise her eyes toward Lucinda.

"What do you mean, no?" says Lucinda.

Elle still doesn't look up. "I mean that I have spent my entire life arranging things so women could get back what we lost. So you and your Sisters could have what your mother and I never did. I'm not going to let you ruin it for us now, just because you think you know better. You don't."

"But we can't afford to wait," Lucinda says. At any time, Adi's father could put the pieces together and start going after Sisters and their families. Even a day could mean the difference between freedom and apprehension. Between keeping their daughters and having them ripped away.

"I don't—" Lucinda begins. But before she can finish her sentence, Elle springs up. There's a bright flash, and then everything goes black.

26

Emeka is sitting at his desk, reviewing the confession from Bernie Murillo when the *ping* of an incoming notification sounds on his mobile.

Message from Gina Rodriguez.

He's been looking at the confession for far too long, reading it word by word. Trying to tease out the truth from the fiction. Or rather, trying to identify the shadows where the truth should be but isn't. His overlay was activated while Bernie wrote out the confession, purple lotus blossom blinking in and out of view as her hand changed positions.

Does Adi know this person? Does Micah?

I was Dr. Das's technical assistant at the time of Celeste Harlow's birth. I programmed Celeste's implant and disabled hormone alerts.

Emeka recalls Rodriguez's story from this morning and her friend Dylan's query. There's no way Celeste was the only victim of this scheme. His stomach turns. Was someone like Bernie involved with Micah? He pushes the question aside and continues reading.

After Celeste's unfortunate death, Dr. Das requested that I apply a data mask so the cause and location of her death would not be uncovered.

For a moment, Emeka tries putting himself into Dr. Das's position. How must she have felt, being responsible for the death of someone she'd known her entire life? And the next thing she had to do was to cover up that death. The guilt must have been overwhelming. It's not hard to see why she might choose to end it all.

When he spoke with Bernie, he didn't ask about the photogram. That piece of information has been locked away in his mind up to now, and until he knows what the tattoo signifies, that's where it will stay. He did, however, ask Bernie why she would confess. If Ruma was responsible for Celeste's death, and Ruma is now dead, then what inspired Bernie's need to clear her conscience now?

The answer was unsatisfactory. "I just couldn't live with myself," was all she said. But there had to be more that she wasn't saying.

Throughout the entire conversation, Bernie did not shed a tear. She seemed detached from the situation, her words deliberate, her movements robotic. "Do you have any family, Bernie?" asked Emeka before she was led to a holding cell downstairs.

Bernie shook her head. "No. Dr. Das, she was the closest I ever had."

Even more of a reason to protect her rather than laying her actions out for everyone to see. Everything about this confession, from the timing to the substance, just serves to further pique Emeka's suspicion. Bernie didn't choose to come here on her own. But, if Ruma Das is dead, then who compelled her?

Emeka clicks to open the message from Rodriguez and a file opens before his eyes. Names, dates of birth, addresses. He scrolls, and scrolls, and scrolls, and he still hasn't made it to the end when his mobile sounds again.

"Did you get the file?" Rodriguez asks. Her voice is eager, and he can nearly see her bright, expectant eyes.

"Looking now."

"Okay," says Rodriguez. She's waiting for something. Something he's not prepared to give her yet.

"I just opened the file," Emeka says. "I'll need some time with it before I can make any conclusions."

"It's a big file," says Rodriguez. "Does that mean what I think it means?"

"I'm not sure yet what it means, Rodriguez. I might need you to run some additional queries. But for right now, sit tight."

"Yeah. Right. Okay," she says. "Sitting tight. I'll find something else to work on." She doesn't disconnect just yet. "This is my first big case," she continues. "I'm just really curious how all the pieces are fitting together."

"You aren't the only one," says Emeka. "I need to do some work before I understand it myself. I'll check back in when I know what I need. You've been a big help," he adds.

Emeka was expecting the list of women with hormone alerts turned off to contain a handful of names. The length of the document blows his mind. Page after page he scrolls, a sea of names passing by and blurring together. It is overwhelming to try and go through each of the names in turn, and so he starts with the names he does know.

First on the list is Lucinda Conroy Das. Just below hers are other names he recognizes: Celeste Harlow. Astor Flynn.

Adi's name doesn't appear on the list, which is no surprise to Emeka. He was there with Abigail at Adi's safeguarding. Years later, he watched through the viewing window as Micah grew in her nursery womb for the nine months before she was born.

Micah. He can see the flower in her palm, floating through the air as she popped the imaginary bubbles at the arcade. He types her name into the search field. Deletes it. Types it again. Better to know than not to know. He presses enter.

Your search returned 1 result.

His mobile rings.

"Daddy?" Adi says when he answers. Her voice drips with distress. "Please don't be mad."

27

BLACK. COLD.

Lucinda's eyes snap open. Still, she sees nothing.

Her lungs beg for air, but she can't take a breath.

Moving, floating. She can't control the motion, can't stop it.

She jerks her head, rolls her body. Finds the surface and the gray light above it. Swims up.

She barely makes it to the surface before her lungs force themselves open. A huge gasp, and she is just able to stay above water while her vision clears. She turns her head to take in her surroundings, the base of her skull throbbing. Aunt Elle's ice-blue eyes flash in her mind as she treads to stay above water.

What happened?

Can't think about that now. The current carries her downstream. The water is deep here, mostly free of rocks and debris into which the water could smash her, but the shallower rapids are up ahead. She aims herself toward the closest bank and kicks with her long legs, scanning the steep side for a handhold.

The water moves too quickly. She approaches a low branch and strains to reach high enough to grab it. Her fingertips brush the damp twigs. She inches closer to the side, at the same time trying to avoid tree stumps and rocks that have piled up along the edge of the water. She lunges next toward the bank, grabbing at a woody stem only to have it come off in her hand. "Shit!" She keeps moving like a projectile down the surface of the river, ever more aware of the approaching boulders.

Up ahead the thick loop of a tree root, exposed over time by erosion of the soil around it, hangs low to the water. She reaches up, stretching her fingers outward and kicking with all her strength. Her arm wrenches from her shoulder when her fist finally closes around the root. She nearly loses her grasp as the pain shoots up to her fingertips. She manages to swing the other arm around and lift her legs out of the rushing water, relieving the strain on the injury.

She pauses there, hanging from the side of the riverbank, gasping to catch her breath. Her eyes search the steep wall for roots, protruding rocks—anything she could use to propel herself upward. A shiver moves through her body, caused only in part by the icy water that moments ago submerged her.

Hot tears form in Lucinda's eyes. She's never truly known this woman, has she? Aunt Elle, the woman she trusted like family her entire life. Evie, the idol on the pedestal. Now, together in her mind as some kind of evil caricature. After a lifetime of being drawn toward Aunt Elle for comfort, she needs to move as quickly as possible in the opposite direction.

Lucinda blinks. Her features harden.

She steadies her feet on a boulder at the water's edge and holds the root with one hand. With her uninjured arm, she reaches out to grab another root and test its stability. After a few failed attempts and more than a few sickening jolts of pain through her arm, she reaches the top and collapses flat on her stomach, back heaving as she struggles to catch her breath.

With effort, she sits up. Her arm screams in pain when she reaches up to tap her glasses and query the time and location. Her stomach sinks. They're not there, of course. She needs to go back to the house, to retrieve her things. She shakes the thought from her mind. Elle might be there. Or she might be coming this way, trying to finish what she started.

Her eyes clear, a renewed flush of adrenaline burning in her veins. Elle might have been tracking her, watching as she struggled in the water, waiting as she climbed the embankment. Lucinda cranes her head around, ignoring the pain as she looks and listens for any sign of another person. It's hard to hear anything over the sound of the rapids far below, but she sees nothing. No movement, no color. Just stillness, in brown and green and gray. Even so, that could change. She needs to move. She takes care with her steps to avoid as many twigs as she can, doing her best to watch both the ground and the woods around her.

She makes her way downstream. Better to increase the distance between her and Elle. Better to get closer to a populated area. Her left arm is wrapped around herself, both to try and retain some of her body heat and to support her right arm, which hangs at an unnatural angle.

There is still a cover of clouds overhead, but the rain has stopped and there's plenty of daylight left. Lucinda moves briskly toward where she thinks she should be going, though without any navigation assistance she can't be certain. Her mind wanders as she travels, settling on that night, years ago, when she was led to believe her mother left her to drown.

Tears fill Lucinda's eyes and her face crumples as an unexpected whimper escapes her lips. "Oh, Mama," she says aloud. "I'm sorry, I'm sorry, I'm sorry." She repeats the futile refrain again and again as the tears flow freely—tears of regret this time, not anger. All the time Lucinda spent angry because her mother had been too hard on her—Lucinda was doing the very same thing, wasn't she? She railed against her mother every step of the way while upholding the values that were given to her by the same puppeteer that controlled Ruma and everyone else close to her.

And now Ruma is gone, and—

The tears stop as abruptly as they began.

—And Elle doesn't seem the least bit sad about it. She showed no remorse about any of it. Celeste, Bernie, Ruma. "If that means using those two as leverage…" Lucinda remembers Evie saying about Micah and Adi. She's become so completely detached; it really is one big decades-long game to her. A game in which the pieces are the Sisters, the Mothers, and the Daughters whose rights she set out to protect all those years ago.

She was unpredictable, and that made her a liability.
A liability.

She winces as her hand shoots to the pocket of her sweatshirt, just as soaked and even more cold than the rest of her clothing. Desperately, she pats around and then reaches her hand inside. She removes a closed fist and opens it to reveal her mother's folded-up glasses. The battery indicator light is flashing red. Almost dead. But not quite.

With shaky fingers, she unfolds the device. The glasses feel foreign on her face, having been specially fitted to her mother's. She resists the urge to activate the overlay, fearing the battery will run out before she can reach the part of her conversation with Elle she wants to hear again. They were in her pocket the whole time, anyway. The camera wouldn't have recorded anything.

The earpiece dangles from the arm of the glasses. She winds it around and pushes it into her ear, then uses the side controls to seek backward. Without video, she has to rely on her ear. She presses the back button, listens for a moment, and then presses it again several times in quick succession. When the audio starts again, her hand freezes in midair, fingertip poised next to the navigation controls as a honey and milk voice seeps into her ear.

The air leaves her lungs, and her pulse quickens as she tries to process the words she's hearing, the voice she never expected to hear again. "We can't just abandon these girls."

And then another voice, just as familiar. "Who said anything about abandoning them? They've got a leader, thirty years in the making."

"Lucinda's not ready."

"Lucinda doesn't have a choice."

"That's not up to you," says her mother's voice, quivering and uncertain. Scared.

The other voice comes back, cold as stone. "Ruma, are you serious? It's always been up to me."

Everything goes silent. Lucinda strains to hear another voice, another noise, anything. Oh, no. She pulls the glasses off and turns them over desperately in her hands. Lights off. Battery dead.

"Shit!" she says, ignoring the pain and shoving the impotent device back into her pocket as a wave of unease sweeps over her insides.

28

"I DON'T KNOW WHAT TO SAY," SAYS EMEKA. HE'S SITTING with Adi on a bench outside the Bureau office building. Adi looks down at her hands. Micah wanders, sullen, around the perimeter of the adjoining playground. "My daughter and granddaughter have been hiding their involvement in an underground extremist organization that breaks the law and led to a woman's death. And now I'm investigating that death. Does that sound about right?"

Adi sighs. She blinks, sending salty globes down her cheeks. "See, Daddy, this is why I didn't tell you. I knew you wouldn't understand. Everything's so black and white to you. The law, or against the law. Good or bad. Right or wrong. There's no room for anything else."

"The law is there for a reason," says Emeka. "It's my job to uphold it."

Adi's tears keep falling. "I know, Daddy. But did you ever stop to think what that reason is? And what women lose when we are told we aren't allowed to create life as our bodies were designed to do?"

"Lose?" Emeka asks. "Four-fourteen was put into place to protect women and babies."

Adi's laugh is sharp, humorless. "Dad, you can't be serious. Four-fourteen was put into place to legislate women's bodies and to protect the bottom line. Medical technology companies that are behind artificial wombs, safeguarding procedures, and implants have government contracts that pay out in perpetuity, and medical costs are static because the uncertainty associated with childbirth is reduced to zero."

"Isn't that a good thing?" Emeka asks.

"Sure," says Adi, anger replacing the sadness in her voice. "If you believe childbirth is risky in the first place. The risk of childbirth was reduced to virtually zero with continuous monitoring and medical technology advances before Four-Fourteen was ever introduced."

"Adi, this entire investigation started with the death of a woman during childbirth."

"Because she didn't have access to the high-quality medical care and monitoring that was available a century ago—care and monitoring that might have detected and corrected whatever had been wrong long before it became a problem." Adi sits back and takes a deep breath. When she speaks again her voice is calmer, more level. "I'm sorry, Dad. It's just—we've had a lot of time to think about this."

"You've been brainwashed," says Emeka. "These people, they somehow got hold of you and Micah, and they've been feeding you these conspiracy theories so you'll go along with whatever crazy plan they've concocted."

Adi levels her eyes at her father. "Daddy," she says, "You know me better than that. If anyone's brainwashed, it's you, blindly going along with the letter of the law, without questioning who's suffering because of it." Her voice falters; this is the first time Emeka can ever remember her speaking against him, and it's as if she said more than she meant to.

"Adi, we're talking about the health and safety of your *daughter*. What if something like what happened to Celeste Harlow happens to her?"

"That's why we need help, Daddy," Adi says, desperation in her eyes. "You have no idea how many people are out there who could become pregnant, now or in the future. The Society's founders had the best intentions. Their plan was a good one, but it got away from them. There are too many of us now, and not enough resources and support. We need help," she says again. Her eyes fill once more as they lock with Emeka's. "I need help. Micah needs help. I'm afraid of what's going to happen when people find out about her."

Adi starts and looks down at her mobile. "Sorry," she mumbles, swiping at her eyes as she picks up the call. "Hi, Astor," she says. Concern overtakes her features as she listens. "When did you last hear from her?" she says, and after a moment, "My dad is here. Give me a minute. I'll call you back."

She levels her eyes at her father. "Looks like we need a different kind of help right now," she says. "Please tell me your Bureau clearance lets you track someone's location."

29

She walks and walks, she has no idea for how long. Hours, at least. Probably in the right direction. She doesn't remember Aunt Elle and Uncle Clark living so far out of town. But, then again, she's never walked it before.

A man's voice calls through the trees. "Lucinda?" Her heart jumps into her throat. Safety, or danger? Who could know she's here? She freezes.

"Lucinda, it's Detective Abuto," the voice says. "Emeka." And, after another pause, "Adi's father."

His voice sounds tender, his light accent softening his words at the edges. But is it sincere?

"I'm alone," the voice says. "Adi was worried about you. She was afraid you'd gotten yourself into trouble when you weren't back in time, and you didn't answer your messages. I've been tracking your implant."

Adi asked him to find her?

Lucinda sent a message to Adi and Astor this morning. The message was vague, but she's sure glad she sent it. The question of whether he's on her side or not will have to wait. For now, she needs his help.

"You're safe," says the detective. "I'm going to keep talking. You just follow the sound of my voice, and I'll get you out of here."

Lucinda takes a deep breath, and her eyes dampen once more. She sees the man's dark form picking through the brush, holding his mobile in one hand. His shiny leather shoes squelch in the ground, still spongy from the morning's rain. "Here," she almost gasps, lurching toward him. "I'm here."

He catches her just before she collapses to the ground, sobbing.

"Okay, there," he says. "Let's look at you." He takes her hand and straightens to his full height; she stands tall, though he still towers over her.

Lucinda jerks away when he places his hands on her shoulders. "Sorry," she mumbles. "I hurt my arm. I think it's dislocated."

"Lucinda, you're a mess," he says. "What happened to you?"

She opens her mouth searching for something to say, but she can't find the words. She looks down at her body, but tears blur her vision. What parts of the truth are safe to tell him? What parts of the truth does she even know? "I need to get home," she says.

"You need to get to the hospital," says Abuto. He removes his suit jacket and places it gingerly around Lucinda's shoulders. "Come with me," he says, gesturing over his shoulder. "I have a car just over the hill."

The car is already warm when Lucinda sinks into the seat. "Why don't you take off that sweatshirt?" he asks. "It must be freezing."

"No, thanks," says Lucinda, hugging the soaked shirt closer to her body. She can't risk leaving it behind, losing what it holds.

The ride back to the city is silent. From time to time, fresh tears fill her eyes and run down her cheeks, but her thoughts are rushing too quickly, and she can't concentrate long enough to engage in conversation. What happens next with the Society? What is she supposed to do about Elle? She's still trying to reconcile the Elle she knows with the cold, calculated woman who just tried to kill her. What else is she capable of?

The car rolls through the hills and then gradually into a more densely populated landscape. As the warmth from the heater at last begins to penetrate her clothing, a new weight settles on Lucinda's chest. She's always felt responsible for her Sisters, but now the stakes have been raised. The responsibility, the need to protect her Family, feels more concrete. She's got to move from following the plan to creating it. This work is risky. Real lives are at stake. If it doesn't work, she'll have no one to blame but herself, no one to turn to for help cleaning up the fallout.

She might not make it through with her life and her freedom.

And then, who will help Serafina as she grows up and tries to make sense of it all? Certainly not Elle.

She misses her mother fiercely. If Ruma were here, maybe she could offer some reassurance that Lucinda's doing the right thing, after all—despite what Aunt Elle thinks. All those years of resentment have faded into a guilty regret. Sure, her mother put too much trust in Elle, but considering everyone who has followed Evie over the years without ever even seeing her in person, she can't blame Ruma for doing the same.

What Lucinda would give to apologize to her mother, to give her a sincere hug for the first time in, how many years? She wipes her damp face and dripping nose with her waterlogged sweatshirt, sniffing and shaking her head.

Rather than shaking away her regret, the movement only reminds her of the pain in her skull.

Finally, the car pulls up in front of the hospital and the detective turns toward her. "Lucinda, why were you visiting Clark and Elle Baker?" he asks as she moves to open the door.

Her mouth opens, but no sound comes out.

"Your mobile devices are at the Baker home," he says, gesturing to the map on the screen of his mobile. "I've been working with Clark to investigate the circumstances surrounding the death of your friend, Celeste. I know you and your family have always been close with the Bakers, but it doesn't add up that you'd have taken the trek out to visit them today of all days and ended up wet, injured, and alone in the forest."

Lucinda swallows and averts her eyes. She needs to get out of this car. The glasses seem to throb in her pocket, a dull echo of the twin aches in her head and shoulder. "Thank you for the ride," she says. "Thank you for coming to find me. My arm is killing me, though. I need to get it looked at."

The detective stares for a moment longer. His eyes are warm with understanding. "Lucinda—" he begins, but then he stops and motions for her to get out of the car. "Get yourself fixed up," he says. "But our conversation is not finished."

Lucinda swallows. The detective has the same eyes as Adi and Micah. A pang of guilt stabs her gut and Aunt Elle's cold gaze flashes in her mind. *You'd be amazed what some people will do to avoid harm coming to their loved ones.* "I think you should check on Adi and Micah," says Lucinda quietly before turning to get out of the car. As she walks through the doors of the hospital, she casts a glance over her shoulder to see Abuto still watching her, his face an indecipherable mask.

30

Lucinda's words still hang icily in the air as Emeka waits for Adi to answer his call. After interminable seconds, she does.

"Daddy?" she says. "Did you find Lucinda? Is she okay?"

"She'll be fine. I need you to get to the Bureau office," he says. "Pack some things. Take Micah and tell no one. If I'm not there yet, ask for Rodriguez. Micah knows her. She'll keep you safe."

"Okay." Her tone is urgent and clear, the same voice she used the day Micah fell off the play structure and broke her arm as a youngster. He can picture her assembling a bag, calm and careful. Only what's necessary and practical.

When he arrives at the office, Adi and Micah are already there. Micah twirls in his office chair, the bored look on her face contrasting with her mother's furrowed brow. "What's going on?" she asks Emeka in low tones just outside the cube.

"I can hear you," Micah drones from the chair.

Adi sighs and glances toward her daughter. "She's pretty mixed up. And she doesn't want to talk about it."

Emeka doesn't need to remind Adi of her role in causing those mixed emotions. "I need to do some more looking before I say anything," he says. "But I need you to tell me more about this Evie person before I can even get started."

Adi shrugs, looking off to the side. "There's not much to say," she says. "I told you this morning everything I know. I remember Ruma saying a week or so ago that Evie was the one who convinced Annette it was time for a change in the Society. Evie moved the Society from education to action, I think she said."

"But you have no idea who she is?"

"I didn't even know she was still alive until yesterday," says Adi. "Lucinda told us Evie called her to take her mother's place as leader."

"Us?" asks Emeka.

Adi's cheeks flush. She looks down at her feet and inhales. "Astor and me," she says.

"Astor?" asks Emeka. "Astor Flynn?"

Adi's eyes meet her father's again. "Do you know her?"

"Her name keeps coming up," he says. Astor is the one person Emeka hasn't questioned in this case.

"She is one of the originals," says Adi. "She and Lucinda and some of the others have known each other their entire lives. Their moms were close friends back in the day, and they were the first ones to follow Evie's words."

"The first to falsify their safeguarding procedures."

"Yeah," Adi says. "The movement grew and grew over the years, and new people"—she swallows— "kept getting recruited. But the originals have always had a special bond." Her face is downcast, and he gets the sense she never fully felt a part of the group.

Yet somehow, she let them convince her to subject Micah to their ways anyway.

He needs some space to think. "Know what? Why don't you two go grab a snack? Just put it on my account."

Micah reluctantly yields the seat to him in exchange for his swipe card. "Oh, your boss came by," she says on her way out. "Said something about the keynote tomorrow."

Tomorrow? Already? Well, that will have to wait. Just until he figures out how to find this Evie person.

Once they've left, he can think clearly about what Adi has just said. Ruma and a group of her close friends began this Society in earnest around the time Lucinda was born. Some quick math reveals Lucinda was born shortly after Ruma finished medical school and began practicing. When he questioned Lucinda, she spoke about the group of close friends she grew up with. Celeste and Astor are no surprise. But she mentioned another name as well, one that comes back to him as he sits with his fingers perched above the keyboard.

Myles Baker.

Myles, son to Clark Baker and Elle Vincent Baker.

Elle Vincent, she would have been called back in school, before she married Clark and added his last name onto hers. Ruma's closest friend.

He is up and out the door to the cube before Adi and Micah even get back. "Rodriguez," he calls as he approaches her desk.

She looks up at him, blinking as if her eyes are tired from staring at the screen for too long. "Abuto," she says. There's something sad in her eyes. "I was just about to go find you."

"No time," he says. "I need to head out. Can you do me a favor and keep an eye on Adi and Micah? I'm sure you can keep Micah busy with a spreadsheet or something."

"Actually, that's what I wanted to —"

He's already turned toward the exit. "Sorry, no time," he says over his shoulder. "I'll call you."

31

BY THE TIME THE CAR APPROACHES HER STREET, THE PAIN medication has taken full effect and Lucinda's thoughts are a jumbled mess.

Serafina and Zavi. Celeste. Astor. Adi and Micah. Elle. Mama.

Mama.

There was something about Mama, wasn't there?

Unpredictable. A liability.

A liability to whom?

To the Garden, of course, Elle's voice answers in her mind, as clear as if they were sitting here together. Cold, calculated, matter of fact. The voice of someone who doesn't mind sacrificing one life, or two, or…how many? for some warped idea of choice. "But only the choice *you* want us to make," Lucinda croaks.

"Pardon, Lucinda?" says the car's AI voice.

Lucinda goes silent, eyes flicking from side to side as if she knows the answer is right there. If she could just focus.

Her sweatshirt is still damp, though she's been out of the river for hours. Balled inside her pocket, her hand clutches something hard. She absently rubs a smooth edge with her thumb, back and forth, as she's done countless times in the last few days. The glasses, she remembers. Dead. This device knows things she does not.

The car has barely stopped before she scrambles out the door and into the building. She stands in front of the elevator doors, punching the *Up* button repeatedly until the doors slide open. She mutters an apology to the group of women she nearly bowls over in her rush to get inside.

The numbers climb and her fingers open and close around the folded-up piece of plastic. Can't forget. Mama.

She bursts through the doors before they even finish opening. Heaves her apartment door open and stumbles inside. Places the glasses on the quick-charging mat on the kitchen counter. Paces into the living room and then back to the kitchen, unable to wait but unable to do anything else. Can't contact anyone, or be contacted, with her mobile still in Aunt Elle's basket.

A beep from the mat indicates the device has enough battery life to be turned on; she forces herself to wait another five minutes before she removes it from the mat. Makes herself a coffee. Snacks on a hard-boiled egg from the fridge. It smells okay, though she can't remember the last time she boiled eggs. Has it been that long, or has time just passed impossibly slowly since Celeste's death?

It feels urgent that she review her mother's feed, but her fingers hesitate before activating the device. Her hand trembles next to her ear. What is she afraid of? It's a foolish question. Somewhere under the layers of grief and denial and pain medication, she already knows the answer.

The overlay flickers to life and she sees Elle's face, short hair blowing forward in a strong wind. She seeks backward in time, watching in reverse. Elle's stony face as her mouth soundlessly moves. A door closing, a backward descent down a narrow staircase. The numbers above the elevator doors counting down. The apartment where Lucinda grew up. Her father's face, soft and loving. A black flash signifies the beginning of the recording.

Lucinda swallows and presses play.

"I'll be back," her mother's voice says, unmistakable.

Her dad sits on the living room sofa, eyebrows in a knot. "Where are you going?"

"Oh, Elle's in town for a meeting. She just wanted to catch up."

Dad's face relaxes a little. "Oh, good," he says. "Maybe you two can do something fun, take your mind off things."

"Love you," her mother says without comment. "I'll see you in a bit."

Her father smiles and blows her a kiss. "I love you," he says, and turns back to the program he was watching on the wallscreen. The next time he saw her, her body would be broken and she would be gone.

Out of the apartment. Up the elevator, painted fingernails picking at dry cuticles. Up the staircase, out onto the blustery roof. Elle is already there.

"Okay," says Ruma, approaching the smaller, fairer woman. "What's your plan? What do we do now?"

"Now, you go," she says. "You need to get out of here. Protect yourself. If you don't, they're going to lock you up."

Ruma's head is shaking. "Elle, I can't do that. We can't just abandon these girls."

"Who said anything about abandoning them? They've got a leader, thirty years in the making."

Lucinda's heard this part of the conversation, but in the woods, she wasn't able to see Elle approaching her mother. Wasn't able to watch—to feel—Ruma backing away. Elle's tone is icy, her expression placid.

"It's never been your choice," says Elle.

Ruma's voice quavers. "It's been the two of us," she says. "All these years. We did this together. I helped you because I trusted you. I believed it was the right thing to do."

Lucinda recognizes Elle's humorless smile from a few hours ago. "Ruma, honey. It was the right thing to do. But I needed you. That's all. Sure, I hoped you'd grow up and be able to handle the tough decisions, the difficult situations. But deep down I knew, you've never been strong enough. You have to have known that, too. That's why we used Lucinda in the way we did. So she would be strong enough to handle it."

Used? The single word breaks through the fog of opiates, sending a surge of endorphins through Lucinda's body. Her eyes clear, her mind wakes up. "Used?" her mother says. "You're talking about my daughter. The little girl you used to take for sleepovers and spa days and nature hikes. We didn't *use* her. We *raised* her. *I* raised her. And I raised her to be the compassionate and giving person she is. Not a sociopath like you."

Elle's forehead creases in mock concern. "Oh, Ruma. See? That's the problem. That's the kind of thing I'm talking about. You're letting your emotions get in the way of what you know needs to happen. You can't accept things for what they are. The Society needs a strong leader who won't get all morally self-righteous when a sacrifice needs to be made."

"Sacrifice?" Lucinda has never heard this shrill version of her mother's voice. "Sacrifice! These are human beings, Elle! Little girls, babies, young women! They are people, not sacrifices." The same thing Lucinda said to Elle just hours ago.

"For the good of the many," Elle says without a hint of irony in her voice. "You were there the first time those words were uttered. You agreed with them back then. The meaning hasn't changed, so what has?"

"One of our Sisters is dead, that's what. And she's left her daughter without a mother." Lucinda can hear the tears in her mother's low voice. "And you call her a *sacrifice.*"

*"*And you knew that was a possibility all along." Elle pauses, steeples her hands in front of her forehead. "Ruma, I don't think we can do this after all," she says.

Ruma is silent. The visual field moves from left to right. She's looking around, no doubt realizing how close to the edge she's gotten. Was Ruma as terrified living this as Lucinda is watching it? Elle takes a step closer.

"I don't think I can trust you to do what needs to be done. I think you're going to use that big, beautiful conscience of yours to do something very foolish."

Ruma's head shakes. "No, I –"

"You're going to ruin everything."

"Elle, I –"

"Everything we've worked so hard for, for more than half our lives."

Move! Lucinda wants to shout. Left or right, or even straight ahead. Her mother was larger than Elle, taller, thicker. She could walk straight through her. But she doesn't.

Lucinda knows how this ends. Maybe Ruma didn't believe Elle would do it. Maybe she'd been so conditioned over forty years of friendship to defer to Elle that she didn't even consider fighting her. Maybe, in some self-sabotaging part of her mind, she thought she deserved it.

"I hope Lucinda can rise to the occasion," Elle says. "I hope she can do what's necessary. I hope she can do what you couldn't."

And with that, Lucinda's visual field fills with gray sky. Occasionally, a familiar bright flash of fabric flaps into view. She barely registers her mother's scream over her own sobs. It's as if, this time, Lucinda's the one falling.

Cruelly, the feed doesn't stop. Lucinda's heaving sobs slow as she watches the events that follow. Her collapse, Abuto's arrival, Elle's brisk exit from the building's front door.

Lucinda stops playback at the point where Elle bends down to comfort her. Aunt Elle. Evie. Mastermind. Leader. Murderer. She sits in a paralyzed silence, resisting the nausea that fills her chest. What is she supposed to do now?

When the door opens, she nearly jumps out of her skin.

"Shit!" says Lucinda with a start as Zavi walks through the door.

"Lucinda, what happened to you?" Zavi says, rushing to her side as the door closes behind him.

She looks down at herself. Her clothing is muddy and torn, her long hair a rat's nest of tangles and debris. She can barely see through the puffy, tear-filled mess in the space where her eyes are supposed to be. Her arm is immobilized in a sling, though mercifully the pain has lessened to a dull throb. "Don't touch," she croaks out. "I'm sore all over."

"What the hell happened?" Zavi asks again, this time with more urgency.

Lucinda stares down at the glasses she's ripped off her head and flung onto the table's glass top. "Elle," she says.

Zavi freezes. "Elle?" he asks. "Aunt Elle? What about her?"

"Well, she killed my mother, for starters." Lucinda is surprised by the steadiness of her voice. "And she cracked me over the head with a rock or something and pushed me into the river."

"No," Zavi whispers, pulling out his mobile. "No, no."

"Watch if you want," says Lucinda. "It's all recorded on my mother's overlay. You can see for yourself. Then I dislocated my shoulder trying to get up the riverbank." She looks at Zavi for the first time. He is flicking a finger around on his mobile. His face has gone white. "Wait, what time is it?" she asks, craning her neck to see the clock in the kitchen. School has been over for an hour already. "Zavi, where is Sera?"

When Zavi's eyes meet Lucinda's, his pupils have nearly eclipsed his violet irises. "Elle picked up Sera from school." He holds out his mobile, open to the school's communication portal. *Dismissal Log*, reads the screen. At 11:13, Elle signed Serafina out for an appointment.

"What appointment?" says Lucinda. "There is no appointment. *Where did she take her?*"

"Lucinda, why would your aunt have taken
Serafina?"

Lucinda swallows, takes a deep breath, and looks
Zavi in the eyes. "So she can keep control of the Garden
Society." Zavi stares at her blankly. He's not getting it, but
she can't explain now. They need to find where Elle has
taken Serafina and get her back. Lucinda snatches Zavi's
mobile out of his hand and opens the *Contacts* screen.

"She's not going to hurt her," Zavi says before the
call connects. "Right?"

Lucinda doesn't answer. Twenty-four hours ago,
she'd have said there was no way Elle would hurt either of
them. Now she knows the woman is capable of anything.

Elle's voice on the other end of the line apologizes
for being unavailable. Of course she wouldn't answer.
Lucinda hangs up and tries Clark instead.

"Zavi, what a surprise," says Uncle Clark on the
other end. Lucinda can hear the smile in his voice, and she
wants to wrap her hands around his neck.

"Not Zavi," she says, talking right over Clark's attempt at a warm greeting. "Clark, where is Elle? I need to
find her right now."

"Lucinda, what's wrong?" he asks. "I'm still at work.
I haven't talked to your Aunt Elle since this morning, but I
assume she's at home, finishing up with her day. Is everything okay?"

"She's definitely not working. And nothing is okay."
Would she have gone back up to her house with Serafina?
Not unless she wanted to be caught. "I can almost guarantee

she's not at home, Clark. Now, I need you to think. Where would she go if she needed to hide?"

"Hide? Lucinda, what are you talking about? What on earth would Elle need to hide from?"

He's so earnest. He has no idea what Elle's been up to. "Clark, I can't get into it right now," she says. "But Elle has Serafina, and I need to get her back. Can you think of anywhere she might go? If she were in trouble? Can you call her and see if you can figure out where she is?"

Clark stumbles over his words, but the alarm in his voice has ratcheted up a notch. "*Has* Sera? What do you— trouble? What kind of—why would she take Serafina? I'm very confused, Lucinda. What is going on?"

The blood courses through her veins so fast, she can smell the iron. "Clark, I promise I will explain this all to you after I get my daughter back. But for now, can you please just stop asking questions and help me find her?"

Clark takes a deep breath. "Yeah, okay. One second." After a brief pause, he says, "I tried checking her mobile location. It's not shared with me."

Location. "Wait," Lucinda says, as much to Clark as to herself. "I might have an idea." She tells Zavi to pull up the *Guardian* application, installed on both of their mobiles when Serafina's implant was placed. From here they can check Serafina's vital health statistics. And they can check her location.

"Come on, come on!" Zavi bounces in his seat as the map loads on the screen in front of them. Then, his eyebrows knit up in confusion and he slides the device toward Lucinda. *INACTIVE*, reads the notification.

Impossible. "What the hell does that mean?" Lucinda swipes the time slider back to 11:13, the time Elle picked up Serafina. Slowly, she slides to the right, watching as the yellow beacon crawls out of the city, then picks up speed moving south of town, and just … blinks out. Bile rises in her throat, and she wants to scream.

"What does what mean?" asks Clark. Lucinda had almost forgotten he was on the other end. "Serafina's implant status is inactive," says Lucinda. "They headed south of the city and her implant just stopped sending tracking data."

"Wait, south of the city?" says Clark.

"Yes." Lucinda's response is terse. "The opposite direction of your house."

Clark is silent for a moment. "Fucking Nathan," he spits at last.

"Nathan?" says Lucinda.

"Who's Nathan?" Zavi says at the same time.

"Nathan Mackenzie," Clark says, his voice laced with disgust. "*Doctor* Nathan Mackenzie. He's a friend of your Aunt Elle's—"

"Don't. Call her that," says Lucinda.

Clark breathes deeply and begins again. "He's a friend of Elle's from way back. She insisted I recommend him for his job, as a matter of fact. He's the medical director for my division. Responsible for making sure medical protocols are standardized, implants are gathering the right data, that kind of thing."

Clark needs to get on with it. "What does this Nathan guy have to do with my daughter?" she demands.

"I don't want to be talking to you about this," Clark says. "It doesn't feel right."

"Clark, I'm an adult and Elle has my daughter. If it's relevant, I need to know it. I don't care how it feels."

"Right. Okay. Well, those two had some *thing* going on, back before Elle and I met. The two of them were never apart. When I first got together with Elle, a day didn't go by that they weren't messaging back and forth or having conversations behind closed doors. At least a few times a week they had dinner with Nathan's mothers, followed by little sleepovers they both swore were innocent." Clark's voice grows distant yet more bitter. "'Working late and lost track of time,' was always the excuse. They had some naturalist group they were trying to promote back then. One day, they just stopped talking about it, and then they spoke to each other less and less. Nathan married Kyle and I thought they'd outgrown their little fling. Maybe they just got better at hiding it. Anyway, the only people I know of that live out that way are Nathan's mothers. They hosted our engagement party there, a hundred years ago. If Aunt—I mean Elle—wanted to get away, I'd bet money she's there."

Nathan. Wasn't that who kept texting Elle when they were out at dinner? "Do you remember the address?" Lucinda is almost pleading. What are the chances he would, if the last time he was there was nearly forty years ago?

"No," he says. Tears form in Lucinda's eyes and her heart feels like it's clawing its way out of her chest. "But I can get it. Hold on."

Lucinda catches her breath. Her eyes meet Zavi's over the table, and they both stand, ready to leave the house to go find Serafina. Lucinda hands Zavi's mobile back to him and goes rushing about, checking the countertops and bedrooms for anything she might need to bring. She comes back empty-handed other than a jacket and a change of clothes for Sera. What else could she need? Her eyes dart around the apartment, settling reluctantly on her mother's battered glasses. The thought of leaving them here, sitting on the table, troubles her. She grasps the device as if it might burn her, then shoves it back into the pocket it's been occupying since the day of her mother's death.

Clark is back on the line, reading off an address he must have found in some government database as Zavi and Lucinda board the elevator. "Wait. You're not going down there on your own, are you?" asks Clark.

Of course they are. What else would they do?

"My office is on the way for you," he says. "Pick me up. I'll go with you. We can call the police on the way down."

No way. Lucinda has gotten into this situation by placing her trust in the wrong people. Clark's ignorance of Elle's secret life seems genuine. But even if he doesn't know what kind of person Elle is, and what kinds of things she's done, he could very well try and protect her. Besides, they've already wasted enough time.

"I'm not going to do that, Clark," Lucinda says. She disconnects the call without another word.

As the car pulls out of the parking bay and, hopefully, toward her daughter, Lucinda can't help flashing back to the view from her mother's overlay. Her hands clench in her lap as a single question plays on repeat in her mind, one she can't bear trying to answer.

Elle had no problem letting Celeste die. She killed Ruma with no hesitation and threatened to use Adi and Micah against the detective. What is she willing to do to Serafina?

32

EMEKA IS IN THE CAR, HEAD LOST IN A JUMBLE OF THOUGHTS. He'd intended to head up to the Baker place and question Elle, but when the warrant came through and he checked her location on his monitor, he found her implant was offline. How did she manage that?

He changed course to Clark Baker's office instead, intending to bring him in as a person of interest. If his partner was involved in this secret society at the highest levels, surely he had to have known something about it. He's the Director of Population Science, after all. The perfect job if you want to cover up population science crimes.

On his mobile, a notification sounds. "Incoming message from Dr. Ruma Das."

That's impossible. Ruma Das has been dead for days now. He accepts the message, not sure what he expects to find. At first, he is confused by what he sees. It looks like the feed from an overlay, but it takes a moment for him to recognize Josiah Conroy and the apartment he shared with Dr. Das. The video continues. A brown hand adorned with jangling gold bracelets—Ruma Das's hand—reaches for an elevator keypad. She brings Emeka to a staircase and out onto a rooftop. A woman stands there, small and blonde and confident, and wearing a black dress and heels.

Emeka watches, transfixed, as the last minutes of Ruma Das's life unfold in front of his eyes.

He watches until those same heels click past Ruma's body and Elle Vincent Baker kneels to comfort the daughter of the woman she's just killed.

Just as the feed cuts out, an incoming call startles him. It's Lucinda's voice, low and rough, that greets him when he answers. "Did you watch it?"

"I did." How many times has she watched it? Enough times to know exactly how long to give him before calling.

"She has my daughter," says Lucinda. "She pushed me into the river, and then she came down to the city and she took my daughter out of school. We're going to find her now. Can you help us?" Her voice cracks. "We need help."

"Of course," says Emeka. "Of course I'll help. Do you have any idea where she might have taken her? There's a problem with Elle's implant and I can't track her location."

Lucinda sniffs. "Serafina's implant shows on our app as inactive. But my uncle, Clark—he gave me the address where he thinks she is. That's the only thing we have to go on, so that's where we're headed."

"Okay, send me the location," says Emeka. "I'll head that way too, and I'll call the local law enforcement."

"Okay." Lucinda takes a breath. "Okay." Her voice is small but less panicked.

"Lucinda, I want you to listen to me. I want you to stop before you get to this place, and I want you to wait for me."

"But—"

"I know you want to see your daughter. Trust me, I do. But you need to let the police do what they're trained to do, so nobody gets hurt." There's silence on the other end. "Lucinda, can you promise me to do that?"

Deep breath. "Okay," she says. "But hurry. Please hurry."

33

Uncertainty stretches the already long drive. Is Serafina okay? Are they even going in the right direction? Lucinda keeps the panic at bay by recounting to Zavi all that has happened since he left for work this morning.

"I just can't believe Elle would do that," says Zavi after Lucinda describes the interaction between Elle and her mother. "So it was her who convinced your mother to leave you when you fell in the river?"

Lucinda feels a pluck at her heart once more, for all she's unfairly laid at her mother's feet all these years. "Yeah," she says, voice full of gravel. "Said it would prove to my mother I was stronger than I thought."

"Think it worked?"

Lucinda shrugs. "Honestly? I think it just drove me away from my mother and brought her further under Elle's control. Once you've let your boss convince you to leave your child to drown, it's hard to take a step back."

Zavi looks up Nathan Mackenzie as the overcast sky continues to darken and the car turns onto a local road. "Parents are Sonequa Gordon and Natalie Mackenzie."

Lucinda turns toward Zavi. "Gordon?" she asks. "Like Annette Gordon?"

After a few taps on the screen of his mobile, Zavi says, "Annette's daughter. Actually, it looks like she was the last person to be born naturally. Last until Serafina, that is." He squeezes Lucinda's knee.

There is silence for a moment. Zavi's foot taps absently on the floor. Lucinda picks at her cuticles. "She wouldn't do anything to hurt Sera," Zavi says.

He says it as a statement this time, rather than a question, but neither of them can be sure. "She loves Serafina," she says. "And Sera's an innocent little girl. I have to believe Elle wouldn't hurt her." Lucinda swallows down her doubt. What else can she do?

Elle took Serafina to scare Lucinda. That must be it. She had to have known Lucinda would make it out of the river, just as she did all those years ago. Elle only wanted to get Lucinda out of the way, so she could get to Serafina and manipulate Lucinda into doing what she wanted. She wouldn't hurt an innocent little girl out of spite.

Lucinda keeps repeating this to herself as they crawl southward on the freeway. She can only hope it's true.

34

EMEKA INTENDED TO SPEND THE DRIVE RESEARCHING Nathan Mackenzie's parents, their home, and what Elle might have in mind if, indeed, she brought the girl here. He has only been on the road for a few minutes, though, when he is interrupted by a call.

"Mackenzie," he says when he picks up.

"Detective Abuto." He sounds laser focused today, the opposite of his distracted demeanor last time they talked. With a hint of panic in his voice, the doctor says, "I have urgent information for you."

"Oh?" asks Emeka. "What information is that?" Emeka has already learned about the Society and Elle's part in it. He knows Mackenzie covered up information about a cluster of girls who, like Celeste Harlow, aren't safeguarded. He knows Elle is likely on her way to Mackenzie's mothers' house with a kidnapped little girl.

Other than satisfying Emeka's curiosity about why an esteemed physician would risk his career and his reputation on this woman and her scheme, he's doubtful Mackenzie has anything useful for him.

The doctor takes a deep breath. "Clark Baker just called me. He told me his partner, Elle, she took a little girl."

"And?"

"And... well... and I know where to find her." Mackenzie's stutter betrays his cognitive dissonance.

"I'm listening."

The tension in Emeka's shoulders gives way a bit when Mackenzie reads off the address to which he's already headed. Turns out, Mackenzie's mother called him when Elle and the girl showed up on the doorstep of his childhood home.

"Did you talk to Ms. Baker?"

"No, but my mother said they were there, doing a puzzle in the family room. I called you right away." The line is silent for a moment before the doctor adds, "I told Mama not to tell Ellie I'd called, not yet. I think something is wrong with her. She may be having a psychotic break."

Convenient setup. If Elle is crazy, anything she says about Nathan can be questioned. "Any idea why she would bring the little girl to your parents' house?"

"No, I have no idea," says Mackenzie, and his voice has lost all uncertainty. He's lying. "But I think I might be able to convince her to turn over the girl. Detective, I'm worried she's dangerous. I don't want my mothers or that little girl getting hurt."

Mackenzie is trying to save himself, but that doesn't make him wrong.

"Stay on the line," Emeka says. "I'm almost to their house, and I may need your help."

35

LUCINDA'S NAILS ARE DIGGING INTO HER PALMS WHEN THE car stops just short of the address Clark gave them. The area is not as isolated as Elle and Clark's place, but it's too sparsely developed to be considered the suburbs. Copses of naked trees serve as the border between houses, each sitting on several acres of land. The gray sky is darkening, and the sun is a bright smudge behind the clouds as it approaches the horizon.

"Almost there," says Detective Abuto when she calls from Zavi's mobile. "Local law enforcement is preparing. Stay back until you hear from me."

"You have to let them do their jobs," says Zavi, pulling Lucinda close to him and away from the car door. "If they see you outside the house, they'll know they've been found." She loosens her white-knuckle grip on the handle but can't bring her body to relax.

"I just wish I had some binoculars or something," she says. "Like, I don't even know for sure this is the right place. What if it's not? What if she's gone somewhere else completely? What if she's done something to Sera?" Her voice is bordering on hysterical. Blood rushes through her veins like microscopic knives.

The house sits atop a small hill. Lights are on. People are moving around. But they're too far away for Lucinda to make out any details. Is Sera one of the blurs passing back and forth in front of the windows? It's dinner time, she realizes. Her stomach turns at the thought of some strange person feeding her daughter. Or even Elle, who might as well be a stranger.

Sera was probably thrilled to see Elle at school. She wouldn't have questioned why she was being picked up early. She couldn't have known the terrible things Elle had done. What is she thinking now? Is she asking to go home? Is she asking to talk to her mama? Is she crying?

Tears are falling down Lucinda's face when she pulls the handle and moves to push the door open. "I can't just—" she begins.

"Look!" Zavi says, catching her wrist. He pulls her back toward him once more and points up the hill.

Black figures are moving toward the house. A lot of them.

Lucinda sinks back into her seat, unblinking. Now all she can do is wait and hope.

36

FOR THE SECOND TIME TODAY, EMEKA IS SURROUNDED BY trees and leaf litter because of Elle Baker. The cold breeze carries hints of damp pine sap. His senses are sharp, alerting him to movement in all directions.

The warrant came through while he was en route, and local law enforcement has been watching the house and setting up their offensive ever since. The dark provides plenty of cover, but still, Emeka stays back a dozen or more feet from the tree line as the soundless swarm of the tactical team approaches the house.

His heart is steady, masking the excitement of pursuit he always feels in situations like this. He hasn't eaten since breakfast. His stomach growls as he stands and waits, a mosaic of body camera feeds on his mobile's display and Nathan Mackenzie's voice in his ear.

Emeka had assumed Elle Baker was desperate, but from what he's heard in the last fifteen minutes, she might be as unhinged as Nathan suggested. "These girls," she has said several times. "They have no appreciation. What I gave to them. What I risked for them. And they think they don't *need* me? Lucinda wouldn't be where she is without me. None of them would."

From his place in the woods, Emeka watches Elle pacing back and forth in front of the windows.

"They want to just give up the whole Society, and why? Because one person died. Well, two. But Ruma brought it upon herself. And anyway, that was the whole agreement! What else does it mean, *For the good of the many*? It's all about acceptable sacrifice. We are so *close*, Nathan. Just a little farther, and we—"

Nathan has to raise his voice to get a word in through Elle's ranting. "Don't you think maybe it's come too far now?" he asks. "With Ruma and everything, don't you—"

"Oh, don't you dare go all remorseful on me now," she spits. "You agreed Ruma had to go. I was just the only one with the guts to do the dirty work." So Elle wasn't the only one involved in Ruma Das's murder.

Emeka's mobile screen shows the officers in position and ready to go in. They're waiting on a signal from the sergeant standing next to him, and that sergeant is waiting for Emeka. He still hasn't seen the girl, though, and he wants to know she'll be out of the action when they go in. *Convince her to get the girl somewhere out of the way,* he sends to Mackenzie through the surveillance application he's using to monitor the phone call.

"What are you going to do with that little girl, though?" he asks. "I'm sure she's missing her parents, and mine aren't really set up for a little girl, you know."

A faint voice sounds over the line. "When will it be time to go home?"

"Not too long, baby," Elle says, some distance from the microphone. Then she turns back to her conversation with Mackenzie. "She's going to learn from Mama," Elle says. "She's going to learn what it means to honor those who came before. Something Lucinda apparently didn't learn well enough herself. Serafina will be good. Do you know the first thing she did when she got here? She saw the picture of

Gramma Annette hanging in the stairway and her eyes lit right up. She knows. She'll be better than her mother." Elle pauses. "Lucinda's gone, anyway."

"Gone? What—?" Nathan begins.

Stay focused. Lucinda's fine.

"Never mind," Nathan says to Elle. "Did you have dinner already? You know Mama always has a frozen pie ready to slice up for dessert."

"Oh, that's a wonderful idea. Serafina, sweetie, why don't you go into the kitchen and ask Mama Gordon for a slice of her special pie?"

He hears the child's faint acknowledgment and barely catches the smear of her figure in his binoculars as she bounds into the kitchen. Elle stays in the living room, pacing. She's beginning to repeat the same deluded narrative that Serafina is going to be the new beginning of the Garden Society when Emeka finally gives the signal.

The black figure on the front porch reaches over and silently tries the doorknob. Locked. Emeka's eyes flit back and forth between that officer's body camera and his binoculars, trying to follow what happens in real-time. The officer positions herself in front of the door, and the two officers at her flank take up positions just out of sight.

What's happening? Mackenzie types as Elle continues on her rant. She seems to have forgotten she's talking to anyone at all. *Should I tell my parents to get the girl out the back?*

Emeka sees the message, but just then the officer at the front door knocks. Elle stops talking, stops pacing. She looks out the window in the direction of the woods. Can she see him, all the way out here? Another knock. "Is there somebody at the door?" Emeka hears one of Mackenzie's mothers call from a distance.

"Elle?" Mackenzie says. "You there?" He has been keeping the conversation going, but now his voice has a troubled edge.

Stay calm.

What is happening? Are my parents in danger?

"Where are you?" Elle's voice is cold, otherworldly.

"Me?" asks Mackenzie. "I'm at home, in my apartment. What do you mean?"

"You sent them for me."

"Who? Elle, who would I have sent? Is someone there?" his voice trembles.

"You know someone's here," she says, her words like knives. "I thought we were in this together, Nathan. To the end. Why would you do this? We're almost there!"

Emeka signals, and two loud bangs fill his earpiece. That's all it takes to get the door to swing open, and on the body camera feed, Elle appears, as up-close as he's ever seen her. Her ice-blue eyes are filled more with rage than with fear. She's not afraid to be caught. She's furious about it.

"Come in from the back," the officer, now standing in the living room, says into her communicator, but before the officers can get in, Elle is running through the house in the same direction Serafina's just gone.

Emeka's view is a piecemeal of several different angles on the same scene, each as troubling as the rest. There is shouting. Orders to raise hands and move away, to sit in a seat or drop to the ground. Elle heeds none of them. She heads instead to the kitchen counter with the familiarity of someone who's known this place for years.

There is screaming, this time from Serafina. Her tiny body is dwarfed by the rustic wooden chair where she sits, fork midway between plate and mouth. There are no words, just the sound of fear and disbelief. Mackenzie's mothers sit on either side of the little girl, and their arms are thrust in front of her.

"Ellie," one woman says. Her voice is level, but her face betrays her fear.

"Please think about what you're doing," says the other, tears streaming down her face.

But Elle doesn't respond. Their pleading just adds to the tumult until one of the officers yells for them to be quiet.

Elle's eyes are wide and determined as she selects the biggest knife from the block, then swivels her head back and forth in search of a route. She's surrounded by officers, but it's tight quarters. She extends the knife out in front of her as the officer who first knocked at the door tries to bring her around. "Ms. Baker," she says. "Think about what you're doing. You don't want to hurt anyone. You care about these people, and they care about you. You don't want to hurt them. And it's our job to protect all of them. If you try and hurt someone, we're going to have to hurt you."

Elle ignores her and locks eyes with Serafina. "Sera, sweetie," she says. Her voice is clear enough she almost sounds lucid. "The Society is going to be yours one day. With your grandma gone, and your mama gone, you will be able to take over. You want that, right? You want to be a leader like Grandma and Mama?"

Serafina sniffs. "I— I guess so?" she says. "Where's Mama? I want to go home now." Giant tears roll down her cheeks. "I want Mama!"

"Don't you want to stay with me and Mama Gordon? We can teach you how to be the best leader."

One of the women begins to raise her hand in protest, and the other quiets her with a look.

"No!" Serafina yells. "I want Mama and Daddy!" She drops her fork on her plate, stands up from the table, and bolts out the open door to the woods outside.

Elle dashes toward the door, still wielding the knife. The officers shout for her to stop, but she hasn't registered a single thing they've said, and this is no different. Before she can make it to the door, the pop of a taser brings her to the floor.

One of Mackenzie's mothers stands and looks around at the officers, as if for permission. "Go!" says one, gesturing toward the door. "Find the girl."

"Did you shoot her?" the other woman says after her partner leaves. She's the only civilian still in the home with the officers and Elle.

"She's just been tased, ma'am," says the officer who fired. "We'll have her up and out into the car in just a minute."

"Then what's all that blood?" the woman asks. She's shrinking away from Elle's collapsed form on the ground, lifting her feet to avoid the pool that spreads impossibly outward from it. "What's all that blood? Tasers don't make you bleed, do they? Why is she bleeding? She's not supposed to be bleeding." She's nearly screaming.

"Elle?" Mackenzie's voice sounds in Emeka's ear. He'd forgotten the two were still on the line together. "Elle, are you okay? Detective, what's going on?" He asks, on the verge of panic. "Is she bleeding? What's happening?"

Emeka tells Mackenzie to disconnect the call. "We will be in touch," he says. And then he watches on his screen as Elle Vincent Baker's body is rolled over. Mackenzie's mother howls in horror. The knife Elle was holding protrudes from her neck at an odd angle. Her face is smudged with blood, but her eyes look as they always have, ice-blue and unblinking.

37

NOT TEN MINUTES HAVE PASSED SINCE THE DOOR TO THE house was forced open, two sharp cracks traveling down the hill and through Lucinda's closed car windows. A short time later, two more figures emerged from the woods and rushed inside. Aside from that, the house looks unassuming and peaceful. Lucinda feels like crawling out of her skin imagining the horrible things that could be happening in there. She sits forward in her seat, her face nearly touching the windshield, and tries in vain to catch a glimpse of anything other than vague blobs of color through the windows.

"Zavi, what if she did something to her?" she asks for what feels like the hundredth time. "What if she tied her up in a closet, or what if she locked her in a basement, or what if she killed her? Zavi, what if she killed her?" The waiting is too much, and it doesn't matter what comforting words Zavi says, because no one will know what Elle has done until she is brought out of that house in custody.

Sirens sound in the distance. "What is that?" Until now Zavi has been the calming presence in the car, but now there is panic in his voice. "Why are there sirens?"

"They're far away," Lucinda says. They can't be coming here.

But the wailing grows closer, and then red lights illuminate the leafless branches surrounding them, and when the ambulance passes their parked car, she can no longer pretend it's not meant for someone inside that house at the top of the hill. She feels sick. "Oh no." An image comes into her mind before she can stop it: her little girl lying on the ground, pale and lifeless, her long black hair splayed out in all directions.

Frantic, she tries Detective Abuto. He doesn't answer. Is he one of the dark-clad figures inside the house? She should have pressed harder to find out how he was going to protect her daughter. She should have asked more questions. Why did she trust him to keep Serafina safe?

Her eyes are glued to the house as if with a hard enough look she could see inside it. She doesn't see the two figures running down the street, one in hot pursuit of the other, until they nearly collide with the car. "Sera?" she cries, opening the door and rounding the car in a single motion. "Sera, come here!" Tears stream down her face as the little girl stops, mid-sprint.

"Mama," Sera says. A smile breaks through her tears as Lucinda kneels on the damp pavement to receive her.

"Come here, baby." Serafina runs to Lucinda, who encircles her daughter in her arms, inhaling the sweet musk of her hair.

Zavi is there, too, kneeling in the light from the car's headlamps, enveloping both of them in his warm arms. He holds their daughter at arm's length and looks her up and down. "Are you okay, sweetheart?"

"I'm fine, Daddy," Serafina says, and then she smiles and throws her arms around his neck. She looks fine. She sounds fine, too. Hopefully, it's not shock. Hopefully, she's too young to understand whatever it is she's been through today.

"Let's get you home, then," Zavi says. "It's almost bedtime."

Zavi takes Serafina into the car to buckle in for the trip home, and Lucinda stands to face the other figure, the woman who was in pursuit of Serafina as she ran down the dark, abandoned street. But the woman has already turned and is running even more quickly back up the hill to the house.

They need to get Serafina home. They have to find out what happened and make sure she's okay. Maybe even take her to the doctor. A vise tightens around Lucinda's chest. Ruma was her doctor. Lucinda will need a new doctor now. Because Elle killed Ruma.

Elle, who is in that house right now, where someone, for some reason, needed an ambulance. Lucinda has to know why. She catches Zavi's eye through the car window as he fastens their little girl into the car. She's safe now. "I'll be back," she says. She follows the woman up the road before Zavi can raise a word of protest, running as fast as her feet will take her.

The front door is blocked by an officer. "Can't come in here," he says.

"I — I know them," says Lucinda, panting. "My daughter was here. She— She was kidnapped." Surely that, if nothing else, gives her the right to know what's happening in there.

The officer crosses his arms. "Can't come in, sorry."

Lucinda cranes to see inside. Two women stand in the living room, an uneasy energy surrounding them. On the wall leading up the staircase hangs a familiar portrait. The woman who chased Serafina turns in Lucinda's direction, and there is no question that this is Annette Gordon's daughter. Same light skin and caramel eyes, even the same strong and confident posture. The last natural-born person before Serafina, Zavi said. Lucinda would be in awe if she weren't so exhausted.

Past the women, at the other side of the house, is a concentration of uniforms. A familiar face stands taller than the rest. "Detective Abuto!" she calls, waving a frantic arm over the officer blocking the door.

The detective's grave face turns toward her.

"Oh, no," she says once more, this time so softly even she can barely hear it.

After some words with the officers, Abuto comes in her direction. "It's okay," he says. "Let her in."

The officer moves aside with little urgency, and she pushes past. Emeka meets her in the living room. Fresh tears are already forming in her eyes when they meet the Detective's. She doesn't know what happened, but one way or another, Aunt Elle is dead.

"Where do we go from here?" Lucinda asks Detective Abuto.

She's standing on the front step of the Gordon-Mackenzie home. It takes all her will to keep her eyes on the detective and not look past him into the house where Elle's body is still being tended.

Abuto looks back at her with sad eyes. "Cases don't close themselves," he says. "And they don't just disappear. I'll have to compile all the information I've gathered and hand it over to the Council Attorney. They'll decide what to do with it."

Lucinda swallows. "What information?" she croaks. "Are we going to be arrested?"

"Well, you know," says the detective, "with the leaders of this organization gone, one might be convinced it was the two of them who were responsible for Celeste's death and" —he gestures vaguely— "and everything else with you and the other members of your group. I'll do my best to convey that in my report." After a moment, he adds, "Of course, I also have my own girls to protect."

A tear forms in Lucinda's eye. She is now responsible for protecting all the girls. The air is silent for a moment, but Serafina's presence pulls at Lucinda from the car, where she and Zavi have been waiting. The little girl is turned toward Lucinda, but her eyes are blank. Lucinda looks down at her hands, sees them twisting against each other, and doesn't bother trying to stop them. "I don't know what to do," she whispers.

"I can't pretend I know either," says the Detective. "But whatever it is, you'll want to do it soon. I will take my time completing my report, but I can't delay it for very long." Lucinda lifts her eyes to meet his. His look is serious, but he adds nothing else. "Go on now, get that little girl home and tucked into her own bed. She's the most important thing right now."

Lucinda takes a deep breath, turning toward the car. Serafina's eyes focus and her lips twitch up into a smile.

Behind her, the detective calls her name once more. "I'm sorry, Lucinda. About your mother and your, um, aunt."

Fresh tears glisten in her eyes. She remembers back to the table they shared at that long-ago awards banquet. Toasting with Emeka even as she recruited Adi and her unborn daughter for the Garden. "I'm sorry, too," she says. "For all of it."

"Mama, can I take off my bracelet now?" Serafina murmurs. Her head is in Lucinda's lap. Zavi sits silently in the front seat. Lucinda's heart has dropped further with every mile they've drawn closer to the city. She can't bring herself to imagine what comes next in the nightmare her life has become.

"Baby, I thought you were asleep," says Lucinda. "What bracelet are you talking about?"

The little girl thrusts her wrist upward, revealing a metal band Lucinda's never seen before.

"Where'd you get this?" Lucinda asks.

"Aunt Elle gave it to me," she says. "When she picked me up at school. Where is Aunt Elle, anyway? She told me we were going to stay with the nice ladies. Mama, she was kind of scaring me. Is she okay?"

Lucinda swallows, looking for a way to unclasp the bracelet. "Just rest," she says. She pats Sera's hair once the band has finally hinged open. "We'll talk about it tomorrow." Sera settles in, and soon her breath is heavy. "Zavi," Lucinda whispers, passing the bracelet forward. "What is this?"

"A bracelet?" he says. "Weird-looking bracelet for a six-year-old."

"Actually," says Lucinda. "Hold on. Let me see that." She pats her pockets and realizes her mobile is still at Elle and Clark's place. "Hand me your mobile."

She opens the *Guardian* application, and there it is. The blinking beacon representing Serafina's location. She watches the map as the dot travels with them, north up the freeway and away from the house in the woods.

"What is it?" Zavi calls back.

"One minute," she whispers, gently lifting Sera's hand and placing the bracelet back over her wrist. Right over the location of her implant. "Ha!" she says when the beacon disappears again. She presses her lips together reflexively when Serafina stirs in her lap. She removes the band once more and passes it back to Zavi. "It must be some kind of signal blocking band. Sera said Elle gave it to her when she took her from school."

Zavi turns the band over in his hands. "I didn't know these things really existed."

"Me either," says Lucinda.

The car rolls on and Lucinda stares out the window, streetlamps flying past her unfocused eyes. Her shoulder is aching; she forgot her medication in the rush to find Serafina. The back of her head has begun to throb, too. She winces, reliving those last moments with Elle. The unexpected strike to the head, the fall into the cold water. The crunch of the ligaments as her body was wrenched in the opposite direction of her arm.

She looks down at her sleeping daughter, sleek black hair cascading down the front of the seat. A sob escapes her throat before she knows it's coming.

"Hey, hey," Zavi says, reaching an awkward hand back between the seats to pat her leg. "She's safe now. Elle can't hurt her anymore." He pauses, then squeezes her knee and adds, "She can't hurt you, either."

And that's enough to put her over the edge. The tears fall faster than she can wipe them away, as images of her mother and Celeste play on an endless reel in her mind. It's all she can do to shake her head when Zavi asks if they should pull over and have some water. "No," she chokes out. "I'm fine." Sera needs to be home and in bed by now. She's been through enough today, and they shouldn't disturb her even more.

Eventually, after wiping her face on the sleeve of her sweatshirt for the dozenth time, she catches her breath. "I don't know what to do," she says.

"Do, about what?" Zavi asks, but he must know what she means. The state of the Garden Society is uncertain at best right now. Countless mothers and daughters have been left vulnerable. Women who have counted on Lucinda and Ruma all their lives.

"About Sera, and the rest of my Sisters. My mother's gone. Evie—Elle, whatever—is gone. I'm on my own. What am I supposed to do?"

"Do you need to do anything?" Zavi asks. His eyes are on the road, his face indecipherable.

The simplicity of the question floors her. Does he think she should leave them to fend for themselves? "The Society is on the verge of being discovered. If I do nothing, my Sisters and I—not to mention our daughter—are in very real danger. We could all be arrested. Or force-safeguarded. Or both. Or I don't even know. And then everything we've

all been through for the last thirty-plus years will be mean-
ingless. I'm their leader now. I might not be the one who put
them in this situation, but I'm all they've got left. I can't just
abandon them."

Zavi takes a deep breath but says nothing. Adi's
words sound in her head, and her mother's. The voices of her
Sisters travel to her through a decades-old bond. *For the
good of the many.* After everything they've all been through
in the last two weeks, the words ring differently.

For the good of society, yes.

But also, for the good of her Sisters.

For the good of their daughters.

You are the voice of the next generation.

*I don't see how you can keep the Society safe without
risking yourself.*

"Zavi." Lucinda swallows. Clears her throat against
the lump forming there. "Can you get Sera to bed?" she
asks.

The only movement from the front seat is the flick of
his violet eyes as they meet hers in the rearview mirror. He
takes a deep breath. "Lucinda, how long has it been since
you slept? You've had a long day. Don't you think you
should get some rest, too? Whatever you're thinking, can't
it wait until tomorrow?"

"It can't," she says. A new resolve shines from her
golden eyes. "I'm sorry. I don't know how much time I have
until Detective Abuto files his report and they come after me.
Until they find out about the others and come after them, too.
But I know it's going to happen, and I need to get ahead of
it." Her voice softens. "These women and girls, they've put

their trust in me. I don't know if it's going to work, or even if I can pull it off. But I owe it to them to at least try."

"Lucinda, what are you going to do?" Zavi's eyes glisten. There is fear there, and the realization that, even if he tried, he wouldn't be able to stop her.

"That's what I've got to figure out. I'm going to do what I can to protect them. And her," she says, running her thumb along Serafina's impossibly smooth cheek.

Zavi is silent for a moment. When he speaks there is a vulnerability to his voice. "Do what you need to do," he says. "But can you promise me something?"

Lucinda looks into her partner's gaze. If she speaks, she'll cry.

"Promise me you'll try to remember to protect yourself, too."

Lucinda looks back down at their little girl, snoring softly on her lap. "I'll do my best," she says. Another promise she hopes she can keep.

Lucinda paces the floor in the birthing suite. It's the first time she's been back here since Celeste's death and, despite the late hour, she doesn't even try to sleep. Time after time, her eyes drift to the center of the main room. The Sisters cleaned up well and the sofa was replaced, but all Lucinda can see in that spot is the bloody mess that was left after she failed to save her Sister. From death. From the Society which both gave them life and took it away. From Elle, who once her façade finally broke, turned out to be the most dangerous foe they could face.

Astor is behind the closed door of the bedroom, where she's been working all night—contacting media outlets, appealing to the Society's Council members, and coordinating with their Sisters. The room has been quiet for a while now. Hopefully, Astor finished up and took to the bed for some rest.

The shades are drawn into the same floral tapestry she memorized over the course of her third trimester. As back then, Lucinda feels like a caged rat. Her every impulse tells her to get out, to stand in the open, to suck the crisp night air into her lungs. Not yet, though. She has to get it just right. Just hold on until morning. She can almost feel the weight lifting.

Her mother's long fall replays in her mind, as does the conversation with Elle this morning at the river. She wanted to send the videos to her Sisters. She wanted them to see who they'd truly been dealing with all these years, to see what she'd been through.

"What's to gain from doing that?" Astor asked last night. And she was right. Evie isn't the Society. She never has been. It was always Ruma and Lucinda. The Mothers looked to Ruma, and the Sisters to Lucinda, as a model for what the Society represented. Evie only created the framework for them to exist. And now it's time for Lucinda to choose her own path. A path that allows for her and her Sisters to be free. One that will lighten the weight on her shoulders.

She mutters as she walks, rehearsing the same lines over and over again. She was self-conscious when she began, but she's been at it for hours and now she doesn't even realize she's doing it. The halo of outside light around the shades becomes lighter, and Lucinda continues wearing the same path around and around the floor of the suite.

"Brava," says Astor after she finishes another practice round. Lucinda jumps. She didn't even notice her Sister come in. The sleeves of Astor's sweatshirt are pulled over her hands, muffling her applause. She tosses an arm around Lucinda, leaning so their heads touch. "It's great."

"Really?" asks Lucinda. She relaxes against Astor. For the first time since she can remember, the two of them are aligned, moving in the same direction, with the same goal, and it brings unexpected relief.

"Yeah," says Astor. "Really. It's perfect."

Lucinda breaks away and goes into the kitchen, searching in vain for something she can stomach. She settles on a flavored seltzer water from the dispenser inside the refrigerator. "Do you think they'll come?" she asks as Astor joins her.

"I do." Astor presses a few buttons on the autochef. "And if they don't, you still know you're doing the right thing. And you know I'll help you with the Attorney's Office as much as I can." Two warm bagels pop out of the autochef's delivery compartment. Astor butters them both, takes a bite of one, and thrusts the other in Lucinda's direction. "Eat it. You need it," she says around a mouthful of bread.

The women's eyes lock and Lucinda can see back through the years, before Astor's face was hidden behind that cold and untrusting facade. Some of the earnestness has returned, and Lucinda hopes it's here to stay. "Thank you, Sister," she says. Saying more would invite emotion she can't afford to spare, so instead, she brings Astor in for another hug.

A short time later they're in the elevator, gazing at the expanse of the upper gardens through the slim glass column for what could be the last time. Without even thinking, Lucinda presses the red *HOLD* button. The mix of emotions swirling in the small compartment is palpable. This place is as much a home to her as her parents' apartment across town, as the sky-high balcony at her place. Only here, among the smell of oxygen and earth, with her hands in the ground, did she ever feel completely free.

Free. The word hits her like a lead ball. What a limited freedom it's been. She was only ever free to be the person Elle and Ruma created. Free to serve her purpose within the Society and propagate it without question. Free to teach her Sisters, as long as the message was pre-approved.

She thinks back to the day Serafina was born. Ruma rushed the new family out of the suite, eager to show off the very first Garden Society baby. The proof of concept. Her Sisters lined the pathways, palms extended to reveal an unending corridor of purple lotus blossoms to her augmented vision. The baby grunted in her arms, and Lucinda was growing ever more anxious to get home so she could practice the hours-old skill of feeding her baby. As they waited for the car, an officer approached them. Lucinda was horrified, certain they'd already been found out. She can still feel the relief that washed over her body when the woman just complimented the baby and went on her way.

Lucinda snapped at her mother that day. Something about how she never felt good enough for Ruma. "You were perfect today," her mother whispered to her as they parted ways. It was her way of apologizing, but it just reinforced to Lucinda that her value was as First Daughter, the first Society member to give birth naturally. As Ruma's daughter, she never seemed to register.

Astor squeezes Lucinda's hand.

"Sorry," Lucinda says, blinking and taking a swipe at her nose with the back of her hand. "Sorry. I was just re-membering."

"You don't have to be sorry," says Astor, leaning her cheek on Lucinda's shoulder. "We have a lot of memories here. We'll be back one day."

"Maybe," Lucinda says. "But by then, everything will be different." For now, she can only hope Adi's plan works and she doesn't regret what she's about to do.

38

EMEKA SITS IN THE CAR, WAITING FOR SOMETHING TO happen. His mobile sits next to him on top of a paper copy of the case file he finished compiling late last night. Not that he needs it. It will be sent electronically as soon as he presses the button.

A call comes in. Rodriguez again. The *Missed Calls* total increases to *22*.

Give me til morning, Lucinda said last night. He re-reads her last message. It came through in the wee hours, but he was up anyway, worrying over Adi and Micah and how he could possibly both do his job and protect his family. He didn't ask what Lucinda had planned. It's better if he doesn't know. But based on where they are, he has an idea of what's to come.

Be at the Council steps. Keep an eye on our girls. Just in case.

On his mobile map, the beacon representing his granddaughter blinks yellow as the distance between them closes. While he's not technically supposed to track anyone without a warrant, he rationalizes this exception he's granted himself in the name of Micah's safety.

Across the street, people gradually arrive and gather on the sidewalks near the building, in the courtyard out front, and eventually on the steps. At first, they appear casual, standing around and chatting. Through his overlay, Emeka catches glimpses of purple from time to time as the women gesture in accompaniment to their conversations.

As the top of the hour approaches, the group begins to organize. Gradually, their conversations stop, and they turn toward the steps. The haphazard groupings disperse and form into straight lines, packed tightly together. Micah, Adi, and Astor join, and it's only for his surveillance equipment that he keeps from losing them. On his mobile, the green rectangle of the courtyard is dotted with little yellow beacons. Micah's beacon, the one he's selected to watch, blinks with the regularity of a beating heart.

Filmographers from media outlets pepper the sidewalks around the perimeter of the group. Pedestrians, sensing something out of the ordinary is about to happen, stop and train their cameras—first on the crowd, and then on the landing atop the tall stone staircase in front of the building.

There is a clock built into the building's face, a circle of Roman numerals etched into the stone. The hefty minute hand has been ascending for the last half-hour, and at last, it clicks into place at the XII. The courtyard becomes a near-blinding sea of purple lotus blossoms.

All the beacons on his display screen vanish.

A handful of people dressed in varying shades of black and gray emerge from the building and gather around either side of the landing. Council members. Almost in unison, they open their hands to reveal photograms. The rest of the Council filters out through the doors and stands on the top landing, looking around and murmuring.

Emeka's heart is pounding. He swipes at his forehead with his handkerchief, and it comes back damp. He scans the crowd once more to be sure Adi and Micah are safe. They all stand, unmoving.

And, just when he is wondering how long this suspense will last, someone moves through the crowd and climbs the stairs. Her long, black hair shimmers like a crow's feathers in the morning light, the shine forming the only contrast with her all-black outfit of leggings and a long-sleeved shirt. The resolve in her face is still there; if anything, it's strengthened since last he saw her. At the top of the steps, she turns to face the women who have gathered below. She opens her palm and stands motionless for a moment, her eyes moving over the crowd as if to make eye contact with every single person in it.

Then she turns toward the front of the building and begins to speak.

39

THE ENERGY IN THE CROWD BUZZES BEHIND LUCINDA AS SHE turns to face the Council. She nods to the Council members on either side of the landing. They're putting themselves at great risk by standing where they are.

Everyone here is at risk. But at least, today, it's a risk they chose for themselves.

She saw the cameras rolling as she approached the entrance to the building. Will Zavi be watching? Will her father? She messaged them both a few minutes ago and then turned off her mobile in case they responded. She couldn't bear to worry about their reactions.

Black slacks and jackets face her, as do high heels and colorful blouses. She lifts her eyes to meet theirs and answers their expressions—curiosity, impatience—with one of determination. She can still feel the ghost of Astor's arm around her shoulders, her words encouraging. She is speaking for them all, and she is ready.

Lucinda swallows and takes a deep breath, and then she begins.

"The day I was born, an experiment began. A group of women gathered together and made a decision that would carry enormous opportunity, and also enormous consequences, for everyone you see in front of you.

"Their intentions were pure. They disagreed with a law that was oppressive. A law that classified women and our bodies as a problem rather than the beautiful, natural, life-giving miracles they are. Their mothers and grandmothers had fought against Ordinance Four-Fourteen using every legal tool at their disposal, but ultimately the will of a small number of powerful people—most of whom were men—and their allies won out.

"These women tried to persuade the ruling party through so-called legitimate avenues. After years of having their efforts stonewalled, they saw only one path to recourse: to take matters into their own hands. Our foremothers gave their daughters the opportunity they would never have—to bear their children as nature intended. Unfortunately, the methods they used endangered the very people they were trying to free.

"Our Mothers broke a law, albeit an unjust one, by not having us undergo reproductive safeguarding when we were born." A murmur rises through the crowd, and Lucinda raises her voice above it. "They used our bodies as a tool through which to rebel, and their rebellion forced us into a life we did not choose for ourselves. Our mothers gave us reproductive choice but robbed us of so much more. And the life of hiding and secrecy our Mothers chose for us has had devastating consequences for us all."

Lucinda takes another deep breath, steadying herself against the upwelling of tears she can feel in her throat. "Just a little more than a week ago, my close friend, Celeste Harlow, died bringing her new baby girl into the world." The assembled Council members look around at each other, eyes wide, but this time no one speaks. "Then, just a few days later, my mother—the person who set this ball in motion the day I was born—lost her life in the name of our Society."

Her voice remains level despite the tears rolling down her cheeks.

"Our mothers wanted to give us the choice to create and carry new life. They did not give enough thought to the dangers that would come along with that ability. Behind me stand my Sisters, the women of the Garden Society. There are women among us who, like our mothers, yearn for the opportunity to grow their child in their womb, to nourish their infant at their breast." Astor's face comes into her mind, and a lump settles in her throat. All these years, as she's been trying to talk Astor into what the Society wants for her, she's been denying Astor's story. She swallows down the emotion and continues. "There are also women who would prefer safeguarding and nursery wombs, and others who don't want to have a child at all. As adults who are in control of our bodies, we have all the knowledge and maturity we need to make that decision, and we believe it is our decision to make."

"Today we present ourselves to you. We are your partners, your daughters, your colleagues, your friends. We ask for your understanding, your amnesty, and your help. Our mothers' decisions were not ours, but neither are the decisions of a nameless, faceless Council from a century ago. We humbly ask you: please, help us create a world where a woman's body is her own. Where decisions about her reproduction are made based on her desires, not on some government spending model or risk profile.

"Our mothers risked a lot for us. My mother and my Sister, Celeste, paid the ultimate price. Some might say their actions were misguided. But their aim was lofty: to create a world in which our daughters can make their own reproductive choices. After a lifetime of hiding, we are coming back to these steps, where it all started. We cannot change what has already happened, but with your help, we can change what is to come.

"You might believe we live in a world of mutual respect. Women and men, people of all skin colors and cultures and abilities, individuals of any sexual orientation or gender identity—all are accepted and treated with fairness. But you must also be aware that this has not always been the case. The equality movements of a hundred, two hundred years ago and more, made the society of today possible. I come to you today, on behalf of my Sisters, to tell you there's more work to be done.

"In case you're wondering why our Mothers didn't just play by the rules and appeal for the change they saw necessary, let me remind you that they tried that. Back then, their voices were not heard. Furthermore, no great social change has ever happened because everyone played by the rules. The rules, after all, were made to keep the oppressed group oppressed. Only by going outside the rules and showing the world what can be done can we change the world in our favor.

"When you return to your chambers, an article will be awaiting your consideration. As your fellow citizen, I ask that you please vote yes on all counts. So that my Sisters can remain safe. So that your partners and daughters and all our future generations can have the choice that was stolen from our mothers and grandmothers. Look out at the faces you see here. Four-Fourteen holds back women in our society, and we are here telling you a change is due. Please, help us make it."

Lucinda holds her gaze steady, though she would rather be looking anywhere but at the Council members gathered in front of her. Behind her, she can hear the rustle of clothing and she must resist the urge to turn around and watch her Sisters disperse. The women to her right and left, Council members who have just outed themselves to the rest of the legislators, stand stock still, expectant eyes upon the rest of their colleagues. She half-expects someone to come for her, to force her hands behind her back and take her away. Nobody does. Not yet, anyway.

Gradually the bewildered Council members filter back into the building, first the main body and then, more tentatively, the women flanking the sides. The silence in the courtyard gives way to the sounds of an ordinary morning: conversations between groups of pedestrians, father and child calling out to one another, cars rolling along the street on either side.

At first, Lucinda can't move. Her arms and legs have lost all sensation, and she doesn't know where she'd go anyway. She is still staring across the now vacant landing when Astor's voice drifts up the stairs. "Told you they'd come."

Lucinda turns to see her Sister approaching up the steps. Astor wears a worn smile, weathered yet with a cautious relief shining through. "They came," says Lucinda. After all this time resisting tears, her eyes are too tired to cry.

"They came," Astor says, taking Lucinda's free hand in her own.

"Will it make a difference?"

Astor breathes deeply. "I honestly don't know. But It's in the Council's hands now. There's nothing else you can do. Regardless of what comes next, you did more for us than Evie ever did."

"Maybe," says Lucinda. "But we will owe it to her and my mother if the law changes. Without them, there wouldn't have been the Society, and without the Society, none of this could have happened."

Astor squeezes her hand and says nothing. Maybe she'd say the law didn't need to be changed in the first place. Or maybe she'd be happy for her Sisters to have the right to choose, even if it wasn't something she wanted in her life. However she feels, Lucinda is glad she's here. Grateful her oldest friend is by her side once more.

The day is picturesque. The sun has taken the edge off the morning chill, and the sky is a cool blue, kissed with threads of white. A few sailboats are already out on the river. Lucinda has a sudden urge to be out there with them. To be in the water once more, this time of her own free will, floating face-up and bobbing lazily with the waves.

"Oh. Here," Astor says, reaching into her pocket and removing a dark matte band.

"You got them," says Lucinda. In the blur of the last 24 hours, she forgot she showed Astor the bracelet Elle gave to Serafina.

Astor lifts her wrist. "Bernie had a stockpile of them in her apartment. I never knew what they were until you showed me the one Sera had." Astor winks. "Thankfully she never changed her key code after we broke up. I gave one to every Sister."

"That many?" asks Lucinda.

"Yeah," says Astor. "Looked like she'd been building up the stash for quite some time."

That must be what Elle meant when she said they could disappear if the Society were exposed. Lucinda is glad she didn't let Elle talk her out of her plan. Lucinda convinced the detective to hold off until this morning to submit his report. But after he does, there will be no turning back. If Lucinda had folded, if she'd let Elle convince her to sit back and do nothing, they'd all be scrambling to hide now, and who knows for how long. But if her plan works and the Council grants her Sisters amnesty, they'll never have to hide again.

"Put that on," says Astor, but Lucinda shakes her head.

"Protect yourself," she says. "Keep our Sisters safe. If they need to find someone, I'm okay with it being me."

Astor turns to face Lucinda, still holding her good hand. When Lucinda can bear to look her Sister in the face, she sees the tears gleaming in Astor's eyes. "Thank you," Astor says.

So much packed into those two words. So much history, so much pain, so much love. "Thank *you*," is the only thing Lucinda can say back. "Go," she says. She squeezes Astor's hand and releases it, looking away to blink the tears from her eyes. "Get out of here."

Astor looks at Lucinda for a moment, then brings her in for a hug. "I love you, Sis," she says. "I'll let you know when I hear."

Lucinda stands, frozen in time, as Astor walks, down the dozens of steps, across the courtyard, and out of sight without a single glance back.

40

MICAH'S SOMBER FACE APPEARS IN THE CAR WINDOW, startling Emeka. His eyes have been on Lucinda at the top of the Council steps, her voice surrounding him through the car's speakers. She sounded sure of herself. Ready to take responsibility. Ready for what comes next.

Whatever that is.

Emeka checks his mobile as the window lowers. Micah's location beacon still registers as inactive. Rodriguez hasn't called since the women began assembling on the courtyard.

"I guess that's that," says Adi's voice from behind Micah. Her hand is on the girl's shoulder, and Emeka notices a sleek black band around her wrist.

"Papa?" asks Micah. The fear makes her look like a little girl again. "Is Lucinda going to get in trouble?" She swallows and ventures, "Are *we* going to get in trouble?"

Emeka takes a deep breath. "I can't say for sure, sweets," he says. "I wish I could." He raises his eyes to his daughter. "Do you have a plan?" he asks.

Adi shrugs. "I made some calls," she says. "And we have these." She indicates the bracelet and, looking down, Emeka sees that Micah wears one too. Signal interrupters. How did they get their hands on those?

"Probably best if you leave it at that," he says. He's got to keep some professional distance. The link between him and these two will certainly come out, and he's likely to be questioned. If he doesn't know anything, he won't have to choose between protecting his family and his career.

"All right," Adi says. She leans in so her forehead nearly touches his. "I'm sorry, Daddy," she says, tears filling her eyes.

Emeka forces a smile. He takes both of their faces, one in each hand. "My girls," he says. "Take care of each other. We'll see what comes of today."

Micah grasps his hand and holds it to her cheek. "Love you, Papa,"

"I love you, too, sweets. And you, too," he says, looking into Adi's eyes. She stares back into his as if trying to read his thoughts. "Go on, now," he says. "I'm certainly going to have some questions to answer when I get to the office. I'd prefer not to be any later than I already am."

Adi, tugs on Micah's elbow and they turn away. Emeka raises his window once more and sets the car on the short trip to the office. Once in motion, he activates the sub-mission portal on his mobile. His finger hesitates for a moment before tapping the button marked *SEND*.

And then it's done.

The bustle begins when he steps off the elevator. Far from the silence that usually greets him, allowing him to sit undisturbed in his cubicle, organizing his thoughts and plan-ning his day, he is confronted with a wall of buzz as he makes his way through the maze of pathways to his desk.

At first, no one directly addresses him, but the snip-pets of conversation he hears remove all doubt that his report and what just happened on the Council steps are the main topic of conversation. Do they know about Adi and Micah yet? Surely someone must.

"Abuto," Rodriguez's voice cuts through the rest of the noise just as he's settling into his firm but familiar chair. "I've been trying to get ahold of you since last night," she says.

"You know I don't like to talk shop off-hours," he says, trying for his most authoritative tone. He doesn't feel authoritative, though. Doesn't feel like a guy who's been at this job longer than Rodriguez has been alive. He feels twenty-three again, just waiting for everyone else to figure out he's not the gifted young detective they were promised.

"Bullshit," says Rodriguez, pulling up a chair across from him and sitting backward in it. She lowers her voice and leans in. "I read your report," she says.

"Credit to you for helping me compile much of it," says Emeka.

"Oh, there was quite a bit in there I didn't compile," she says. "Plenty of things I knew nothing about."

She's right. Lucinda in the woods. His conversation with Nathan Mackenzie. Elle, or Evie, or whatever her name was. Was that just yesterday? Adrenaline and lack of sleep have warped his sense of time. "Okay," he says. "Fine, you're right. What was it you needed to talk with me about?"

"Well," she says, folding her hands together on his desktop. "I was trying to warn you that Micah was on the list. I don't know what I thought that would accomplish. But you know I like the kid. I guess I just thought it'd be better if you heard it from me before you saw it on the spreadsheet."

"I appreciate that, Rodriguez," Emeka says.

"The way you laid out the case, though, these women," —she raises her eyes to meet his— "even the ones who were there when the Harlow woman died, aren't to blame."

Emeka sits back in his chair. He agonized over that report. He spent hours writing, erasing, rewriting, and erasing again. Trying to strike the right balance between objective and protective. As the detective on the case, he witnessed firsthand the attitudes and orientations of the women in the Society. They believed they were doing the right thing. They were taught to believe they had no choice. Their destiny, their purpose, had been determined by the women before them. Their mothers, and Ruma, and Evie, and even Lucinda to some extent, had raised them on the idea that the Garden Society was going to solve a problem in the world, but not without their help. They were given a certain responsibility without any instruction about how to use it.

And, of course, he had his daughter and granddaughter to consider.

"The way I see it," he says, "those who hold the blame are dead now. If Ruma Das and Elle Baker were still alive, there would be a need for a different kind of conversation. But, through a series of tragedies, we have lost them. And without them, it's hard to know where to place the accountability."

"What do you think will happen to them?" Rodriguez asks.

"I don't know," says Emeka. "It's not my place to decide how to try a case. We've got prosecutors for that. I just put together the information and hand it over."

Rodriguez nods. "Well, good for you," she says. "It must have been hard for you to hand over the names of your family members without knowing for certain what will happen to them."

Emeka's eyes lower to the photo of Abigail, Adi, and Micah that sits on his desk. "I've been a part of the system for most of my life," he says. "I've just got to trust it will work the way it's designed to work."

For the rest of the day, though the tension in the office remains, his colleagues keep their distance. For the first time since Celeste Harlow's death, he's able to divert his attention back to his other cases.

When he finally arrives home at the end of the day, he sinks down next to Abigail on the sofa. "In all my years on the job, I never expected I'd be investigating my own family." When he repeats the tired line he said to Rodriguez, the one he only half-believes, Abigail adds the part he didn't say before.

"Mmm-hmm. Trust the system to do its job. That, and hope the girls are somewhere they can't be found, in case it doesn't."

Abigail's voice brings Emeka out of that house in the woods and into the ballroom. Everything that's happened feels more like a dream than reality, and after spending all night driving back from the city and then compiling his report, it's a miracle he can keep his eyes open.

"Nervous?" she asks.

Silverware clinks against plates. Stiff fabric rustles together. The lights are mercifully low, hopefully hiding the circles under his eyes. The dimple in Abigail's left cheek deepens as she smiles her most disarming smile. "What makes you think that?" he asks.

"They made your favorite salmon, and you haven't touched it," she winks.

He looks down at his full plate and grins faintly. "Well, then, maybe I am a little nervous," he says. Not nervous to speak to his colleagues, though. His mind has been so busy on the Harlow case and the cascade of events it set off that he hasn't had time to be nervous for this address. All he can think about is what will happen now that he's filed his report. He's worried for Adi and Micah, and even for Lucinda. He enjoyed her company at the awards banquet all those years ago, and he really feels for her today. She was manipulated by the two women she thought she could trust, and he hopes prosecutors go easy on her.

Now, though, he needs to focus on what's before him. Up at the podium, Director Araleus begins introducing him, playing the highlight reel of his accomplishments during his years of service, ending with the recovery of Serafina just last night. She doesn't mention Adi and Micah's involvement in the Garden Society, but she doesn't need to. It's all in the report.

Applause rises from the crowd as the director finishes, and all eyes look to Emeka. Either word hasn't gotten around, or it hasn't colored their respect for him. Either way, he's thankful it's not a hostile crowd. Not yet, anyway.

He kisses Abigail on the cheek and walks up the aisle.

The ballroom is filled with black ties and long dresses, sparkly jewelry and cufflinks, many familiar faces and plenty of unfamiliar ones. A few flashes of bright purple shine out as hands come together. They're everywhere, now that he knows to look for them. He's grown so accustomed to keeping his overlay activated, he forgot to turn it off. He reaches up and silences the display with a tap. After the week he's had, he doesn't need any more distractions.

The applause stops and he looks out over the crowd. The attendees settle in their seats, expectant eyes trained on his face. He takes a sip from the glass that was placed on a shelf inside the podium for him.

"Forty-six years," he begins. His accent has grown very faint over that time, but it comes through strongly with these first words. "I've been a detective for forty-six years. That's twice as long as I wasn't a detective. I guess you can say I've grown up in the Bureau. And I was asked to speak to you, presumably to tell you all the things I've learned during my long, and some would say successful, career.

"And I have learned so much during these last forty-six years. From you people sitting here, and from those who came before you, some of whom are long gone. I've learned how to be a better detective, and I've learned how to be a better man.

"But I must be honest with you. Most of what I've learned hasn't come from being a detective. The most important teachings of my life, those which have shaped who I am and how I view the world, have come from the women surrounding me. So tonight, rather than talking about how to take down a report efficiently or how to remember all three thousand sixty-seven pages of the procedural handbook"— chuckles from the crowd— "I'd like to share with you some things I never could have learned inside the four walls of the Bureau offices."

He takes another sip. His ease surprises even him.

"My grandmothers, Ifeoma and Nneka, back in my home country of Nigeria. They were my first teachers. Each brought a special spice to the family blend, and together as sisters more than in-laws, they taught me respect and empathy. They taught me the value of knowing others, and of listening to their stories. They also taught me that if you harass the chickens, you get the shoe." Emeka shines a wide, reminiscent smile and more laughter comes from scattered tables.

"My mother, Adaora, taught me much, but foremost was the value of family. Though our nuclear family was necessarily small, I come from an intergenerational home. My mother showed equal love and thought to the elders and the younger generations. She was thoughtful in her interactions, and she strove to understand even those with whom she disagreed.

"My SS2 history teacher, Miss Mildred. She taught me the value of perseverance, even through the most difficult of challenges, and it is certain that if not for her I would not be standing here with you today.

"Some of you know I was quite the amateur sleuth as a youngster. For those who don't, I will simply say that Miss Mildred's teachings were top of mind when I persisted in finding a group of missing girls when the local police had given up on them. My work caught the attention of the Bureau, all the way on the other side of the world, and I was brought here for training as soon as I finished secondary school. I still remember the name and face of each girl, those who made it through the ordeal but were deeply scarred, and those who sadly didn't make it at all. From these girls, I learned that good doesn't always win, and I committed myself to spend my life tilting the balance in the right direction."

As Emeka has spoken, his senses have taken him back decades and shrouded him in the comfort he always took from his caretakers back home. He finds his table. Abigail smiles at him and nods, ever so slightly. It's all the fuel he needs to continue.

"My lovely partner, Abigail. She's been by my side for so long, it's hard to remember life without her. Chief among the lessons she has taught me are patience and unconditional love. It's a lesson she exemplifies by dealing with my nonsense every day, and it shows also in her relationship with our beautiful daughter, Adi, and our amazing and precocious granddaughter, Micah." Abigail lowers her eyes as he speaks, bashful for the attention, but he can tell she's beaming under the brim of her fancy hat. Emeka takes another sip. His hand is steady, though he feels a jolt of adrenaline in anticipation.

"And those two girls," he says, smiling to himself, "have taught me nothing if not that, sooner or later, the younger generation will throw a curveball that will challenge everything you thought you knew before.

"They've taught me not everything is black and white, true or false, one way or the other. I've learned from them that sometimes the rules and structures that have long underpinned your beliefs must be challenged, because even something that seems right on the surface, might be wrong underneath. Knowing Adi and Micah, and coming to know their very good friend, Lucinda, has forced me to take a step back and look at a part of my world I have always simply taken for granted."

At the mention of Lucinda's name, the crowd perks up. Eyes that strayed during the descriptions of his foremothers refocus.

"I am a man of integrity. From my earliest days, I have been concerned with one thing above all else, and that's to be true in all my dealings, both personal and professional. I've always made the best possible decisions with the information I had at the time, and I've changed my thinking when new information was presented. Maybe, though, it's true that I have failed to exercise my critical thinking skills, allowing myself to take for granted that I'm always on the right side. Allowing myself to think there is a single right side in the first place.

"Today I am met with a challenge, a dilemma not addressed anywhere in the procedural handbook. What do we do, as investigators, when we come to know that a law we've sworn to uphold was not instituted in good faith?

"If I could ask my dear grandmothers, and my cherished mother, how to manage this dissonance, I'm certain they'd tell me to follow the compass I'm so blessed to have inherited from them. I know that's what my dear Abigail would say. This compass tells me that right now is a time to sit back and listen. As a man in this world, I fear I have failed to fully know these women who have taught me so much. I have failed to consider what it means to be born with an ability, only to have it stripped away without a thought. I have failed to consider the basis under which these practices were performed in the first place.

"I can argue that as a law enforcement officer it wasn't my job to take any of these things into account. But instead, I will argue it is my job as a human—as a father, a son, a student, a grandson, a grandfather, and a partner—to see injustices for what they are. And, as someone whose entire life has centered around ensuring a just world for everyone, it is my job to call out these injustices and help do something about them."

There are no wandering eyes in the ballroom anymore. Every eye in the house stares in his direction, wide and alert. There are some nods as he speaks, some eyebrows furrowed or raised, but largely everyone is stock still, expressionless. Abigail, however, wears a warm smile. It's the smile she wore the day he was promoted to Senior Detective, and when Adi accepted the award at her work banquet all those years ago, and when she watched Micah's first school play. It's all the validation he needs.

"I know you probably expected me to say something quite different here, to share some bits of detective wisdom I've gained over a long career. But you can get that anywhere. This room is full of excellent professionals, and you can learn more from them than you could ever learn from this old man. And, as I hope I've already convinced you, everything of value I've ever learned has come not from within the context of my profession but from a woman I adored.

"So, I urge everyone in here, if there is a girl or a woman in your life who has taught you something, if you bring a little piece of her everywhere you go because of the lessons she gave you, please talk to her when you leave here. Call her, or send her a message, or commune with her spirit if she's no longer with us. Ask what she would do with the choice to carry her own child if she'd had it available to her.

"Because that's what she deserves. To be consulted. To have a say in what happens with her body. Not to be subjected to a mandate created by politicians a century ago out of what amounts to convenience. I know I will be asking, and I will be listening. And I will continue learning from the women in my life, and I will advocate for their voices to be heard.

"I hope you will, too."

Emeka does not linger at the podium when he finishes. He doesn't expect applause, doesn't want to stand and look dumbly out over the astonished crowd as they whisper to each other and try to decide whether to stand or sit, whether to clap or just look awkwardly down at their dinner plates.

He simply walks toward Abigail, his anchor tonight and always, and takes her hand as she stands to receive him. The sounds of the ballroom are drowned out by the shine of her smile and by her voice in his ear, whispering, "That was perfect."

41

BREAKFAST IS IN THE AIR. LUCINDA'S STOMACH IS HOLLOW, and for the first time in days, she's not repulsed by the thought of eating.

"Did you hear?" asks Zavi, walking around the back of the sofa and proffering a plate piled with steaming eggs, hash browns, and sausage.

"Hear what?" Lucinda yawns, sitting up from her half-reclined position. She slept a hard, dark sleep for most of yesterday and last night, but the events of the last two days still have her achy and tired. At least now she's been reunited with her pain medication.

"The Sisters in the Council," says Zavi. "They did it."

Lucinda is fully awake now. She turns to face Zavi, blowing on a forkful of eggs before eating them.

Zavi switches on the wallscreen, onto which appears a woman with dark, perfectly wavy hair and flawless makeup sitting at a desk. Next to her on the screen is an image from yesterday, of Lucinda standing on the Council steps with a sea of purple flowers stretching behind her. "The temporary declaration," the woman is saying, "is aimed at protecting the so-called *Garden Sisters*, whose appearance yesterday on the Council steps left Council members—and the rest of us—stunned."

The woman moves on to a different news story, and Zavi mutes the screen. Lucinda's hands begin trembling and she has to put her plate down for fear of dropping her food onto her lap.

"Hey, hey, this is good news," Zavi says, seeing the tears streaming down Lucinda's face.

"I know, I know," Lucinda says, wiping under her eyes with her fingertips. It's no use. "I'm just so fucking *relieved*," she says, letting the tears flow freely. Lucinda never expected this day to come. She never pictured a day when her mother would be gone and she would be leading the Society out of the shadows. She certainly never imagined anything would materially change because of something she did.

"Astor messaged me too, just a few minutes ago. Her sources say it looks like they have the votes to approve a rewrite of Four-Fourteen."

Lucinda wants to get up and run around. She wants to hug Zavi and squeeze him tight. She wants to step out onto the balcony and yell. Instead, she covers her face with her hands and lets the emotions run through her. Zavi stands behind the sofa and drapes his arms around Lucinda's neck as she sobs. Lucinda reaches up and squeezes his arms, leaning into him and relaxing as her heart rate slows back down to normal. "Thank you," she says, closing her eyes.

"For what?" he says. "You're the one who did it all. I'm proud of you."

"For trusting me. For supporting me. Even when it was scary."

Zavi squeezes her, kisses her on the cheek, and says, "That's what I'm here for. I told you before, I knew what I was getting into when I married you."

Lucinda smiles, looking out the window on the far side of the room. For all that she wants to melt into Zavi's arms, her stomach is beginning to wake up along with her mind. She breaks free of the embrace and takes her plate. She shovels the food into her mouth, trying to remember the last actual meal she had.

She's only half-finished when a knock on the door interrupts her. She sits up, shoulders back and eyes alert.

"Who's that?" Lucinda asks, eyeing Zavi.

"I don't know," he says with feigned innocence. "Who could it be?"

"Anyone home?" says her father's voice through a crack in the door, and Lucinda is reminded of her aching shoulder when she attempts to jump over the back of the sofa. He's had Serafina since yesterday, in case Lucinda's speech prompted the authorities to try and find her.

"Ouch!" she says, but the pain doesn't stop her from bolting toward the door.

"Mama!" Serafina says when Lucinda pulls the door open. Sera wraps her arms around Lucinda's legs, burying her face in her mother's clothes. "Papa took me to the beach! The water was cold."

"Hi, baby," Lucinda says, patting the back of the little girl's head. "Yes, even the beach gets cold in winter." Fresh tears fall from her eyes as she looks up to her father and brushes a lock of curly brown hair from his eyes. "Hi, Daddy," she says, and he wraps his arms around her and doesn't let go for quite some time.

"You did great," he whispers into her hair. "I am so proud of you."

Lucinda breathes in a million childhood hours, sandalwood and peppermint and guitar chords and piano riffs. She smiles, then lets him go and kneels to look into Sera's golden eyes.

When the little girl speaks, an entire life Lucinda never got to have for herself unfolds before her eyes. "Papa said it was safe to come back."

Lucinda smiles even as her face breaks and the tears flow down her cheeks. "Yeah," she says around the lump in her throat, bringing her daughter in close. "Yeah, baby. You're safe now."

"Lucinda." A deep voice floats down the corridor toward the smiling pair.

Lucinda straightens, pulls Serafina behind her, and says, "Okay, sweetheart, get inside. Why don't you tell Daddy what you and Papa did last night."

"Daddy!" Serafina says. She runs into the apartment, and Lucinda closes the door. Whatever is about to happen, she doesn't want Serafina to be here for it.

Her father's arm drapes protectively around her injured shoulder, and she braces against the squeeze, turning to face the approaching man. Tall, dark-skinned, watery old eyes. Shiny black shoes.

"Hello." There's an apology in his eyes. "I'm going to need you to come with me."

The carpeted hallway blurs momentarily. When her vision clears, she meets his eyes. "Okay," she says. "Can I just finish eating my breakfast?"

Emeka considers her for a moment. "Yes. Yes, of course," he says. "I'll wait."

"What's going on?" asks Josiah. "I thought the decision this morning was good for you and your, um, group."

Abuto clears his throat once more. "The decision by the Council was to temporarily hold harmless the non-safeguarded women and girls and their mothers until the ordinance can be reconsidered or rewritten. The prosecutor made her decision separately."

"And her decision was…?" asks Josiah. Lucinda's shoulder screams as he tightens his grip.

Lucinda isn't imagining the tinge of regret under Abuto's confident façade. He looks down at his mobile and reads. "To bring charges against Lucinda Conroy Das, leader of the Garden Society, for accessory to manslaughter, for the death of Celeste Harlow."

"That's ridiculous!" Josiah begins.

"Daddy, it's okay," she says, stepping forward and out of his grasp. "Just me?" she asks Abuto.

"Just you. At this time no other charges are sought."

Lucinda takes a deep breath, fighting the urge to hug the detective. She at once feels tired, energized, and more hopeful than she's felt in a long time. Astor, Adi, all the rest of the Sisters who were there the morning of Celeste's death. They're all safe. Women everywhere might soon be able to enjoy a choice that hasn't existed in generations.

The apartment door opens. "What's going on out here?" asks Zavi. He steps out next to Lucinda. His stance is protective, though it won't do any good. Serafina clings to his leg, looking up at the detective with wide eyes. Lucinda lifts her chin skyward and closes her eyes. She doesn't want to see their faces when they learn what's about to happen. She just manages to keep the tears in.

When she looks again, all eyes are on her. No one's going to do it for her. "Serafina," she says, kneeling once more. "This man is Micah's grandfather."

Serafina smiles, offering a shy wave. "I remember you," she says. "You came to talk to Mama."

"Yes," says Lucinda. "He is also a detective." Sera's eyebrows knot, but she stays silent. "He says I need to go with him for a little while, baby, okay?"

"Okay," Serafina says. Her voice comes out in barely more than a whisper. "Will you be home later?"

Lucinda swallows back a fresh batch of tears, seeing the wetness forming in her daughter's eyes. "Maybe not to-day. But I'll be home as soon as I can, baby. I promise."

She stands once more, avoiding Zavi's eyes as she leans toward him and places her hand on his waist. "I'm sorry," she whispers in his ear. "This is how I protect them."

Zavi wraps his arms around her. He kisses the top of her head, inhaling and holding his breath. "We'll figure things out," he says at length. He pulls back and squeezes her hand, then guides Serafina back into the apartment with a hand on her back.

Josiah follows them inside, looking back to his daughter with mournful eyes. "We're going to fight this," he says.

Lucinda blinks and a few involuntary tears cascade to the floor.

She'll be fighting, alright. It's all she's ever done. Raised in the shadows, fighting against an old enemy that was never hers. Against a law that was unjust. Against her mother, against Astor, against that rushing river. Sometimes against her very own instincts.

She was born to fight, and she's not going to stop now. But today, the fight is hers. It's time to stop fighting *against*. Time to start fighting *for*. She knows her purpose, and she knows what's at stake. And she won't stop until she wins.

Author's Note

Ahh! Did it feel as good to read those last words as it did to write them? If you loved *When We Were Mothers*, please take a moment to leave a review. Reviews help other readers find books, and they also help me become a better writer. You can help get this book into the right hands and spread the word about Lucinda and the Garden Society!

"But, where can I read the next one?" you might be asking. If you're dying to know what happens next, head on over to www.niccikadilak.com/connect, where I share publication updates and special exclusives like character art and deleted scenes. Sign up now, and I'll send you some questions you might like to use for your book club. And, of course, as a member, you'll be one of the first to know when the next book is available. See you there!

Acknowledgements

To my amazing husband, who is genetically wired to be Supportive No Matter What: Thank you for enduring my rants and reading my drafts and doing your best to keep the kids at bay while I finished "just this one thing" so many times.

To my children, who made me into the mother and person I am: You challenge and enrich me and are wise, kind, and empathetic far beyond your years. When you say you're proud of me, it just makes me that much prouder of *you*.

Mom and Dad: From brain surgeon to teacher to writer, you've always supported my choices. I never question your love for me or your pride in my accomplishments. Pat and Susan, you two read some of the first trash—I mean, *stories*—I ever wrote. Your support and feedback has been integral to every stage of this process, and I hope you know just how much I appreciate you. Jen, Carol, and Aunt Angie, your supportive positivity feels like being wrapped in a warm blanket.

To everyone listed above, and more whose names are not here: I hit the family jackpot with you.

To my writing instructors and consultants, and everyone I met through Jericho Writers and the Ultimate Novel Writing Course: Amanda Saint, your feedback, "Real people don't talk like this!" broke me out of the world of scientific papers and into the world of creating real, authentic characters; Elsie Granthier, Martin Ouvry, Ellie Robins, Rachael Herron, thank you for being so generous with your knowledge and enthusiasm at every stage.

To my beta readers, ARC readers, and street team: The list has grown so long, I can't possibly include everyone here, but wow. From my own sixth and eighth grade teachers to my kid's fifth grade teacher; from acquaintances to colleagues to fellow writers to my dear friends. You came out in force, and I am here for it.

Jen, you're one of my oldest friends and your opinion means a lot to me. When you told me you liked the book, I knew I was on to something. Lauren, you're such an amazing friend, vent partner, and cheerleader. Nancy, Becky, Martha: You are perfect, and I'm glad you all came into my life at a point when I could appreciate the balance and perspective your friendship offers. Jess, I love being your everything-consultant and wouldn't have it any other way; thank you for believing in me enough to shout my name from the rooftops. Victor Chidiebere, thanks for being a wonderful "amigo." You've been endlessly helpful and encouraging, and I've learned so much from you—especially about the weather. Suzann, Caleb, and Steven, your editing intuition is enviable. This book wouldn't be nearly as good without you.

Thanks also to my amazing cover designer, Kari Brownlie, and illustrator, Ryan Webb. EJ Shin, thank you for helping conceptualize the cover long before I knew what this book was. Jacob Duncan, your character work is finally going to see the light of day! All you artists are brilliant beyond measure.

Thanks to every single one of you, and to many more I haven't mentioned, for riding this bumpy road with me.

-Nicci

About the Author

Nicci Kadilak is an educator, author, journalist, and mom whose personal essays have been featured in publications such as *Zibby Mag*, *MamaMia!*, and *The Motherload*. Before becoming a full-time writer, she was a K-12+ teacher, tutor, and school administrator. She could never fully leave the education world, and she still takes regular work as a consultant. She holds a bachelor's degree in neuroscience (with a minor in math) from Boston University and a master's in education administration. When We Were Mothers is the first of many novels Nicci intends to publish–though hopefully the rest take fewer than four years to write. Nicci lives with her husband and three children outside Boston, where she writes and produces a local news publication.

CPSIA information can be obtained
at www.ICGtesting.com
Printed in the USA
JSHW020710180123
36280JS00002B/12

9 798986 064741